LUST IN T

I watched Bibi shuck off her clothes and shake her hair free, the silky blonde strands flowing down to her shoulders. Then she hiked up her short chemise over her shoulders, showing off to best advantage her high thrusting breasts which, if slightly smaller than Lottie's, looked just as rounded and soft and were capped by rich rosebud nipples which pointed out impudently from the centre of her small circled areolae. I gulped hard as Bibi wriggled out of her knickers. My eyes swept over her smooth flat belly and the delights that nestled immediately beneath.

Now, I may have been mistaken, but I was convinced that she deliberately flaunted the firm dimpled cheeks of her exquisitely formed bottom as she walked slowly down the bank to the side of the stream and called out: 'I say, everyone, the water is quite deep here. Who's coming in with me?'

'I will,' cried out Lottie and she ran down the bank to hold hands with her friend. Together the naked girls ran into the stream . . .

Also in paperback from New English Library

The Pearl: volume 1
The Pearl: volume 2
The Pearl: volume 3
The Pearl Omnibus
The Oyster: volume 1
The Oyster: volume 2
The Oyster: volume 3
The Oyster: volume 4
The Oyster: volume 5
The Oyster Omnibus
Rosie – Her Intimate Diaries: volume 1
Rosie – Her Intimate Diaries: volume 2
Rosie – Her Intimate Diaries: volume 3
Rosie – Her Intimate Diaries: volume 4
The Rosie Omnibus
The Black Pearl: volume 1
The Black Pearl: volume 2
The Black Pearl: volume 3
The Ruby: volume 1
The Ruby: volume 2
The Ruby: volume 3

Erotic Memoirs: Volume I

Lustful Youth

Anonymous

Introduced and edited by Jeremy Allandale

NEW ENGLISH LIBRARY
Hodder and Stoughton

This edition first published in 1996 by Hodder and Stoughton
A division of Hodder Headline PLC

A New English Library paperback

10 9 8 7 6 5 4 3 2 1

British Library Cataloguing in Publication Data

Erotic Memoirs. – Vol. 1:
Lustful Youth
823 [F]

ISBN 0-340-66033-3

Typeset by
Letterpart Limited, Reigate, Surrey

Printed and bound in Great Britain by
Cox & Wyman Ltd, Reading, Berks

Hodder and Stoughton
A division of Hodder Headline PLC
338 Euston Road
London NW1 3BH

This is for Valerie and John.

INTRODUCTION

Johann 'Johnny' Gewirtz was born on November 7th, 1869, the eldest son of Graf (or Count) Benjamin Gewirtz, a well-to-do Austrian aristocrat who owned substantial estates in Galicia, an area north of the Carpathians which includes the cities of Cracow and Lvov now divided between Poland and the Ukraine but which until the end of World War One was a province of the Austro-Hungarian Empire.

Like most noblemen in the large, rambling Empire, the Count's family home was in faraway Vienna and he rarely visited his properties, leaving the management of his affairs in the hands of a local overseer. However, unlike many absentee landlords, he did make occasional visits to his house in Pinczow where, as we read in his memoirs, the fifteen-year-old Johann was to enjoy one of his major experiences in '*l'art de faire l'amour*'.

The young Johann's father and his Dutch-born wife Gertrude were both inveterate travellers and such staunch Anglophiles that soon after they were alerted to Johann's frolics with Magda, the young chambermaid in the Gewirtz house in Pinczow, their son was sent to finish his schooling at Harcourt Academy, a small private school in the Cotswolds run by Dr Nicholas Austin, a progressive Victorian educationalist who eschewed the 'muscular Christianity' of the time.

After three years at the Harcourt Academy, Johann (or

'Johnny' as he was happy to be known by his British schoolchums) completed his education at Merton College, Oxford, where he gained a first-class degree in Modern Languages (perhaps not an overly difficult task for a natural linguist who was equally at home in German, Polish, Dutch and English) and, later, at the University of Berlin where he gained a further degree in philosophy.

Assuming the title on the death of his father in 1894, Johann embarked on an Epicurean lifestyle of wine, women and song throughout the capitals of Europe. Whenever he visited London, the house his parents had bought in the 1880s in Green Street, Mayfair was the scene for many lavish dinners and receptions and the Prince of Wales was known to have attended several wild parties thrown by his young friend Count Gewirtz of Galicia, one of which in the summer of 1898 was recorded in great detail in *Cremorne Gardens*, one of the underground journals which circulated amongst *louche* men-about-town at the turn of the century.

Johann Gewirtz began writing his memoirs in the Spring of 1911 at his villa on the French Riviera whilst recovering from a serious attack of pneumonia. With his consent these were published in English and French by his raffish friend Lord Glynn (the second son of the Duke of Middlesex) who was in need of funds to keep up his sybaritic lifestyle in Paris. Such was the success of the book that in less than a year more than 90,000 copies of the English edition were sold to American and British dealers in gallant literature, which earned Lord Glynn enough to continue in his hedonistic ways – much to the fury of his father who was anxious for him to return home and get married in order to produce an heir to the family fortunes.

However, for both author and publisher, their happy

existence came to an end in August, 1914. A true cosmopolitan, the Count was devastated by the outbreak of the First World War and soon afterwards moved to Zurich where he had prudently banked most of his liquid assets after the death of his parents at the turn of the century. There he bought an apartment and, taking out Dutch nationality, Count Gewirtz saw out the war from neutral Switzerland, much of the time in the company of a bevy of pretty girls, including the beautiful young French actresses Louise Roussette and Claire Kerner.

He began travelling again in 1919 but, unable to adjust to the turmoil of post-war Central Europe following the break-up of the Hapsburg Empire, the pleasure-loving Count left for America. On the voyage across the Atlantic, he befriended a Jewish diamond merchant from Antwerp named Abraham Aiginsky and, impressed by his commercial acumen, agreed to finance Mr Aiginsky's plan to set up shop in New York. This proved to be a wise investment although the Count, who was never greatly interested in business, was happy enough to allow himself to be bought out by a grateful Mr Aiginsky in 1923 for three times his original ten-thousand-dollar investment. He proceeded to make a second fortune on the stock market in the boom years of the 1920s and again thanks to Mr Aiginsky (with whom he remained close friends) he sold most of his shares well before the Wall Street Crash in October, 1929.

In 1930, the restless Count decided to settle again in Vienna but, disgusted by the rise of Hitlerism in his native land, he divested himself of his remaining European interests some twelve months before the 1938 Anschluss (the Nazi invasion of Austria) and returned to America with his long-time companion Frau Marlene Schleich, the widow of a wealthy Austrian industrialist, whom he had secretly married back on his sixty-seventh birthday in 1936. The following summer they left Vienna for London and sailed on the *Queen Mary* for New York in September, 1938 where the Count lived quietly until his death a few days short of his eighty-ninth birthday in November, 1958.

A less devil-may-care man than Johann Gewirtz would never have allowed such intimate personal details about his sexual escapades to be published. And I would imagine that his many acquaintances all over Europe who took part in these lusty adventures must have been shocked that the Count made no attempt to shield any person with a pseudonym in his erotic narrative.

Perhaps he sought prior permission to use people's real names although it is difficult for anyone in the 1990s to believe that even the closest friends of the Count would allow him to reveal their identities in his totally uninhibited confessions. Yet it should be remembered that there were no tabloid newspapers at the time and the attitude of mainstream journalists was summed up by the editor of *The Harmsworth Magazine* in 1898 who wrote with pride: '*I claim for the newspaper press of Britain that it refrains from publishing news calculated to needlessly injure or offend.*'

This fawning attitude to the upper classes allowed King Edward VII to holiday in Biarritz every Spring with Mrs Keppel during his reign and makes it quite feasible that the *jeunesse dorée* of the era believed themselves to be members of such an exclusive insouciant coterie that no-one outside their charmed circle would ever hear a whisper about the Count's privately-printed autobiography.

Nevertheless, when copies of the book first appeared, I wonder whether any character regretted allowing himself to be named in its pages, for without doubt the lusty writing contains some of the frankest descriptions of a wide variety of sexual activities to be found in any gallant literature of the times. We are indeed fortunate that this account of the Count's ribald reminiscences will not only amuse and intrigue the contemporary reader, but will also confirm the fact that there was an opposite side to the starched, unyielding respectability which appeared to characterize European Society a little over one hundred years ago.

Here is writing that is lively and explicit in its detailed celebration of sensuality and which informs us that, beneath those swelling bodices and under that solemn waistcoated worthiness, there co-existed an eager and inventive sexuality that refused to submit to the conventional manners and *mores* of the era.

Jeremy Allandale
Associate Professor of European History
University of Arizona
February, 1996

Mutato nomine de te, fabula narratur
(Change the name, and the tale is about you)

Horace [65–8 BC]

CHAPTER ONE

It appears to be the usual practice of an author of autobiography to introduce himself by writing a short introduction and an *apologia* to any offended by its appearance. But I decline to offer any such regrets to any who profess themselves shocked by my decision to put into print these unabashed memoirs culled from memories of my youthful voluptuous adventures from the age of fourteen in Stettin [*Szczecin – Editor*] and Vienna and then from my exhilarating stay at the Harcourt Academy, an English boarding school situated near the leafy village of Fulbrook in Oxfordshire. So, without further ado, let me open this narrative at the very beginning of my life.

I was born shortly after noon on Tuesday, November 17th, 1869 at 46 Zweigstrasse, Vienna, the colourful capital of the Empire and, according to my mother (who had no need to be anything but truthful in this matter), I protested long and strenuously against my entry into the world.

According to her account of my birth, I comported myself with a singular ingratitude towards the gift of life and its bestower, although I was greeted with much greater joy than were my sisters Anna and Emilia.

[Anna Gewirtz (1863–1935) lived in Milan after marriage to the Italian landscape artist Arturo Volpe in 1882, whilst, after a passionate affair with the Prince of Wales, in 1891 Emilia Gewirtz (1866-1940) married an English

diplomat, Sir Randolph Newholme-Palmer, and spent most of the rest of her life in South America where her husband served as the British Ambassador first to Chile and later to the Argentine Republic – Editor]

Indeed, as far as my mother was concerned my birth was a sort of atonement and means of redemption. Cruelly enough, my grandfather Gewirtz found it impossible to disguise his annoyance at my poor mother for bringing 'only girls' into the family, but the disgrace into which she had fallen in his eyes was happily effaced by my appearance, though of course my own service was wholly unconscious and undeserving!

Was this not a truly barbarous mode of behaviour in my grandfather, to withhold his favour from a daughter-in-law until an heir to the Gewirtz name had been produced? For are all of us, men and women alike, so convinced in our hearts of the greater value of the male? As I write these opening words, I have on my desk a copy of *The Times* sent to me from England by my old chum Teddy Crawford about the violent disturbances in London by the Suffragettes who have broken shop windows in the West End and physically attacked leading political figures.

Whilst I deplore the use of violence by the more politically extreme, I must say that I find it difficult to understand the logic in giving the vote to a semi-illiterate agricultural labourer (decent enough fellow though he might be) and denying it to graduates of Oxford and Cambridge Universities who happen to be of the female sex.

Be that as it may, I do not intend to write about my carefree childhood years about which there is little of interest to record except to note that, although I was a delicate child, after entering my teens my health improved with remarkable rapidity. How hardy can an organism become which initially has to be pampered like a hothouse plant! For since those early years I have shown myself to be blessed with a constitution of almost explosive vitality and I am certain that this happy state is due to the love and tender care of my parents, which was closely rivalled by the devotion of my nurses and all the other servants in our homes in Vienna and Pinczow.

Indeed, my initial introduction to *l'art de faire l'amour* was made through the courtesy of a pretty young chambermaid employed by one of the leading physicians in Vienna, Doctor George Hildebrand. Carl, Doctor Hildebrand's youngest son, was my closest friend at the school I attended in Vienna and when the Hildebrand family invited me to spend a fortnight during the summer vacation at their house in Stettin, I begged my parents to let me go. My mother was chary about giving permission but my father said robustly: 'My dear Gertrude, don't wrap the boy up in cotton-wool. Johann is fifteen years old and he could hardly be in better care than with Doctor Hildebrand and his family.'

'Yes, I am aware of that, Benjamin,' retorted my mother with a worried frown. 'But Frau Hildebrand has told me that Carl and Johann would have to make the train journey back from Stettin to Vienna by themselves.'

My father shrugged his shoulders and replied: 'Well, so what? Frau Hildebrand will see them onto the train, they will be travelling in a first class carriage and we will be on the platform to meet them when they arrive at the Hauptbanhof [*the main city railway station – Editor*].

To my great delight, my mother gave way and, as the train to Stettin left at the ungodly hour of six o'clock in the morning, on the evening prior to departure I was dispatched to the Hildebrand household with my luggage.

At the Hildebrands' dinner-table, Carl and I tucked

into our delicious *escalopes de veau* whilst we talked excitedly about the fun we would have at his parents' house in the beautiful hilly, wooded suburbs of the bustling port of Stettin which belonged to Dr Hildebrand's late parents and was now occasionally rented out during the winter months, although the family always spent some time there during the warm summer months.

However, I found it difficult to listen to Carl's conversation during the meal for I could hardly take my eyes off Sonia, the buxom young maid who brought the dishes into the dining-room from the kitchen. The attractive dark-haired girl was wearing a low-cut white blouse and displayed the largest, curviest breasts I had ever seen: they were squeezed into the tightest of bodices, creating a deep cleavage between the rounded globes – the effect of which caused me some discomfort as I pulled my trousers across the stiff little shaft which was pushing up out of my drawers.

Desperately, I tried to clear my mind of her arousing presence, but when Sonia passed by Carl's seventeen-year-old brother Bertolt, my cock began to throb painfully as she bent down to retrieve his table napkin which had fluttered down to the floor and in so doing gave me a grandstand view of the creamy spheres of her bosoms. When this happened a second time, it occurred to me that Bertolt was not as clumsy as he seemed and I nearly spent then and there when I saw Sonia smooth her hand across his lap when she replaced the linen cloth between his trembling thighs.

As it was, I made an excuse to leave the table as soon as I could and walked briskly to the bathroom where I stood in front of the WC and pulled open my flies to release my erect cock which sprang out of my trousers like a Jack-in-the-Box. I clasped my pulsating prick in my hand and furiously fisted my hand up and down the shaft until a surge of pleasure coursed through my body and a glistening jet of sticky white liquid shot out of my knob and splashed down into the toilet bowl.

I had only been spending for the last month or so although, unlike so many of my unhappy schoolfellows, I had no feelings of guilt or shame about masturbating, for on my thirteenth birthday my father had left on my bedside table a copy of *A Young Person's Guide to Human Procreation* by Professor Louis Baum of Berlin which ridicules the commonly held view that tossing off leads to the most dreadful physical and mental infirmities.

To paraphrase the Professor's argument in an admittedly rough and ready style, ninety-nine per cent of boys play with themselves and there is absolutely no medical evidence to suggest that the practice has ever had any bearing whatsoever upon anyone's physical or mental health in later years or on any person's ability to reach a ripe old age.

Indeed, common sense tells us there can be no possible harm caused by young people rubbing their cocks or cunnies. To the best of my knowledge no boy has ever caught any nasty infections through wanking and no girl has ever suffered an unwanted swollen belly through finger-fucking!

Not that any such philosophical thoughts were in my mind as I stood in the Hildebrands' bathroom panting with exhaustion from my frenetic tossing-off whilst I wiped my prick, stuffed it back into my drawers and buttoned up my trousers before washing my hands and rejoining my host and his family in the drawing-room. However, as we had to rise so early in the morning, Carl and I were sent to bed at the stroke of half-past nine. A divan had been set up for me in Carl's bedroom and

Doctor Hildebrand himself came upstairs to turn off the oil lights.

'Good night, boys, don't stay up half the night talking to each other,' he advised us with a smile as he closed the door. But, of course, Carl and I were both too excited to sleep and on a clear summer night such as this the room was bathed in the light of a full moon. So, once he heard his father's footsteps descending the staircase, I could clearly see Carl immediately jump out of bed and pull what looked like a large envelope out from under his mattress.

Then, clutching the envelope in his hand, he came across to sit on my divan and whispered: 'Here, I've something special to show you, Johann. I found this envelope last week in Bertolt's bedroom when he asked me to go upstairs and bring a book downstairs for him. Go on, open it.'

I looked at him with a puzzled expression and said: 'Last week, you say? Well, I'm surprised that Bertolt hasn't realized by now that the envelope is missing and complained to your parents about how something has been stolen from his room.'

'Look what's inside the envelope, my friend,' chortled Carl as he dug me in the ribs with his elbow. 'Then you'll see why my brother daren't say a word about his loss!'

Naturally, I was now extremely curious and, opening the unsealed flap, I put my hand inside and drew out a second envelope which had been mailed to Monsieur Bertolt Hildebrand, Postfach 893, Vienna.

'Why was this sent to a post office box number and not to the house?' I enquired and Carl gave me a mischievous wink as he answered: That's a very good question and the postmark will provide you with the answer.'

What on earth did he mean? I thought with a slight

touch of irritation. But when I glanced down at the envelope, I drew in a sharp breath when I saw that this smaller hidden envelope had been posted in Paris!

'*Gott in Himmel*, don't tell me that Bertolt has been buying naughty French postcards,' I gasped excitedly and Carl chuckled: 'The envelope is open, Johann, so you can pull out what's inside it and see for yourself what my brother has been up to.'

I hesitated only for a moment before following his advice and found myself staring at a magazine called *La Vie Secrete d'Un Jeune Milord Anglais*. It was printed on expensive shiny art paper and I stared in amazement at the front page which consisted of the lettering of the title and a photograph of a shapely dark-haired girl and a handsome fair-haired boy lying on a bed in each other's arms. The girl was naked except for a pair of frilly knickers although her breasts were covered by the upper arm of the youth who himself was clad only in a pair of brief drawers.

My hands trembled whilst I riffled through the pages and goggled at a series of coloured photographic plates of this uninhibited couple, each ruder than the next, which ended with the lascivious pair enjoying a lusty fuck. Then I turned back to the first page and stared open-mouthed at a photograph which showed the bare-breasted girl on her knees pleasuring her partner whose drawers were now round his ankles and was lying back on the bed. He had a seraphic smile on his face, which was hardly surprising because the girl was now holding his thick erect shaft in one hand and his hairy pink ballsack in the other.

My command of French was good enough to translate the few lines of text underneath the picture and I muttered to myself: "Mademoiselle Juliette of Montmartre gives Lord Arthur his first lesson in fucking."

'And what a fine teacher she is! I wish Mademoiselle Juliette were on the staff at *our* school!' I added hoarsely as I gazed at the next photograph in which Juliette's head was bent low and her generous red lips were pressed against the large domed helmet of Lord Arthur's prick.

'There wouldn't be enough room in the classroom for everyone who wanted to be taught by *her*,' laughed Carl as he rubbed his stiff cock which was sticking up under his nightshirt. He slid his other hand across and, laying it on my bursting prick, he went on: 'My! What a size your shaft has swollen up to since you started looking at Bertolt's magazine. Let's see which one of us has the biggest tool and is ready for a lesson with Mademoiselle Juliette.'

We pulled up our nightshirts and frigged our throbbing erections in an ecstasy of delight which ended with us standing side by side in front of the fireplace and tossing each other off, aiming each other's sticky jet of seed into the grate.

Then we climbed back into bed and I sighed: 'Ah well, that was very nice and I'm not saying I don't enjoy a good wank, but I'm damned sure that actual fucking would be much more satisfying.'

'Of course it would,' grunted Carl, pulling the blankets over him as he rolled over on to his side. 'But, unfortunately, I don't think we're going to find that out for some years yet.'

However, as we were to find out, Carl's gloomy forecast was to be proved wrong, and far sooner than either of us could have reasonably expected . . .

Doctor Hildebrand woke us up at the ungodly hour of five o'clock the next morning and we were so tired that we dozed for much of the eight-hour train journey. I woke up shortly before luncheon and observed that besides Carl and myself, our party consisted of Doctor and Frau Hildebrand, Bertolt, and two servants, Frieda the cook and the aforementioned Sonia whose buxom bosoms had caused me such great agitation the previous evening.

We arrived at Stettin to be met at the station by a charabanc [*a horsedrawn wagon with seats – Editor*] that Doctor Hildebrand had wisely ordered to complete our travels. It was my first visit to Stettin which is a true seaport although it lies inland on the densely wooded slope of the Uralian-Baltic range and extends over both banks of the River Oder, whose many arms divide some parts of the city into islands. The wide, sluggishly moving tide flows directly northwards through the busy 'Old Town', bordered on either hand by docks, wharves and warehouses which on the right bank are then replaced by level meadows.

The Hildebrands' rambling old house was idyllically situated on the outskirts of the city in five acres of grounds, with a small tributary of the mighty Oder running along its western boundary. However, Carl and I readily agreed to share a bedroom to save our maid work (for, as Frau Hildebrand explained, Sonia would only have a local girl who would come in three mornings a week to assist her in her duties), and we assisted Bertolt and the coachman in unloading the many valises into the house.

Some kindly neighbours who lived in a house about three-quarters of a kilometre away had left food in the larder for us, and Frieda made a tasty leek and potato soup followed by a nourishing meat *Strudel* for dinner and we ended this simple but delicious meal with a dessert of fresh fruit.

Both Carl and I were now exhausted at the end of a long day and we were both more than ready for sleep by the time we stumbled up the stairs to our large bedroom which conveniently had its own adjoining bathroom. Indeed, we were both so tired that, after cleaning our teeth and washing our hands and faces, we did not bother to put on our nightshirts but slipped into our beds in the nude and very soon the pair of us fell into a deep slumber.

I was the first to wake and as usual my prick was standing up majestically demanding the usual attention from my fist. It occurred to me how nice it would be to look at the pictures of Juliette and Lord Arthur whilst I frigged my throbbing tool, and so I glanced over to Carl who had secretly packed Bertolt's French magazine and had hidden it under his mattress.

Slowly stroking my pulsing erection, I quietly rose out of my bed and padded naked across the room to where my friend was still fast asleep. However, with Carl still in his bed, I could not lift the mattress high enough to pull out the magazine so, rather than disturb him straightaway, I decided to wait for a few minutes for Carl to wake up by himself.

A brisk morning breeze swept through the bedroom and I walked to the window which I shut before tip-toeing back to Carl's bed where, being without the benefit of a nightshirt, I was now quite cold and so I raised the bedclothes and slipped into the bed beside him. There I quickly discovered that his penis was in the same condition as my own and I gave a soft chuckle as I took his hand and placed his fingers around his hot stiff shaft. Carl's eyes fluttered open for a moment but he was still half-asleep when I grasped his wrist and moved his hand up and down his erect prick whilst I pumped away on my own tingling todger. We spent simultaneously, our cocks spurting their gummy essence over the sparse curls of hair around the bases of our shafts and onto our bellies.

'Damnation! We've made the sheet sticky,' whispered Carl, but I peered down and grinned: 'It hardly matters, you must have had a wet dream last night so it would have to have been changed anyway!'

'Oh yes? Well, let me tell you—' he began, but before my chum could finish his riposte he was interrupted by a loud knock on the door and, to his horror (and mine!), Sonia came into the room with two early-morning cups of tea for us.

Poor Carl dived beneath the covers whilst the maid put down the tray on the dressing table and then she went over to the window to pull the curtain fully open and said cheerily: 'A very good morning to you, Master Johann, I hope you slept well. You'd better get up now because it's a quarter to eight and Doctor Hildebrand asked me to tell you and Master Carl that breakfast will be served at nine o'clock sharp.'

'Thank you, we'll be down in time,' I stammered as, holding my tea, Sonia approached our bed where she deposited the cup on the side table.

Of course, when she got closer to us she immediately saw through Carl's inadequate camouflage and with a saucy giggle she asked brightly: 'Who on earth is sharing your bed, Master Johann? Come on, you don't have to be shy, let me have a look.' And before I could prevent it, she threw back the bedclothes and discovered that not only was it Carl cowering next to me but that we were both stark naked.

Sonia's cheeks flushed pink and she moistened her lips as she went on with a note of reproach in her voice: 'Dear me, I thought you two lads would have grown out of playing with your own cocks by now and progressed to some genuine rumpy-pumpy.'

'Chance would be a fine thing,' I muttered under my

breath as Sonia opened her blouse to display the tops of her curvy breasts whilst she continued: 'Have you two just been having a wank? What a pity. If you had waited for me, I would have been pleased to toss you off.'

'I wish we had known, but it's not too late, just give me a minute or so and you can rub my cock for me,' said Carl with a gleam in his eye as he began to flog his shaft up to its former stiffness. 'I'll give you fifty groschen if you'll wait till I can get another stand.'

She sat down on the bed and laughed: 'Okay, I won't say no, Master Carl. After all, your brother Bertolt gives me two schillings every week for giving him a good seeing-to on Wednesday and Sunday mornings which is when I can spare the time to pleasure him.'

'*Wirklich*? So my lucky brother has fucked you!' exclaimed Carl, but moving his hand from his limp shaft and replacing it with her own, Sonia shook her head and said: 'No, we haven't actually had a shag, but for the last three months now, every Wednesday and Sunday morning, he'll be waiting for me as regular as clockwork, lying naked on his bed with his cock sticking up like a flagpole.'

I noticed that Carl's own cock began to thicken as Sonia told us how this mutually satisfactory agreement had arisen. It appeared that the fun and games began one Sunday when she brought Bertolt his early-morning tea. When she leaned over him to put down the tray on his bedside table, he gave a tiny gasp and Sonia realized she had kept the top buttons of her blouse undone and the chemise she was wearing had been cut so low that Bertolt could almost see her titties.

'I could see how excited he was because his hands shook so much when I passed him his tea that he spilled most of it in the saucer,' she smiled as she fisted her hand up and down Carl's cock which was now swelling up to its former rock-hard stiffness.

' "Bertolt, you silly boy!" I scolded him. "Now you'll have to put your pyjama jacket in the wash. Take it off now and I'll give it to Ilse when I go back downstairs. With any luck the weather will stay dry today and you should have the jacket back tonight."

'At first he protested that this was unnecessary for there were only a few splashes of tea on the sleeves, but I insisted that he gave it to me there and then, saying that if Frau Hildebrand happened to come into his room and discovered that his pyjamas were not spotlessly clean we would both get into trouble.

' "Oh, very well," Bertolt grumbled, but as he divested himself of the garment, I picked up the book that he had been reading. I raised my eyebrows when I read out the title: "*Die Auster, [presumably this was a translation of 'The Oyster', the classic collection of late-Victorian English erotica recently republished in paperback by the New English Library – Editor]* eh? My goodness, I had no idea you were so interested in natural history, Master Bertolt!"

'The poor boy blushed when I opened the book for he knew that one glance would be enough to see that he had been reading a spicy story all about the fucking which took place during a wild party after a graduation ceremony at a Viennese *gymnasium [a secondary school which prepared pupils for University – Editor]*.

' "Well, this book could hardly be called a learned work," I observed as I threw the volume back on the bed. "On the other hand, it does explain why Ilse has had to wash so many spunky stains off your sheets."

' "There can't have been any stains, I always use my handkerchief," said Bertolt indignantly and then he clapped his hand to his mouth in great embarrassment for he realized he had given the game away, so to speak!

' "Now, now, don't be silly, you don't have to be ashamed about having a good wank, especially when there hasn't been any girl around to give you a helping hand," I smiled whilst I lifted up the eiderdown to take a look at Bertolt's cock and balls. The dear lad appeared to be more frightened than aroused after I yanked up his nightshirt to expose a fine-looking prick hanging over his thigh whilst resting on the sheet below his cock lay a fully developed hairy pink ballsack. My pussy started to tingle when I ran my fingertips up and down his smooth-skinned shaft and so I stood up and unbuttoned my blouse before sliding it off my shoulders – to be quickly followed by my skirt which I unhooked and let fall to the floor.

'Then I threw off the bedclothes and climbed on top of him, straddling his body with my knees on either side of his hips. Bertolt's eyes widened and he gasped in some alarm: "Sonia, what in heaven's name are you up to?"

' "Don't worry, Master Bertolt, I'm just furthering your education," I replied as I slid the straps of my chemise down my arms and freed my bosoms which now swung teasingly in front of his face. Any apprehension he may have had quickly vanished at the sight of my bare breasts and when I dangled them against his chest, just grazing his skin with my titties, his tool thickened up straightaway and began to throb against the inside of my thigh.

'I guessed he wouldn't be able to hold back his spend for too long, so I moved myself down and crushed his cock between my bosoms. Sure enough, I soon felt his shaft begin to twitch and I jerked myself back just as the first jet of semen shot out of his knob. I clasped his trembling todger and once I had finished him off I felt so randy that I let my nipples slide in the milky pools of his seed on his tummy and then I lifted my titties up to my mouth and licked up the sticky emission as best I could.'

Of course, by now Carl and I were both sporting capital stiffies and Sonia took hold of them in her hands as she continued: 'But whilst your brother enjoys being tossed off, he simply adored our little session last Wednesday when I gave his cock its first-ever sucking. I came into his room a little later than usual and he had already taken a bath and was sitting on his bed in his underpants. Bertolt must have been thinking about me because his cock was so stiff that his purple bell-end had reared up above the waistband of his drawers.

' "I see you've started without me," I said, setting down my tray on the dressing table. Then I went across to him and pulled down his pants and my pussy was so wet at the sight of his erect shaft that I bent down and kissed his mushroomed helmet whilst I fondled his balls.

' "Oh my God!" he groaned hoarsely as I dropped to my knees and began to tease his straining shaft by running the tip of my tongue all round the edges of his springy knob. He closed his eyes and threw back his head in sheer ecstasy when I cupped my hands beneath his hairy ballsack and sucked his shaft into my mouth almost down to the root. The feel of my moist tongue slithering around his tool soon brought him up to the point of a spend and when I felt his balls tighten I began to swallow in anticipation, which was just as well because a few seconds later he flooded my mouth with a fierce jet of frothy jism.

'I gulped down every drop of his cum and licked his cock dry before looking up, and with a twinkle in my eye I asked him: "Well, how did you like that, Master Bertolt? You did very well for a novice lover, but if I ever suck your prick again, please try not to spend so quickly."

' "I'll do my best," he sighed with a seraphic smile on his face. "Wow! That was wonderful, Sonia. You must suck me off again on Sunday."

' "We'll have to see about that," I said as I heaved myself up and with the back of my hand I wiped my lips which still had some flecks of his copious emission upon them.

' "Oh, please do, Sonia," he begged as he cuddled my legs. "I'll give you a silver schilling if you will." '

This uninhibited tale excited us so much that Carl now spurted his sunk all over Sonia's hand and almost immediately my eager prick followed suit and a little of the cum which spouted out of my knob dribbled down my cock and onto the sheet.

'Oh dear, I suppose you're doing the washing here and I've already given you some extra work,' I frowned, but Sonia told me not to worry because the stains were not that bad, and ruffling my hair with her hand she added: 'I'm sure I can remove them with a dab of Professor Danziger's cough medicine – it works wonders with soiled linen.'

Carl gave a shudder and said: 'Ugh! Mama gave me a dose of that stuff when I had a cough last month. I'll never swallow another mouthful ever again.'

'Why not, Master Carl? It must be a good medicine,' said Sonia with an infectious little giggle. 'Why, old Muller the gardener feeds the flowers with it and look how well they all came out this summer!'

We collapsed into fits of laughter and after we swore faithfully that we would never tell tales about her, Sonia promised that later during the holiday she would let us see her bare breasts. Then before the lively lass left she showed us a sweet poem that Bertolt had written in her honour which ran as follows:

What dull and senseless dolt I'd be,
If never of felicity
I tasted; and whatever earthly bliss is there
To that of fucking can compare.
I would endure and ne'er complain
An age of grief, an age of pain,
To purchase but an hour's charms
Wriggling in my Sonia's arms;
And hugging her to heavenly rest,
My hand reposing on her breast!
Her arse my own, her thighs my screen,
My cockshaft standing in between!
My bollocks swinging as in fun,
Banging against her jiggling bum.
How soon the blood glows in the veins,
And nature all the power now strains;
Our passion holds triumphant sway,
Till she and I do die away.

After breakfast, Frau Hildebrand announced that she had ordered the driver who had brought us to the house from the station yesterday to return in half an hour to take her back into town as she needed to make arrangements for food to be delivered to us by the provision merchants she used when the family came here. Bertolt said he would like to escort his mother because he wanted to try out his new camera by taking photographs of the docks and shipyards.

'Do you want to join us, father?' he asked but Doctor Hildebrand shook his head and replied that he preferred to read the newspaper he had picked up yesterday afternoon and then he wanted to take a morning constitutional and would stroll over to our neighbours (the Seligsohn family with whom the Hildebrands had been close friends for many years) for coffee, although he would return home for luncheon.

As for Carl and myself, at the good doctor's suggestion Carl ordered Freida to pack a picnic lunch for us and then we sauntered off to explore the five acres of grounds which were attached to the house. The sun was shining down quite fiercely so we decided to walk through the woods towards the road which formed the eastern boundary of the Hildebrands' land and whilst we walked along the path Carl sighed: 'Well, I'm sure we'll have some fun today but nothing will be able to top what happened this morning with Sonia.'

'Oh, you never know,' I said carelessly as we trudged along. My optimistic outlook was soon to be justified for when we reached the road we stopped and watched with delight as a motley collection of wagons slowly toiled up the steepish hill which had to be climbed before they reached the gently sloping tree-lined road which wound down to the town.

Carl called out excitedly: 'Hey, Johann, did you see the notice on that big green caravan? Look, it says *Professor Ardi Gluck's World-Renowned International Circus*.'

'Yes, I can see it!' I shouted back as the driver of one of the smaller carts in the procession passed me a handbill as I jogged alongside his vehicle. I shouted my thanks as I grabbed hold of it and ran back to Carl to show him the pink piece of paper which announced in bold black type the arrival of the troupe which had played 'before many of the crowned heads of Europe' and would perform in Stettin's main park for five days with the first performance tomorrow night at eight o'clock.

'I'd love to go, wouldn't you?' I asked Carl, but then a gloomy thought struck me and I added glumly: 'But my parents don't like circuses very much and perhaps your father is also not too keen on them.'

'Oh no, Papa might not want to go himself, but I'm sure he wouldn't mind buying tickets for you and me,' my pal answered excitedly. 'And I tell you what, with any luck we'll be able to go by ourselves although we would have to ask Bertolt if he also could come with us. I know, let's run back to the house and ask Papa now before he goes off to the Seligsohns.'

'Good idea,' I said. Carl led the way as we ran back through the woods when all of a sudden he stopped dead in his tracks and leaned against a tree, clutching his side in obvious pain as he gasped for breath.

'What's the matter with you?' I asked anxiously when I caught him up. Through clenched teeth he answered: 'Not to worry, Johann, I'll be fine in a minute or two, it's only a stitch though I'll have to stay here for a bit till the pain wears off. Then when I get back to the house I'll have a good crap and I'll be right as rain. Don't wait for me, you run on and if my father's still at home, show him the leaflet. As he is a great one for opening nights, ask if he would like to book some seats for the first performance tomorrow evening.'

'All right, Carl, see you soon,' I answered and trotted back to the house where I met Freida at the back door. 'Hello there, is Doctor Hildebrand still here?' I asked eagerly but, although the cook nodded her head, she replied: 'Yes, Master Johann, the doctor's upstairs, but he left strict instructions that he was not to be disturbed.'

I gnawed my lip in irritation, but then I realized that Doctor Hildebrand would be coming downstairs soon as if he were going for his walk to the Seligsohns. So I said: 'Oh dear, in that case I'll just have to wait for him. Um, may I go to my room for my field-glasses? It will only take me a few moments for I know exactly where I put them.'

'Yes, but please don't disturb the doctor,' she said and so I scuttled upstairs and took out of my wardrobe the Zeiss binoculars which had been presented to me by my Uncle Wolfgang on my fourteenth birthday. Then, on the landing, just as I was about to descend the stairs, I paused when I heard the sound of little gasps coming from behind the door of Doctor Hildebrand's bedroom. I reasoned that the doctor must have fallen asleep, but as it did not appear that these gasps were coming from anyone in distress, I simply shrugged my shoulders as I hurried downstairs.

Now although I was not greatly adventurous by nature, in the somewhat overgrown garden stood a large oak tree with branches like bannister rails that simply invited a boy to climb up it – and this is what I did whilst I waited both for Carl and his father.

It took only minutes to find myself a comfortable perch at the top of the tree and for want of anything better to do, I trained my binoculars on the window of the bedroom occupied by Doctor and Frau Hildebrand – only to be so shocked by what I could see that I nearly lost my balance and tumbled down to the ground.

For on the matrimonial bed, writhing half-naked in each other's arms, were Sonia and Doctor Hildebrand. I clamped the binoculars to my eyes as I gaped at the sight of the buxom maid slipping out of her master's embrace to lie on her back and pull the straps of her chemise down over her arms. The material fell away from her large pendulous breasts which she cupped in her hands, her fingertips brushing the erect red nipples as she lifted her arms to undo the clips in her hair.

This graceful movement made Sonia's bosom lift and the two gorgeous orbs of her ripe young tits jiggled from side to side as she now lowered her arms and wriggled out of her knickers and ran her hand through the curly brown triangle of pussy hair between her thighs. I was eager for a longer look at her cunt but now Doctor Hildebrand rolled over the maid to cover her lissome body with his own stocky frame, so instead I was given a quick glimpse of the doctor's thick cock which was now pressing against Sonia's belly as he slid his hands under her legs to fondle the fleshy globes of her bum cheeks.

My hands trembled as I watched him press his lips to Sonia's tawny titties, nipping and sucking on the inviting stalky paps. She began to twist from side to side when he released his hands from her buttocks and brought them up to rub his palms against her engorged nipples. Then he heaved himself up and plunged his rampant rod into her cunney as their lips met in a passionate kiss as Sonia jerked her lovely bottom up and down in order to absorb as much of the doctor's prick inside her as possible.

I was staring with such concentration at this lusty exhibition that I almost jumped out of my skin when I heard Carl call out: 'Hi, Johann, what are you up to?'

Not surprisingly, my cock had swollen up whilst I had been eavesdropping on his naughty Papa, but it deflated quickly as I took the binoculars away from my eyes and fibbed as I scrambled down: 'Oh, nothing much, I was just taking a closer look at one or two of the bird nests.'

Fortunately Carl accepted this explanation and after I had jumped down on to the grass he asked if I had spoken to his father. I told him that Doctor Hildebrand was still here but he had given strict instructions that he was not to be disturbed. However, we did not have to wait long because the doctor came out of the house only fifteen minutes later, looking a trifle flushed after his frenetic exertions with Sonia. But the mid-morning fuck had clearly put him in a good mood for after we showed him the handbill about the arrival of the circus, he said: 'Yes, of course you and Johann can go to the circus tomorrow night. I'd rather like to go myself but your mother and I have already accepted an invitation to dine with Professor Barber and his wife at their villa over in Stepnitz.

'However, I've a good idea, my boys,' he continued, putting his hands upon our shoulders as we walked with him towards the front gate. 'Herr Seligsohn has installed one of these new-fangled telephones so I will ask him to speak to one of his friends in the city who will obtain two of the best seats in the house for you. No, on second thoughts, we'd better book three seats because I'm sure Bertolt will want to accompany you.'

Doctor Hildebrand was as good as his word and the next evening two coaches came to the house, one to convey the doctor and Frau Hildebrand to their dinner party and the other to take Bertolt, Carl and myself to the circus.

Oh, how we did enjoy the show – so much so that Carl and I begged his father to let us go again, a request to which he kindly agreed without hesitation – and two days later we were back there again for the Saturday matinée performance.

Now whilst I had felt familiar stirrings in my crotch at the sight of the female acrobats in their skimpy sequined costumes and flesh-coloured tights, there was no way that I could have forecast that fate had decreed that this afternoon would be the time of my rite of passage into manhood . . .

We had deliberately arranged for the coachman to meet us for the return trip home at six o'clock, a full hour after the performance ended so that we could spend some time (and even more pocket-money!) at the colourful stalls of the small funfair which surrounded the big top.

Carl wanted to join the long queue at the helter-skelter slide, but I preferred to try my luck throwing balls at the coconut shy, so we arranged to meet up again at the houpla stand at half-past five.

After six unsuccessful throws (truth to tell, all of the wooden balls I chucked at the nuts missed them by miles), I consoled myself by buying a toffee-apple and wandered off around the outskirts of the fair through to where the circus artistes' caravans were parked. There I sat down on a mound of dry earth to eat my apple and whilst I munched away my eyes lit up when I saw the pretty funambulist [*tightrope walker – Editor*], Mademoiselle Christa, walking along the path from the big top. I wondered if she would sign her photograph in the programme for me, and so I scrambled to my feet and began to run down towards her, only to see her climb up the steps and step into a large blue caravan.

'Oh, blast it,' I muttered as I skidded to a halt, but then after a few moments' thought, it occurred to me that she would not be angry if I asked for her autograph. The worst that could happen would be that she would refuse, I said to myself as I walked briskly up to her caravan.

But when I knocked politely on the brightly-painted door, to my great astonishment, far from rebuffing me with an order to leave, Christa sang out: 'Come on in, darling, it's not locked.'

Now some may be critical of the fact that I did not pause and announce myself after hearing this extraordinarily intimate reply, but in my youthful innocence I simply thought Christa knew that her visitor was the boy she had seen scurrying down the path towards her caravan! Be that as it may, I will never forget the thrill when I opened the door and saw the gorgeous girl standing before a long wall-mirror, taking down her hair and brushing the silky auburn strands.

On Saturday nights, the evening performance was not until eight o'clock and Christa had taken off the costume she had been wearing for the matinée. She was wearing only a short transparent vest and this was furled up over her backside, leaving herself naked from well above her hips to her heels!

A strangled little cry escaped from my lips as I stood transfixed, staring at her beautiful bum cheeks, but this was nothing to what happened when she bent down slightly to comb her hair and in the mirror I saw her bare breasts slip out of the tiny garment. Speechless, I gazed at the succulent red berries of her nipples and then my eyes were riveted on the curly thatch of brown pussy hair between her thighs.

Christa put down the comb and pulled off her vest to leave herself completely unclothed as, with a beaming smile, she said: 'Ah, Manfred, I'm so glad you could come round. I hope you're feeling horny, because I'm really dying for a good fuck.'

But then Christa turned round and the smile froze on her face when she saw a strange lad gawping at her stunning nude body!

'Who the blazes are you?' she began when there was another knock on the door. My cock was now sticking out in the front of my trousers like a little bent pole as Christa walked by me, her pert breasts jiggling up and down. Strategically placing herself behind the door, she called out: 'Yes, who's there?'

'It's Konrad from the ticket-office, Miss Christa,' a man's voice answered her. 'I have a note for you from the leader of the orchestra, Herr Manfred.'

'May I have it, please?' she replied as she opened the door a fraction. When she slid her arm out from behind the door, the caller placed an envelope in her hand.

'Thank you, Konrad,' Christa called out as she closed the door and, apparently not caring that she was still standing stark naked in front of me, she tore open the envelope and pulled out a single sheet of notepaper. It took her only a moment to read Manfred's short letter which clearly angered her, for she crumpled his message into a paper ball and threw it down to the floor. Then she stormed over to a table and, picking up a bottle of schnapps, poured a hefty measure into a glass. She downed the schnapps in one gulp and refilled the glass before sitting down heavily on a small stuffed sofa.

'The rotten sod says he thinks it would be best for us both if in future we kept our relationship strictly on a professional footing,' she growled at me, although she was actually speaking to herself for, of course, I had not asked for an explanation of her behaviour.

She finished her drink and then, holding out her glass, said commandingly to me: 'Be a good boy and get me another drink.'

I walked across to the table and with trembling hands brought the bottle over to her. She grabbed it from me and poured out a smaller measure than her previous drinks.

'I'd better not have any more or I'll fall off the bloody tightrope tonight,' she sighed as she sipped this third glass of schnapps. 'Not that Herr Manfred would care a fig if I broke my neck!'

Then she swallowed the rest of her drink and looked boldly up at me. 'Well, what are you staring at, young man? Haven't you ever seen a naked girl before?'

I was still tongue-tied though I could feel my cheeks flame red as I shook my head and stared down at the floor. Christa gave a husky chuckle and remarked: 'My, my, the next thing you'll tell me is that you're a virgin! What's your name, boy?'

'Johann Gewirtz, Fraulein Christa,' I stuttered whilst she rose up from the sofa and walked towards me with a roguish smile on her lips. She raised her arm to place her hands up on my face and smoothed her fingertips down my flushed cheeks as she murmured: 'And am I right, Johann? Look at me, now: is it true that you have never been to bed with a girl?'

'Yes, it's true,' I muttered and then plucking up my courage I went on: 'Although that's not because I don't want to. Unfortunately, I've just never had the opportunity.'

Now Christa moved her hands upwards to ruffle her fingers through my hair and she breathed: 'Ah, you poor deprived lad! But be honest, Johann, are you really ready to take such an opportunity if it came your way?'

'Oh yes indeed!' I answered fervently as she dropped her hands down to my waist and pulled me gently towards her. She ground her belly against my pulsating prick and grinned: 'H'm, I see what you mean. Well now, have you something hidden in your trousers besides your cock? You haven't? Then in that case, Johann Gewirtz, get undressed, the time has come for you to lose your cherry!'

She stepped back and I drank in the proud thrust of her impudent, uptilted breasts crowned by large raspberry nipples which were already pointing out with desire. I shucked off my jacket and caught my breath as I lowered my gaze down over her flat snow-white stomach and to the crisp thatch of chestnut hair nestling between her thighs.

The voluptuous girl took hold of me and pressed her lips against mine, darting her tongue between my teeth as she slipped her hand down to squeeze my throbbing tool. I shivered uncontrollably as she first unbuckled my belt and then unbuttoned my trousers which fell down to my ankles whilst she glided her hand into the slit of my undershorts and drew out my hot, smooth-skinned shaft.

Christa glanced down at my prick as she slowly frigged my twitching truncheon and enquired whether I was sixteen or seventeen years old. Naturally, I did not dare answer truthfully in case she decided I was too young to fuck, so I added eighteen months to my real age and replied: 'Oh, I'm only sixteen but I'll be seventeen in November.'

She nodded approvingly whilst I tore off my clothes and pulled off my shoes and socks and said: 'Well, Johann, you've a nice big cock for your age, that's for sure, and it's certainly time that it was put to good use.

'You won't be a virgin for much longer, my dear, this I can promise you,' she whispered as she pulled me by my cock across the room. We stood in front of the sofa and kissed wildly, our tongues deep in each other's mouths as Christa mashed her soft breasts against my chest. She took hold of my hands and placed them on the jouncy globes of her bum cheeks as she pressed herself against me, but after a short while she broke the embrace in order to pull two soft cushions off the sofa and throw them down on the crimson rug which lay in front of it. Then she lay down on the rug, placing one of the cushions under her head and the other under her lovely bottom.

'Come and fuck me, Johann,' Christa murmured throatily as she spread her legs and ran her hand invitingly between her legs, spreading her puffy pussy lips with her fingers to give me a glimpse of the red chink of her love channel.

At last, the moment of truth had arrived! My heart began to pound as I knelt in front of her and then to my utter dismay, I was overcome by nervous emotion and in a trice my treacherous tool suddenly lost almost all its stiffness and dangled limply down over my balls. However, Christa was wise enough to understand my anxieties and she smiled at me and told me to relax as she reached out and clasped hold of my recalcitrant cock, rubbing it gently until my shaft swelled up again and leaped and bounded inside her rolled-up fist.

She released my prick from the sweet prison of her hand and held me by my buttocks as I lowered myself down on top of her. In one powerful forward thrust (by luck rather than any good judgement, I would be the first to admit) my bursting shaft sank directly into the tight wetness of her cunney right to the root until my balls slapped against her bottom. For a short while we just lay still with my cock tightly engulfed inside her love funnel and I almost swooned away with pleasure as I gloried in an orgasmic ecstasy and then Christa chuckled: 'How does it feel, Johann? As nice as you thought it would be, I trust? Now I want you to fuck me. Push your prick in and out of my pussy, but when the spunk rushes up from your balls, you must immediately pull out and shoot your seed over my tummy.'

I needed no further urging and Christa eagerly lifted herself up to welcome the enthusiastic if inexperienced prick which was sliding in and out of her juicy cunt, clutching at my jerking bottom as she heaved herself upwards to pull me further inside her. She worked her hips in time with my thrusts and the stimulating caress of her cunney muscles around my cock made me buck up and down at an even more frenetic pace and she gasped: 'Slow down, Johann, slow down. I want to spend too, you know.'

I responded to her request by slowing down the pace of my frantic thrusts and I looked down delightedly at my shaft which glistened from its coating of Christa's cunney juice as it pumped in and out of her notch and I noticed how her love lips clung to my cock every time I pulled back as if afraid of losing such a sweet sugar stick.

'Now speed up again and fuck me as hard as you can,' she panted through her tightly clenched teeth. 'Go on, Johann, give me all you've got, you lovely big-cocked boy!'

Nevertheless, it was with some trepidation that I slammed into her squelchy snatch, fucking her as hard and fast as I could. But I need not have worried for now Christa was transformed into a raging wild animal, biting my shoulder as she writhed wildly beneath me until with a long wail she slumped backwards and her breasts and buttocks shook in a rapid series of tiny spasms as she achieved a delicious orgasm. This led to the muscles of her cunney squeezing my trembling tool even more tightly and this sent me speeding up to my own climax. I could feel the sperm rising from my scrotum and, remembering her instructions, I pulled my cock out from her cunt and spurted my emission over her belly before I slumped down on top of her.

My mind was in a whirl as I lay exhausted from my journey across the Rubicon. I have often read that one's first introduction to the joys of love-making can be a traumatic experience and certainly it is one that few of us ever forget, for this first experience in *l'art de faire l'amour* can be thrillingly ecstatic – or a total disaster! In my opinion, success or failure mostly depends upon one's choice of consort which is why I have always urged young people to try and find an experienced partner for their first complete sexual experience. Thankfully, I was lucky enough to be guided by a kind, sophisticated girl who took the trouble to guide me through this important rite of passage.

Indeed, although it was not a propitious time of the month for Christa to let me spend inside her, she praised my performance to the skies saying that she could hardly believe that this had been the first time that my cock had sheathed itself inside a cunney.

'Johann Gewirtz, was this really your first fuck?' she enquired as we hauled ourselves up off the floor and Christa replaced the cushions on the sofa. 'Come now, are you telling me that no girl has ever instructed you on how to pleasure her pussy?'

'No, I promise you I have never made love to a girl before,' I said timidly, and naturally I felt so proud when Christa clapped her hands together and said: 'So you were a virgin and I was your first conquest? Oh, what an honour! Now I'll give you a splendid reward. Lie back and close your eyes whilst I give your lovely cock a nice big kiss. I take it this would also be a new experience for you, eh?'

Naturally I was very happy to let Christa be the first girl to suck my cock and a blissful smile spread over my face as she slipped down on her knees directly in front of me. Holding my flaccid shaft in her hand, she gently squeezed it whilst she planted a delicate kiss upon the tip of my knob and in seconds my prick thickened up to a rampant state of excitement.

'That delicious big cock looks good enough to eat,' said Christa huskily and she proceeded to wet her lips and gulp about half of my eighteen-centimetre-long shaft into her mouth.

'Woooh!' I gasped as Christa washed my helmet with her wet tongue, and then, bobbing her head up and down in a slow, thorough tempo, she began to palate my cock with her sweet, suctioning mouth. She now let go my cock and grasped my buttocks with both hands to move me backwards and forwards as she skilfully sucked my cock, now releasing one hand from my bum to play with my balls as she swirled her tongue around my throbbing column.

If anything, this was even more exciting than fucking the frisky girl who was clearly deriving great enjoyment from this sensuous sucking, sliding her tongue up and down my trembling tool, gently nipping, licking and kissing my delighted cock.

Ecstatic stabs of desire crackled through my entire body as she sucked me off, tonguing my helmet against the roof of her mouth so sensuously that I soon felt the surge of a powerful spend coursing up from my tightened ballsack. This being my first experience of the delights of *fellatio*, I found it impossible to hold back and I cried out: 'I'm cumming, Christa, I'm cumming! Oh God! Ohhhh . . .!'

My hips began to jerk faster and faster and then, with one final thrust, I spurted a stream of sticky jism into Christa's mouth, every drop of which she eagerly gulped down until inevitably my sated shaft shrank down to dangle limply between my thighs.

As I recovered my senses, I looked up at the clock on her table which showed that I had only three minutes to get to the houpla stall if I were not to keep Carl waiting for me. I explained this to Christa as I hastily threw on my clothes, and then I asked her if I could see her again.

'Oh, I don't know about that,' she said doubtfully and, despite my continued pleas, refused to commit herself further, reminding me that in only five days' time the circus would be leaving Stettin for their annual ten-week season in Berlin.

'Well, at least may I write to you?' I asked as she helped me on with my jacket. This she agreed to with a smile and scribbled down the address of the small hotel in which she would be lodging whilst in Berlin.

As I kissed her goodbye my head was still whirling with such excitement that as I closed the door of the caravan behind me, I missed my footing and tumbled down the short flight of stairs. 'Ow!' I exclaimed as I scrambled to my feet and hobbled painfully towards my rendezvous with Carl at the houpla stall.

I shouted out to my chum who was pacing impatiently in front of the stall when I finally arrived. When he saw me limping along as best I could, he ran over and took my arm as he exclaimed: 'Johann, what have you done to your leg? Where on earth have you been? I was worried that you had forgotten where we were meeting up because I've been waiting here a good ten minutes for you.'

I took hold of his arm and apologized for my late arrival as we walked towards the road where the coachman would be waiting to take us home. 'Sorry, Carl, I went arse over tip going down some steps and I think I've twisted my ankle,' I answered with a grimace of pain as I limped alongside him. 'Ouch! It hurts like hell when I put any weight on it.'

When we reached the house, he helped me out of the coach and up the stairs into the bathroom where I soaked my foot in a hot bowl of water. We went to bed shortly afterwards and Carl went to sleep almost immediately, but my mind was still buzzing with the excitement of the evening. In one sense, I had passed into adulthood, but I was level-headed enough to realise that I still had much to learn, not least about the many forms of fucking if I wanted to emulate the feats of great lovers like the lusty Casanova or more contemporary cocksmen such as the British Prince of Wales [*the future King Edward VII – Editor*] and I resolved to broaden my education in this direction as widely as swiftly as possible!

My next chance to do this came the very next morning after I had hobbled downstairs to breakfast. Of course, when he saw me limp to the table, Doctor Hildebrand insisted on taking a look at my foot which was aching quite painfully, and after making a careful examination he remarked: 'Now look here, you two, I know you young chaps are always dashing hither and thither, but let this be a warning to the pair of you to take more care. Johann, thankfully you haven't broken any bones, but your ankle is badly bruised and my advice is that you stay inside this morning and rest your foot till we return from our walk at about noon. By then the bruise will probably have come out and you'll find it far less painful.

'However, for now you must keep the foot off the ground,' he added sternly. 'Did you bring any books with you? No? That's a shame, for I doubt if Frau Hildebrand or myself possess anything you would care to read. What about you, Bertolt? Have you any books you could lend Johann?'

'How about one of the publications you subscribe to?' asked Carl and I held back a giggle with difficulty as he nudged me in the ribs. Bertolt shot him a dark look and muttered that he hadn't packed any magazines in his case, but then Doctor Hildebrand said: 'No matter, only last night I noticed that Herr Danziger, the businessman who rented the house from us last month, left some journals in the study and Johann might find something of interest in them.'

It was a bore having to stay inside on such a bright summer morning, but I could hardly argue with the doctor. So, ten minutes later, I waved goodbye to the entire Hildebrand family who had been invited over to the Seligsohns for a practical demonstration of the telephone.

Frieda and Sonia had a great deal of work to get through, so I knew I would not be disturbed as I walked slowly into the study where I found the pile of magazines left by Herr Danziger.

At first I groaned when I scanned through them, for they all appeared to be concerned with affairs of trade, but when I picked up a copy of *The Corn and Grain Digest*, another smaller magazine slipped out of its pages. My eyes widened when I saw that this was an English periodical entitled *The Confessions of Miranda Morley* and thanks to my Mama (who like many Dutch people was fluent in English and German as well as in her native language) at school I had been top of the class in English for the previous three years and by this time I already possessed a good enough grasp of the language to read this racy magazine.

One glance inside was enough to tell me that this was a publication of the same ilk as the one which Carl had purloined from Bertolt's room. So I hauled myself upstairs back to my bedroom and, lying down on the bed with my leg resting on a pillow, I settled back to enjoy the rude memoirs of Miranda, who was (she assured the reader) an eighteen-year-old daughter of a wealthy farmer down in one of the southern counties of England. I had to read at a slightly slower pace than if the magazine had been in German, but this was hardly a chore for I relished every word of Miranda's naughty story which, after some scene-setting introductory paragraphs, continued in the following fashion:

I'll never forget one particular warm afternoon last June when Jack, the vicar's handsome eldest son, came round to take me out for a walk and (if I had anything to do with it) for a long-awaited romp in the hay, for I hadn't seen Jack since Easter. This was because he was studying at Cambridge University and had arrived back in the village only a few days ago for the summer vacation.

Now I freely admit having a soft spot for Jack who was a nice, gentle boy who wore his riotously curly hair so long that it touched his collar and I should add that the lucky lad had been blessed with a smooth, lightly tanned complexion and large brown liquid eyes which made me shiver when they swept over my body.

But unlike so many young men who are over-eager to force their attentions on one, Jack Dennison was a shy lad and he rarely showed his desire to make love to me. The only exception was on the last evening of his Spring vacation when we had exchanged a long passionate kiss outside the front door of my home after he had walked me home from a dinner party at Squire Neild's mansion.

On this glorious summer afternoon I was determined to overcome Jack's reticence for my pussy was fairly aching for the need of a rampant throbbing tool. It had been five long weeks since I had enjoyed a good fuck with the curate, Reverend Pethick. There had been no chance of any further fun with the raunchy reverendo and, to make matters worse, I had also been cruelly denied the chance to enjoy a romp with the notorious Sir Andrew Bennett when he was suddenly called away to London on business the day before we were supposed to spend an evening together.

This was an especially frustrating state of affairs because Sir Andrew is a young gentleman known (with good cause) as 'Randy Andy' by several other girls of my acquaintance who have met this gay baronet who, according to my dear friend Lady Camilla Windsor, boasts the largest pair of balls in the county of Sussex, although until I have the opportunity to gauge the dimensions of Sir Andrew's scrotum for myself I cannot yet confirm her interesting assertion.

But I digress, for as Jack and I sauntered through the meadow which led down to the small stream which divided our land from the acres farmed by Colonel Fenner, my thoughts were solely concerned with how best I could seduce the bashful boy who I speculated would need only a little encouragement to go further than pressing his stiff cock against me as he held me in his arms during our aforesaid one and only embrace.

A number of these ideas were running through my mind when, to my delight, I realized that Jack's arm had snaked its way around my waist and that he was guiding me towards a small haystack some twenty yards away to our right.

'Would you mind if we rested for a while, Miranda?' he murmured softly in my ear. 'We could lie down on top of the haystack over there and let the warm air waft over us.'

'Oh yes, that sounds like a lovely idea,' I replied, trying so hard to conceal my enthusiasm that it did not occur to me to realize how extraordinarily convenient it was that a ladder had been left at the side of the haystack in question. I should have realized that Jack had given one of our farm-hands a florin [10p – Editor] *to leave the ladder there early that very morning!*

Anyhow, once we had climbed the haystack and made ourselves comfortable, Jack soon showed me that since the kiss on our doorstep back in April, the shy lad had been transformed into a fiery, passionate young man. When I snuggled up next to him and laid my head in the crook of his shoulder, he let out a cry of passion and, lifting me up in his arms, he crushed me to him in a powerful embrace. I was totally engulfed in waves of idyllic bliss as our tongues slithered wetly together whilst his hands moved to my breasts and caressed the firm, rounded globes.

I let my own hand slide down to his lap and I drummed my fingers on the tubular bulge between his legs as he deftly unbuttoned my blouse and helped me discard the garment before sliding the straps of my chemise off my shoulders. My naked nipples rose up like hard little tawny bullets to greet him as I unbuckled the belt around the waistband of his trousers.

'Jack Dennison! You naughty boy!' I giggled when his hand dived down and he began to pull up my skirt, but I made no attempt to prevent him pressing his palm against my pussy. Indeed, I now undid his fly buttons and he lifted his bottom to let me pull down his trousers and pants.

My tongue passed hungrily over my top lip as I thrilled at the sight of Jack's magnificent beefy cock which rose majestically up from a curly thicket of black curls at the base of his belly. I grasped hold of his palpitating, smooth-skinned shaft and squeezed it for a moment or two before reluctantly releasing it to shuck off my skirt and undergarments until I lay naked beside him.

He gazed at my uptilted breasts and let out a choking sigh when I shamelessly smoothed my fingers over my pussy and diddled my fingertips inside my moistening crack – and as if this were not a clear enough signal that I wanted to be fucked, I whispered fiercely: 'I'm ready for you now, Jack. Plunge that thick prick into my cunt and pump out all your frothy jism into my sticky honeypot.'

I lay back and spread my legs apart as he rolled over on top of me and my whole body tingled with desire when Jack pressed his uncapped helmet between my yielding love-lips which opened like magic to allow his quivering shaft to sheath itself inside my welcoming cunney. Soon I had every inch of his cock lying snugly in my tingling snatch and then I worked my thighs upwards, wrapping my legs around his back as he started to piston his fleshy boner in and out of my squelchy slit.

How glorious it felt as his heavy balls slapped against my bum cheeks with each downward thrust and shivers of ecstasy ran through my body as behind my closed eyes I imagined how my hot, dripping quim was absorbing Jack's rampant rod as it slewed to and fro inside my love funnel. I was now so wet that I could feel my cuntal juices trickling down into my arse-hole before seeping into the hay.

What a wonderfully energetic lover dear Jack turned out to be! He pounded away with such strength that he stretched my cunney to the limit with surging strokes of his thick throbbing tool. Every nerve in my body thrilled with rapture during this truly marvellous fuck, but these exquisite sensations were too delicious to last and all too soon I climaxed and Jack's spend followed a few seconds later.

'H-a-r-g-h! I'm cumming! I'm cumming!' I shrieked out as I thrashed around in the dizzy delirium of my orgasm and then, after a quick series of spasmodic twitches, an abundant jet of jism spurted out of Jack's knob and splattered against the walls of my cunt.

He rolled over next to me and to my great excitement, I could see that his lovely cock was still semi-erect and would shortly be capable of a repeat performance. I said as much to him and Jack smiled and said: 'By all means, my dearest, I would love nothing better than to fuck you again, but after such a vigorous coupling, you really must allow me a few minutes to regain my strength.'

This was a reasonable enough request and I lay back as he slid his fingers into the pool of moisture between my thighs and I closed my eyes to relive the excitement of our love-making whilst Jack's artful fingertips popped in and out of my sopping crack. He frigged me so wonderfully that at first I took no notice of the creaking sounds from in front of me – but when they became louder, I opened my eyes and, to my horror, I realized they had been made by a third person who had climbed up the ladder to see what Jack and I were up to.

It was no consolation that the uninvited visitor was one of my father's employees and not a total stranger. I recognized him instantly as Dick Tallon, the good-looking young farm-hand who Jack had bribed to leave the ladder in such a handy place for us.

Richard's face was a picture as he sat on his haunches gaping at the lewd sight of Jack's fingers sliding between my pouting pussy lips. Yet after the initial shock, I found it most exciting to realize that my lover and I were being watched by the blushing seventeen-year-old, and I reached over and began to fist my hand up and down Jack's burgeoning todger.

'So what are you gawping at, Richard?' I snapped at the tongue-tied teenager and then added in a sarcastic voice: 'Perhaps you would like Mr Dennison and I to stay completely still whilst you take a photograph?'

'Don't be too cross with him, Miranda,' said Jack soothingly. 'Richard's probably never even seen a girl's pussy before and he's too overcome with emotion to apologize for disturbing us.'

I giggled and said: 'Yes, I suppose you're right and we do need him to keep his mouth shut, don't we? I know, why don't we go the whole hog and put on a tableau vivant *that he'll never forget?'*

He nodded his head and chuckled. 'What a clever idea, darling! I'm game if you are – but what exactly did you have in mind?'

'Lie back and I'll show you,' I said, continuing to slide my hand up and down Jack's slippery wet length whilst I rose up and knelt between his legs. I licked my lips and

jammed down his foreskin as I leaned forward to kiss his uncapped bulbous helmet, knowing full well that by deliberately arching my hips in this wanton manner my bouncy bum cheeks would be jiggling just a yard or so in front of Richard's flushed face, displaying my backside and my pussy to the delighted young man.

Then I turned my head and said to him: 'Well, you've now had a bird's eye view of my cunt, so you must let me take a good look at your cock.'

I heard the astonished lad gasp in amazement as he realized that, with any luck, he might be invited to fuck me. In the meantime, I busied myself by working over Jack's rock-hard cock, running my teeth up and down the blue-veined shaft, and then sucking the glistening wet knob and flicking my wicked tongue over its slitted end whilst I cradled his hairy ballsack.

'Are you ready yet, Richard?' I enquired as I pulled Jack's cock out of my mouth, but when I turned back again I could see that it was unnecessary for him to answer the question as he had already pulled out a squat barrel-like cockshaft which he was fondling and squeezing in his fist.

I was so fired by the sight of Richard's thick chopper that I wantonly wiggled my backside and pushed my voluptuous white buttocks out even further towards him. Then pulling my lips away from Jack's pulsating prick, I called out: 'What are you waiting for, you silly boy? Or does Mr Dennison have to give you a demonstration on how to fuck me from behind?'

Richard's eyes sparkled and he replied in his broad rustic dialect: 'No, Miss Miranda, t'ain't necessary for Mr Dennison to move hisself, I know all about fucking. But instead of a doggie-style shag, how do you fancy a nice poke up your tight little arsehole instead?'

'No, I think not, thank you,' I said hastily as he divested

himself of his trousers and drawers. 'But feel free to slide your splendid staff into my clingy little quim.'

'Very good, ma'am,' he grunted as he shuffled forward on his knees behind me and as I replaced my lips on Jack's moist helmet I reached out behind me and, taking Richard's truncheon in my hand, I guided it into the cleft between my bum cheeks until the tip of his knob touched my cunney lips.

Then, with the sun beating down on my back, I started rocking back and forth between the two men. I slurped on Jack's twitching tool whilst my bottom rose with every shove as Richard drove home and the contractions of my cunney muscles soon sucked the jism from his cock which pumped out of his bell-end as he heaved his throbbing tool in and out of my dripping crack with all his youthful strength.

As Richard shot his load into my cunt, Jack gave a deep groan and his shaft began to tremble violently between my lips. I realized that he could no longer hold on and pulled his cock out of my mouth until only the tip of his knob was resting on my tongue. Then I gave one gentle tug on his tool and let him watch his seed shoot out over my lips and teeth and when he finished I licked up all his salty spunk and gulped it down.

The three of us would have liked nothing better than to have continued playing these lascivious games, but to do so would have put us in grave danger of being discovered in flagrante delicto *and so reluctantly we dressed ourselves and climbed down from the haystack.*

However, the memory of this sensual afternoon will never fade, for it marked the first time – to use the common vernacular – that I had been "the meat in the sandwich" in a lascivious threesome and I had so enjoyed the lusty game that Jack and I have since invited several other players of our own social standing to join us, including Squire Neild's son, Martin, and the infamous rake Sir Roger Tagholm who in his own words 'would travel through the night from Brighton to Birmingham for a damned good fuck.'

And no, dear reader, I have no regrets or feelings of shame; as the poet says: me tamen urit amor; quis enim adsit amori [Love consumes me yet – for what bounds may be placed on love? – Editor].

I end with the following farewell wish to all ladies and gentlemen:

May you never be in a need of a fuck
Nor yet a prick or cunt to suck.

As can be imagined, after reading Miranda Morley's raunchy essay my shaft was as stiff as a poker and I unbuttoned my trousers and began to slide my cupped hand up and down my erect prick as, closing my eyes, I imagined that Miranda had invited me to participate in her frolics with Jack Dennison. The intensity of this erotic reverie was so great that only moments later, sticky gobs of adolescent sperm churned up from my balls to squirt up from the tiny slit of my engorged penis and my thighs trembled as my cock reared and plunged in my fist whilst the spunky emission dribbled down my twitching tool and coated my fingers.

After I had milked my cock of the last drains of cum, I rose up and staggered to the bathroom where I wiped my hand on a towel. Fortunately, this frenetic wank had not stained my trousers and so after washing my heated face, I limped back to the bedroom and placed *The Confessions of Miranda Morley* under a pile of my underwear in the wardrobe.

I spent the next hour playing various games of patience with the pack of cards that Carl had had the foresight to bring from Vienna and at noon Sonia came in and asked me if my foot was feeling any better.

'It does feel much easier, thank you,' I said and when I pulled off my sock I was able to see that Doctor Hildebrand's prognosis had been correct because there was now a huge blackish blue bruise around my ankle.

Sonia sat down on the bed and smoothed her fingers gently over my foot as she commented: 'Yes, you'll be up and about in no time now that the bruise has come out. Still, it's not much fun to be laid up on such a nice day, though Master Carl will be back for luncheon and he'll be able to play with you this afternoon.'

The Hildebrands returned shortly before one o'clock along with two guests who would stay with us for the rest of the day – Lottie, Herr Seligsohn's attractive sixteen-year-old daughter and her Swedish friend Bibi, a stunning girl who had been blessed with typical Scandinavian good looks. Within only minutes of their arrival, it was quite clear that Bertolt was smitten by Bibi's limpid blue eyes and honey-blonde hair which she wore in long shiny strands on either side of her pretty face.

Before we sat down to luncheon, the doctor examined my foot again and informed the company that the invalid was making such excellent progress that it would not be necessary to issue any further bulletins!

'Nevertheless, you must rest the ankle for the next day or so,' he warned me, but when he saw my face fall, he went on with a kindly grin spreading across his craggy features: 'On the other hand, it wouldn't hurt if you bathed your foot in the brook at the bottom of the garden.'

After we ate a delicious luncheon, Doctor and Frau Hildebrand retired upstairs for a snooze and with some amusement I wondered to myself whether the doctor would poke his wife in the same uninhibited, vigorous manner as when he had fucked Sonia yesterday.

Now though I say so myself, despite the fact that Carl and I were slightly younger than Bibi and Lottie, the girls seemed to find our conversation of genuine interest. This appeared to irritate Bertolt somewhat, especially when Lottie turned to me and said: 'Johann, would you like me to walk down with to the brook with you? You can hold on to my arm so that you don't strain your poor ankle.'

'That's very kind of you,' I replied hauling myself up from the chair. 'But I don't want you to tire yourself out in such hot weather.'

'Exactly so, there's no need to trouble yourself. Carl can take young Johann down to the water,' growled Bertolt, but Lottie went on: 'Oh, it's no trouble. Besides, I would rather fancy having a little paddle in the stream myself, wouldn't you, Bibi?'

'Yes, I think that is a splendid idea,' agreed the beautiful Swedish girl and to my amusement, Bertolt immediately changed his tune and exclaimed: 'Well, I dare say you're right, Lottie, it would be nice and refreshing to cool ourselves off. So why don't we all go down to the brook with Johann?'

The others readily agreed to this suggestion and, after raiding the linen cupboard for towels, we set out for the brook which lay only about three hundred metres away from the house. However, the small stream was secluded from prying eyes in that to reach it one had to walk through a clump of trees and these provided some welcome shade from the rays of the burning afternoon sun.

Now to this day I don't know what made me slip into my pocket the pack of cards with which I had been playing patience before luncheon – but what an excellent decision this proved to be!

For if I had not taken the cards with me, I might not have been able to take part in some forbidden frolics which were so naughty that, thirty years afterwards, just thinking about these adventures makes my cock swell up and throb for relief . . .

CHAPTER TWO

As we were about to leave the house, Bertolt said to Carl: 'You show our guests the way down to the brook and I'll join you in about five minutes.'

This remark rather puzzled me for it was crystal clear that Bertolt was smitten by the pretty girls, but I concentrated on clinging closely to Lottie as, walking with an exaggerated limp, I held on to her as we moved slowly through the trees to a clearing at the side of the slow-running stream.

We took off our shoes and socks and the four of us – Lottie, Bibi, Carl and myself – gaily splashed around in the cool water. 'There, does your foot feel less painful?' asked Lottie, and I nodded: 'Oh yes, I'll be as right as rain but I still want to hold on to your arm on the way back to the house!'

She burst into laughter and gently smacked me on my shoulder as she exclaimed: 'You cheeky boy! Now I am wondering if those blue marks around your ankle really are bruises or whether you painted them on yourself in order to gain our sympathy and win the opportunity to hold hands with me!'

'Certainly not, those bruises are genuine enough,' I replied indignantly, but then I stopped for our attention was drawn to the figure of Bertolt who was walking towards us carrying a silver tray on which rested two bottles of champagne, a jug of orange juice and five large wine glasses. He carefully deposited the tray on the gently sloping bank of the stream upon which we had already left our towels.

'My word, what have you there, Bertolt?' enquired Lottie, and Bibi (who, like many Swedish people, spoke perfect German and English in addition to her native tongue) added softly: 'How very grand! Is there an anniversary or someone's birthday for us to celebrate?'

'No, there aren't any anniversaries or birthdays but I decided we must celebrate the first visit of two charming girls to our home,' said Bertolt grandly and he picked up one of the bottles and began unpicking the wire around the cork.

'Good, the bubbly is nice and cold,' he continued as he pointed the bottle away from us. 'Now, have either of you girls ever tasted the latest cocktail which is all the rage in Vienna? It's quite delicious and couldn't be easier to make – all I have to do is pour equal parts of chilled champagne and fresh orange juice into the glasses.'

[This drink (which originated in the bars of the French Riviera) enjoyed great popularity, initially on the Continent and later in England during the late 1880s after it had been given an enthusiastic welcome by the Prince of Wales and his ultra-fashionable friends in the 'Marlborough House' set. It became known as Buck's Fizz, in honour of Captain William Buckmaster of the Household Cavalry who first introduced it to London Society – Editor]

'Here's to our visitors,' exclaimed Bertolt grandly as he lifted up his glass. 'Bibi and Lottie, I hope this afternoon will be the start of the best summer holiday you have ever had.'

Carl and I echoed his toast and I tasted my first champagne cocktail. It was as delicious as Bertolt had said, and I eagerly accepted his offer of a refill. Then he offered a second refill and after that he opened the second bottle of '74 Château Aigin Premier Cru which he had purloined from Doctor Hildebrand's small cellar.

Now it would be wrong for me to accuse Bertolt of wanting to get Bibi and Lottie sloshed. No, if any such caddish thoughts were in his mind, they would have been directed against Carl and myself, for I am certain that he would have liked nothing better than to make us *hors de combat* and thus enjoy the company of the girls by himself. However, I have no proof for this assertion so let me merely record the fact that after an hour or so of imbibing, the five of us were all feeling very merry indeed.

To be frank, I suppose we were all slightly tipsy, none more so than Carl who foolishly helped himself to a fifth glass of pure champagne after we had finished up all the orange juice. Not surprisingly, once he had settled himself down on the grass and made a pillow of his towel, he soon fell fast asleep. Bertolt looked over at his brother and shook his head as he commented: 'Dear me, it looks as though Carl has had a little too much to drink. Oh well, it will teach him a lesson if he wakes up with a hangover. Are you all right, young Johann?'

'Yes, thank you, I'm fine,' I replied truthfully, for although I might have been a little light-headed I wasn't feeling sleepy. So when Bertolt suggested that we play some parlour games before going into the water for a paddle I perked up and brought out the pack of playing cards which I had slipped into my pocket as we left the house.

'How about a round of whist?' I suggested, but Bibi giggled and said: 'If you like, but Lottie and I know a much better game which we learned last term at school. We were taught by Franz, the son of a local farmer, when we walked across the fields to his home on Saturday afternoons. I'm sure you'll like this game, it's even easier than making a champagne and orange juice drink and can be great fun to play, especially in mixed company.'

'Fair enough,' said Bertolt and I added that I was also keen to join in and said boastfully: 'Are there any prizes for the winner? I am usually lucky at cards.'

'Ah, the beauty of this game is that, in a way, everybody wins,' laughed Lottie. 'Let me explain the simple rules. After I have shuffled the pack, we all pick a card and the one with the lowest has to take off an item of clothing. Then we repeat the procedure and carry on till someone has no more clothes to take off and then continue until everyone except the winner is naked! So how about it, boys, shall we play?'

'Of course,' I said immediately, before Bertolt could gather his breath. 'But this could take quite a long time.'

'Not if we are quick about it,' retorted Lottie. 'Bibi, deal the cards!'

'Two of hearts,' announced Bibi, peering under her card without turning it over. 'I lose.' And when she stood up and unbuttoned her dress and let it fall to the ground, my cock began to thicken as I gazed at the rounded swell of her breasts which were now only partially covered by her silk chemise.

'I hope you're not cheating, my dear,' said Lottie severely as she pulled the card out of Bibi's hand. 'You naughty cat! That's the *nine* of hearts. I thought it unlikely that you would be dealt three deuces in succession! So you had better put your dress back on again.'

'Oh, don't be a spoilsport,' grinned Bertolt, who had been dealing the cards. 'It really doesn't matter too much because Bibi would have lost the next round anyway.'

'How can you be so sure?' asked Lottie, who had drawn

the lowest card in most of the previous rounds but had chosen to undress in a somewhat unorthodox manner, taking off her stockings and suspenders and wriggling down her frilly lace knickers even though she had yet to take off her dress.

Bertolt laughed out loud. 'Because I was cheating too!' he admitted as he shuffled the pack and gave us all a card as he went on: 'But this is an honest deal, you saw me mix the cards yourselves. Look, we'll all turn them over. I'll begin.'

He grimaced as he exposed the knave of diamonds and I also scowled when my card turned out to be the nine of spades, for that was unlikely to be the lowest in the round. However, Lottie's eyes lit up when she turned over her card and a mischievous smile flitted across her face as she exclaimed: 'The Joker! That means ten items of clothing must be removed either from myself or any other player I choose!'

'You never mentioned that rule,' protested Bertolt, but Lottie shrugged her shoulders as she hauled herself up and began to unbutton her dress. 'I think I did, you know. Ask Bibi and Carl.'

'Oh yes, I distinctly recall her saying so,' I chirped up, pulling at my crotch to try and give my cock more room, for now my prick shot up to a fully-blown throbbing erection as I watched Lottie step out of the dress which now lay in a heap at her feet and then pull her chemise over her head to stand stark naked in front of us.

To be quite frank, I had to summon up all my strength to prevent my hand flying to my swollen shaft as I stared at the lovely girl's glorious nudity. A gasp of pure ecstasy escaped from my lips as I gazed at the firm swell of her bare breasts, each creamy globe proudly uptilted and crowned by large pink circled areolae with raised crimson nipples which acted like magnets to my gleaming eyes and also, of course, to those of Bertolt. He stood transfixed with his jaw sagging downwards as he gasped at Lottie who, thrusting her hips forward, almost allowed her curly brown bush of cunney hair to brush against his lips.

'Two choices left,' murmured Lottie in a throaty whisper. 'But I have nothing left to remove, so who shall take my place—'

Prior to my exciting frolics with Sonia and Christa, I had been bashful of even showing my legs to a girl, but now I could hardly wait to strip off and I chimed in: 'Choose me, please. I've hardly lost a stitch and the sun's really beating down. Honestly, I think I might faint if I don't get rid of some of my clothes.'

'But what about Bibi?' enquired Bertolt who, naturally, was far keener to see the blonde beauty unclothed rather than myself.

'Don't worry about me, Bertolt,' smiled the lissome Swedish girl. 'After all, if we all end up unclothed at the same time, the whole point of the game is lost.'

Lottie mopped her brow and said: 'Well, you're right there, but it's so warm that I propose we agree to call the game drawn so we can all get undressed and cool ourselves off in the water. Does everyone agree?'

'Absolutely,' Bibi and I concurred enthusiastically and though I could see that Bertolt was nervous, he also mumbled his acceptance as he unhooked the belt of his trousers. He had only his trousers and underpants to take off whilst I had only lost my shoes and socks in the game, but I was already in the buff whilst he was still gingerly pulling his trousers from his legs as he sat on his towel.

My cock was sticking up uninhibitedly against my belly as I watched Bibi shuck off her clothes. It ached for release when she shook her hair free and the silky blonde strands flowed down to her shoulders.

Then she hiked up her short chemise over her shoulders, showing off to best advantage her high thrusting breasts which, if slightly smaller than Lottie's, looked just as rounded and soft and were capped by rich rosebud nipples which pointed out impudently from the centre of her small circled areolae. I gulped hard as Bibi wriggled out of her knickers. My eyes swept over her smooth flat belly and the fluffy flaxen muff which nestled between her legs.

Now, I may have been mistaken, but I was convinced that she deliberately flaunted the firm dimpled cheeks of her exquisitely formed bottom as she walked slowly down the bank to the side of the stream and called out: 'I say, everyone, the water is quite deep here. Who's coming in with me?'

'I will,' cried out Lottie and she ran down the bank to hold hands with her friend. Together the naked girls ran into the stream and caused a thousand bright shards of liquid sunlight to dance a frantic jig on the surface of the ice-blue water which till then had shimmered as still as a millpond at the break of dawn.

Bertolt and I looked on in awe as the two girls shrieked so loudly with laughter as they splashed each other with water that I thought that the noise would wake Carl. However, when I glanced back at my friend, I saw that he was still fast asleep, and then Lottie called out to us: 'Boys! Would one of you be a dear and pass me my black bag?'

'I'll get it for you,' I shouted back for I was standing only some ten metres away from her towel. Quite forgetting my bad ankle, I covered the short distance in a few swift strides and grabbed hold of the bag. With my stiff cock still standing vertically upwards and pulsing away like crazy, I ran down to the side of the stream where, instead of just taking the proferred bag, Lottie took hold of my outstretched wrist and pulled me towards her until the water was half-way up my shins.

'I'm glad to see that your ankle has recovered,' Lottie grinned as she took the bag from me and rummaged around inside it while she looked at my swollen shaft. She went on: 'And there doesn't seem to be much wrong with your prick either, young man.'

I was sure that I was going to be invited to join them and I could feel some pre-cum ooze out of my knob as Lottie took out something from her bag which she passed back to me, asking me to put it back on her towel. But it was only when I stepped back that I saw that what she had taken out of her bag was a thick wooden tube which had apparently been carved in the shape of a stiff penis, complete with a rounded ridged knob.

Truly, neither Bertolt nor myself had any idea that this curious object was a ladies' comforter, for this was the first dildo we had ever seen, although we soon understood its purpose as the girls came out of the water with their arms entwined around each other's waists. The two of us both watched goggle-eyed as, after shaking most of the water off her arms and legs, Bibi sprawled down on her back on her towel with her legs wide apart whilst Lottie knelt between them. I caught a quick glimpse of Bibi's pink pussy lips before Lottie slid down onto her elbows and placed her face in front of Bibi's open cunney, the fingers of her left hand playing around in the silky saffron pussy hair whilst in her right hand she clutched the dildo.

'Ooooh! Ooooh! Ooooh!' wailed Bibi in delicious agony as Lottie rubbed the side of this imitation cock up and down her pouting crack. 'Be careful, Lottie, or I'll spend all over your nice new toy.'

'But I *want* you to spend, darling,' answered Lottie in a husky voice as she turned herself deftly round to face Bibi's feet and then moved her body upwards to thrust her bare backside in Bibi's face. 'And I'd love you to finish me off at the same time, there's a love.'

Even though I had reservations as to the truth of this statement, Bertolt insisted afterwards that he knew all about tribadism *[lesbian behaviour – Editor]* but *I* was utterly astonished when Bibi rubbed her hand between Lottie's bum cheeks whilst her partner bent down and started to lick the satiny surface of Bibi's thighs, coating them with long, loving swathes of moisture.

Bibi began to pant with delight as Lottie now tickled her cunney lips with the dildo, manipulating the wooden cock with relentless skill around the golden hair of Bibi's sweet pussy, teasing the coltish blonde to distraction until, with a wicked giggle, she briefly inserted the knob-end of the dildo into Bibi's yearning love channel before whipping it out again.

This set Bibi into a *real* frenzy and, holding my painfully throbbing tool in my fist, I moved round to see her cup the globes of Lottie's delectable bottom, parting them and working the tip of her little finger inside her arsehole, an action which provoked delighted cries of gratitude from her bosom friend. Bibi took out her finger, lifting her bum and wantonly pressing her mouth against the dripping lips of Lottie's cunt, clearly probing her slit with her tongue. And, as she did so, Bibi raised her straining, slender legs and clamped her thighs around Lottie's head as the other girl repaid the compliment by licking out Bibi's pussy in exactly the same way.

The naughty pair sighed and groaned as they writhed in this tribadic *soixante-neuf*, playfully tonguing each other's cunnies to the unbearable excitement of Bertolt and myself.

Indeed, Bertolt could no longer contain himself and began tugging on his thick boner which responded almost immediately by squirting out a fountain of frothy seed that spattered all over Lottie's shoulders. Now I myself could no longer hold back and followed suit, but I was careful to aim my ejaculation away from the two girls who were still threshing around in great ardour, totally oblivious to the fact that they were being watched by two masturbating boys.

'H-a-a-r! I'm coming, Lottie, I'm cumming!' gasped Bibi and Lottie now replaced her lips with the dildo, sliding it quickly in and out of Bibi's cunt until she screamed out her excitement as a delirium of ecstatic joy spread from her pussy to every fibre of her body in a gigantic peak of orgasmic lust. Bibi's head fell back and she lay still for a while. Then she repaid her sweet tormentor by nuzzling her lips back between Lottie's puffy pussy lips which I knew were now oozing love juice. Although I could not actually see Bibi's tongue darting in and out of Lottie's hairy quim, a shudder of excitement slid through me as the afternoon air grew scented with the heady aroma of raw sex.

Then I heard Lottie howl with joy as she climaxed copiously in thrilling waves of pure pleasure. The raunchy girls lay panting with exhaustion as they slowly recovered their composure. My cock now started to thicken up again and I began to slide my fist up and down my stiffening shaft. But then Lottie looked up and called out: 'Johann, leave your prick alone. I'm sure *we* have better use for it.'

I was nonplussed by this request but, trembling with nervousness, I somehow managed to propel myself towards the two tribades. I stopped a foot or so away and Lottie took my hot smooth shaft in her hand, saying lightly: 'I suppose you're too young ever to have used this impressive tool for *real* fucking, aren't you?'

'Oh no I'm not,' I said stoutly. 'And I would dearly love the chance to show you how good I am at it.'

'Now, now, Johann, remember the old saying about pride coming before a fall,' warned Lottie as she continued to stroke my twitching todger. 'Still, it would be fun to see if you really can translate those bold words into action.

'Bibi, I have a notion that Johann would love to fuck you rather than me,' she went on thoughtfully as she released my quivering cock. 'Would you like to oblige him?'

'I would love to, but my cunney is rather tender after being stretched by your dildo.' Bibi answered with regret. She paused for a moment and then she said with a smile: 'But I would have no objection to Johann going up my arse. His tool isn't too thick but it's of a good length for bum fucking.'

I wasn't too sure whether or not to take this as a compliment, but then Bibi replaced Lottie's hand with her own soft fingers which glided firmly around my shaft. She said: 'Don't be scared if you haven't fucked this way before, Johann. I know you'll really enjoy sheathing your cock inside my bottom. Lottie will explain how you should go about it.'

With that she turned over onto her hands and knees, pushing out the full, pale *rondeurs* of her superb backside to give me a better view of her wrinkled little rear dimple. Then Lottie bent down and washed my twitching tool with her saliva before taking my shaft in her hand and guiding my knob into the cleft between the delectably rounded cheeks of Bibi's bottom.

Despite this encouragement, I hesitated to push forward for I was genuinely concerned that sliding my helmet into the tiny orifice would hurt the lovely lass. But once Bibi felt the tip of my knob pressing against the ring of her anus, she whimpered with excitement and deftly shifted herself backwards to engulf my fleshy truncheon, inch by inch.

This erotic stimulation sent shivers of ecstasy coursing through my body as I felt the moistened bell-end enter the narrow passage of Bibi's bum-hole. The aroused girl continued to move herself backwards until she was fully impaled on my prick. Then she began to ride my throbbing tool in the most deliciously sensual way for I could see the sensual movements of her buttocks and the stretching of her anus by my cock as she slid backwards and forwards on my delighted chopper.

The blissful smile on Bibi's face when she turned her head round to blow me a kiss showed that she was enjoying this lusty bum-fuck as much as me. I cupped her creamy breasts and squeezed the jouncy globes as my cock bucked and bounced inside the tight sheath of Bibi's arse as if spring-loaded. It now plunged to and fro quite easily when Bibi reached back and spread her cheeks still wider, jerking her bottom in time with my thrusting shaft.

We soon approached the highest peaks of erotic ecstasy and spent together in perfect accord. When the first spurts of spunk shot out of my cock, Bibi's anus constricted and milked my pulsating penis in the most thrilling fashion as I exploded into her.

Bibi purred contentedly as she slid forward onto her tummy for a rest, but when I pulled out my still semi-stiff shaft from her bottom, Lottie made a grab for my tool and said gleefully: 'What a nice, meaty prick! Well now, Johann, I'd like to see how much spunk you have left in your balls, you randy young scamp!'

She began to fist my cock in her hand, rubbing it up and down until it stood up as proudly as before. Naturally, these lascivious scenes had thrilled Bertolt, who waddled forward, sliding his hand up and down his renewed immense erection. Lottie gobbled his knob hungrily into her mouth and began to suck his shaft with great gusto whilst she continued to masturbate me. She lapped at his smooth wide helmet, savouring to the full the salty taste of his cock as Bertolt thrust his slippery shaft deeper into her mouth. Lottie helped him by sliding her lips as far down his cock as she could until his wiry pubic hair tickled her sweet little nose. Bertolt groaned as he shot his load and Lottie swallowed his copious emission in great gulps, pulling him hard into her mouth as he jetted the spunky contents of his big balls right down her eager throat. She sucked on his cock until it was completely drained and began to shrink back to its normal size. He withdrew his flaccid shaft from between her lips.

All the time, Lottie had been fiercely rubbing my cock. Now that Bertolt had pulled out of her mouth, she lost no time in sucking my prick into this vacant space. I moaned with almost unbearable pleasure when Bibi joined in, clambering onto her hands and knees and starting to lick behind my tightening balls. This quickly brought the boiling sperm shooting up from my scrotum and I drenched Lottie's mouth with a second libation of sticky seed which she let slide down her throat with a well-practised ease.

I do believe these insatiable hot-blooded girls would have liked to go on playing with our cocks, but they could see that their young male companions were now totally exhausted. Instead, the four of us lay entwined in each other's arms, Bibi and Lottie letting their hands wander all over our bodies whilst Bertolt and I slumped down, our chests heaving whilst we recovered from our exertions.

The name of the silly fellow who said that women are the weaker sex escapes me, but that lubricious afternoon was the first of many experiences which for me totally disproved this argument. Oh, I grant you that, by and large, the human male is usually bigger and therefore better suited to hard physical work such as coal-mining or laying down miles of railway tracks. But women of the lower classes also undertake tremendous amounts of unsung labour every day, dragging around heavy loads ranging from sacks of potatoes to small children, often after working all day in a factory. And in the evenings, whilst their husbands drown their sorrows in the taverns after eating the meals prepared by their wives, it is these same women who stay at home looking after their offspring.

Truly, a woman's work is never done. With these words, dear reader, I wish to confirm that, after being involved with many women in intimate relationships (admittedly some of short duration but there have also been others such as those with Princess Marussia of Samarkand and Lady Heather Southgate of London which have lasted many years), I have some knowledge of the female sex and I make no secret of my firm support for female suffrage and for the so-called 'wild women' who are currently agitating for this right in Great Britain. Lord Patrick Uxbridge and others of his ilk may deride these ladies as "females who have failed in their rightful physical and mental development" but, in my humble opinion, men have nothing to fear and everything to gain from living in a society based upon the principles of sexual equality.

Eh bien, j'y suis, j'y reste! Forgive my digression, but where else can I ride my hobby-horse if not in the pages of my own autobiography?

To return to the idyllic scene on the banks of the brook at

the bottom of the Hildebrands' garden, at Lottie's suggestion we refreshed ourselves by another dip in the water. Then, after drying ourselves, we decided to get dressed for, though the sun was still blazing down, there was always the possibility of someone coming down from the house and discovering us *in flagrante delicto*.

Shortly afterwards Carl woke up and, not surprisingly, announced that he had a rather bad headache. 'You drank too much champagne, you silly boy, said Bertolt unsympathetically. 'I suggest you go back to the house and rest there out of the sun until you feel better.'

Carl nodded his head and after he gingerly walked away, I threw a pebble into the water and watched the ripples spread out across the silvery surface. I cleared my throat and said timidly to Lottie: 'I know I'm being inquisitive, but may I ask you a very personal question?'

'Of course you may,' she replied gaily and, before I could continue, she sat down next to me and went on: 'Let me guess what it is. I know, you would like to know about my first fuck. Am I right?'

I blushed furiously as I nodded my head silently and Lottie chuckled: 'Oh, don't feel embarrassed, I know how boys love hearing naughty anecdotes and, as I rather enjoy telling them, I'm more than happy to oblige!'

Bibi and Bertolt sat down by Lottie to listen to her story which she began by confessing to us that she had always been attracted to Helmut, a handsome friend of one of her brothers, who often stayed for long week-ends at their house in Linz.

'I was so pleased that Helmut would be at our house for my sixteenth birthday party, continued Lottie with a smile. 'It was not a huge affair and only a few friends from the town had been invited. If I say so myself, I looked rather fetching in a new dress Frau Drucker had made for me. It was an evening gown with a far more daring *décolletage [a low-cut neckline – Editor]* style than my Mama would have wished. Indeed, she had insisted that it should be trimmed with lace, but before I came downstairs for dinner, I took off the dress and unpicked the fringe, and to my satisfaction, when I slipped the dress back on, the cleft between my breasts was now clearly visible – and when I leaned forward I could see the swell of my bosom in the mirror. With a sigh, I closed my eyes and lightly passed my fingertips over my nipples whilst I thought how heavenly it would be to have Helmut Wesolowski's strong hands cupped round my breasts whilst we exchanged the most passionate of kisses.

'It sounds dreadfully boastful, but I know that my dress caused a stir amongst the male guests! There was no dancing after dinner but we played parlour games and I believe that everyone enjoyed a most pleasant evening. At midnight the guests left and we all went upstairs to bed. However, I was still wide awake from all the excitement and so I decided to tip-toe downstairs to the drawing-room and pick up a novel that I had been reading earlier in the day to continue in bed.

'No one seemed to be around, although the lights were burning, but this was not surprising because Schmidt, our butler, never put out the lights until the living rooms were tidied up ready for the morning. So I was not alarmed when I heard someone moving around in the drawing-room, but my heart began to beat faster after I opened the door to see none other than Helmut sitting in an armchair reading a book.

' "Hello Helmut, that must be an interesting book to make you burn the midnight oil," I said and he smiled as he rose from his chair and replied: "I'm not reading Professor Barber's *Advanced Economics* for fun, Lottie.

The truth is that I have so much swotting to do for the University entrance examinations this summer that I have set myself a target of studying for an hour a night every night without fail till the end of May."

' "Gosh, have you really?" I said as I sat on the arm of his chair and leaned forward to look at the graphs and mathematical equations on the open pages of Helmut's book. Of course, I knew full well that this would show off my breasts to him and I was rewarded by a sharp intake of breath from Helmut whose eyes had obviously strayed down to my barely covered titties. He closed the book sharply and said thickly: "*Mein Gott*, Lottie, I can remember when your chest was as flat as mine when I used to see you go out for a morning trot round the park on your pony."

' "Can you, Helmut?" I said softly. "Well, that was some time ago. I'm sixteen years old now and a fully developed young woman." His handsome face betrayed his struggle to keep his composure as I deliberately leaned forward again to expose my snowy-white breasts to his gaze.

'He said nothing, but I could see that he had been affected by my brazen behaviour. I moved off my perch and glided to the sideboard as I said: "It's too late for work, Helmut. Now, my brother told me that you are eighteen in two weeks' time so let's have a nightcap to celebrate our birthdays. Isn't that a good idea?"

'Helmet smiled boyishly and said: "It's an absolutely splendid idea, Lottie. I'll have a small kummel, *[a caraway-seed liqueur extremely popular in Central and Eastern Europe – Editor]* please."

'I poured out two glasses and took them over to the sofa, so that Helmut had to come over and sit there with me. We sat down together, clinked glasses and wished each other a happy birthday. For a while we talked idly of this and that, although I knew that Helmut was simply bursting to take me in his arms. Clearly, he needed some encouragement so, putting down my glass, I moved my hand up to his shoulder and let it rest there.

'As I had guessed, this did the trick! For a moment he looked steadily at me with his soft brown eyes and then slowly he drew my face closer to his and kissed me full on the lips. A surge of delight coursed through my veins and I responded eagerly as we embraced, but then he drew back and, almost choking with emotion, he breathed: "My darling girl, I have an overwhelming desire to make love to you."

'I kissed his flushed cheek and whispered: "And I have a similar desire to make love to you! Why have you not told me this before?"

' "Because you are the sister of one of my closest chums and, in any case, I would be a bounder to take advantage of a fifteen-year-old girl."

' "Your candour does you credit, but I am not ignorant of *l'art de faire l'amour*," I smiled, an answer which was true as far it went, although I knew full well that it gave the impression that I had already made love when in fact I had only ever "petted" with Gerhardt, our neighbour's son who was only three months older than me, and the furthest I had allowed him to go was to let him pull down my knickers and slide his hand under my skirt to frig my pussy with his fingers whilst I rubbed his cock which he had taken out of his trousers.

'Helmut's hands slid gently down my arms whilst he positioned me to receive a further intimate embrace. Then his tongue sank inside my mouth and I felt his fingers close gently over my bosom. Then I gasped as his hands lifted out my bare breasts from their scanty covering and I purred with pleasure as he toyed with them, tracing circles around my hardening nipples with his fingertips and then rubbing them against the palms of his hands until the darling tip-tops stood up in salute like small red bullets.

'Soon he was passing his lips over my pert titties, kissing and sucking my nipples so sensually that soon my pussy began to moisten. True, I was inexperienced but, as he was later to confirm, Helmut had been regularly fucking his second cousin Eva since he was only fourteen years old. I was like putty in the hands of a master builder as he leaned down to caress my trembling knee.

'Of course I knew what was in Helmut's mind, but I made no attempt to stop the handsome boy as his hand worked its way up my thigh and a strangled cry of exultation escaped from his lips when he realized that I had taken off my knickers and his fingers enmeshed themselves inside my silky thatch of pussy hair.

' "Helmut, did you know that the hair of my pussy bush is exactly the same colour as the hair on my head?" I said sweetly and smiled when he panted: "I'd love to see that for myself."

' "Then you shall, my dear," I breathed in his ear whilst I wriggled out of his arms, deliberately letting my hand brush against the prominent bulge which was tenting out in the lap of his trousers as I pulled the nightgown over my head. This was the very first time that I had ever exposed my naked body to a man and, feeling very wicked, I draped myself across Helmut on the sofa, my pussy aching with desire. Like a man possessed, he began to tear off his clothes.

'His slim, youthful frame glistened in the lambent glow of the gas lamps and my heart skipped a beat as I gazed at his muscular shoulders, wide chest and on down to the base of his belly where his cock bobbed up like a thick, curved scimitar. Any inhibitions I might have had about surrendering my virginity fled from my mind as I reached out and encircled his warm, pulsing shaft with my fingers. Although I had never kissed a cock before, I leaned down and licked up a blob of pre-cum which had already formed around the tiny "eye" of the beautiful pink crown. Then I stretched myself out on the sofa and Helmut knelt alongside me, fervently kissing my breasts and belly – and when he pressed his lips in my pussy hair, I lovingly clutched his head, moaning my approval and urging him on, for when I felt his tongue run down my crack the sensations were so divine that I nearly screamed with unalloyed delight.

'Helmut carried on this delicious sucking of my cunney for a while and when he began nibbling on my clitty, it began to fairly tingle with excitement. Then he raised his head and, with a sensual smile playing about his lips, he declared gallantly: "My sweet girl, I could feast on your pussy all night, but of course I would far rather make love to you with my penis. However, if you would prefer me just to bring you off with my fingers and tongue, just say so and you know that I will respect your wishes."

' "Darling, I *want* you to fuck me," I breathed and slid my arms under his shoulders to heave him up over me until I could see his stiff cock hovering between my thighs. To his credit, even in this highly-charged stage Helmut dragged himself back from the point of no return and panted through gritted teeth: "Oh Lottie, you are so delectable that I am dying to fuck you, but are you *quite* certain that I should carry on? Say something now if you want me to stop because I can scarcely hold back as it is and in a few seconds it will be too late to step back. But if I do continue, I promise to be careful not to spend inside you."

' "I want you to fuck me, Helmut," I repeated softly.

"*And* I want to feel you shoot off your spunk-flood inside my cunney. It will be my time of the month in two or three days' time so there is hardly any risk in your doing so."

'I laid my head back and parted my thighs wide as I watched Helmut slide his hand around his thick shaft and position the tip of his knob between my yielding pussy lips. He pushed forward gently and I gave a huge sigh of joy as I felt the ridge of his helmet scrape past the folds of my sensitive inner love lips.

' "Ooooh!" I gasped as the first prick ever to enter the tight notch of my love funnel entered my virgin hole. Thinking he was causing me some pain, dear Helmut instantly pulled back, but I giggled and muttered that this was far from the case! "Don't stop! Don't stop!" I urged him and so he began to push his knob in and out of my quim at a slightly quicker pace.

' "You're sure I'm not hurting you?" he enquired anxiously. I shook my head and assured him that I was greatly enjoying this wonderful experience. In truth, there had been an initial slight discomfort at the very commencement of this first fuck, but this soon passed. My hymen had broken long ago, due perhaps to my energetic bouncing up and down on the saddle whilst riding my pony or more probably to the frigging I had practised with my fingers and the india-rubber dildo I secretly purchased from a seedy stall in the Naschmarkt. *[A famous Saturday flea market in Kettenbruckengasse still in existence today – Editor.]*

'Anyhow, for whatever reason, I experienced no pain as Helmut's proud prick rammed faster and deeper into my squelchy slit. But I shall never forget the shivers of ecstasy that swept through my body whilst his thick prick scythed in and out of my tight little notch! So much so, indeed, that when he cunningly opened my love lips wider by frigging me with the mushroom dome of his helmet, I could not help bursting out: "Oh! Oh! I want much more than just your helmet, Helmut! Shove it all in! Push in further, I need more of your king cock! Ohhhhh!"

'With wanton upward jerks of my hips, I eagerly met each of his powerful thrusts – and this was such a delightful engagement that I wanted to keep Helmut's enormous truncheon inside my sopping channel of love. So on his next forward thrust when our pubic hairs mashed together and every last inch of his superb shaft was sheathed inside me, I closed my thighs and trapped his trembling tool fairly and squarely inside my cunt. Helmut could not really move his cock forwards or backwards because the muscles of my cunney were gripping his shaft so firmly, but I ground my hips round, massaging his palpitating prick whilst dribbles of love juice now began to trickle out of my cunt and seep into the cushion which was underneath my bottom.

'Now he grasped my bum cheeks convulsively and I slightly eased the pressure of my cuntal grip around his prick which enabled Helmut to begin driving in and out at a wild speed. My pussy exploded into a most delicious spend as Helmut's jerking cock gave a final throb and he jetted a torrent of hot creamy spunk inside me. I pushed my pussy up against him, burying his twitching todger even deeper so that all the wonderful white froth bathed the inner walls of my quim and he pumped away until his cock had been drained of every last drop of jism and his thrusts slowed to a halt. Panting heavily, he rolled off me and we lay gasping for breath as we gradually recovered our senses.'

There was a dreamy look in her eyes as Lottie paused for breath and then, looking at my rampant prick which I had almost unconsciously frigged up to a throbbing stand during her raunchy tale, she muttered: 'Goodness me, just thinking about Helmut's gorgeous cock makes my pussy so wet! Still, that's a fine beefy shaft you have there, Johann. How about slipping it into my snatch? Does that appeal to you?'

'Yes, very much,' I answered immediately, and in a trice I was on top of the luscious girl, squeezing her firm breasts, rubbing up the tawny nipples against my palms to make them rise up like engorged little nubs whilst Lottie guided my throbbing young cock into her yearning cunney. Then she wrapped her arms and legs around me and urged me to make it 'hard and fast, Johann – ram your boner into my juicy cunt, you randy young devil!'

I responded excitedly as Lottie opened her legs wide, drew them up and back and clamped her feet around my ribs as I pistoned my prick in and out of her soaking slit. This erotic spectacle was too much for Bertolt (who may well have been miffed that Lottie had not asked *him* to satisfy her needs) who was tugging his hand up and down his own boner.

'Bertolt, come over here and I'll suck you off,' cried Bibi and his face lit up as he knelt down next to her. Without further ado she pulled in his prick between her lips, laving his pole with her tongue as she sucked noisily on her fleshy lollipop.

The sight of the blonde girl palating Bertolt's prick sent me over the top and, with a yelp of happiness, Lottie achieved her spend just as I drenched her cunt with a flood of sticky seed. Simultaneously I saw Bertolt's tight bum cheeks jerk as he thrust his hips forward and ejaculated a copious emission of spunk down Bibi's throat. She swallowed this creamy libation eagerly, milking his cock of the last drops of his salty masculine essence.

'We had better be getting back for tea before someone comes down to fetch us,' Bertolt observed sensibly as he and I towelled off the beads of perspiration from our bodies. We agreed that he was right and, after hastily throwing on our clothes, we set out for the house. Sure enough, we had only walked some fifty metres when Doctor Hildebrand appeared and said genially: 'Ah, there you all are! Good, I'm glad you're ready to return because tea will be served in ten minutes.'

He turned to the girls and added: 'Taking some light refreshment at this hour of the day is a habit my wife and I have copied from our English friends. Myself, I don't drink tea but Carl and my wife now prefer this beverage to coffee. Talking of Carl, he seems to be rather under the weather. If I didn't know he had been with you since lunch time, I would have diagnosed a hangover.'

We smiled to ourselves but of course we did not "shop" Bertolt to his father who might have been very cross had he known that not only would his diagnosis of Carl's condition have been correct but the root cause had been two bottles of his own best Château Aigin champagne!

By the time the girls left us at about six o'clock, Carl had fully recovered from his hangover, although when I informed him what had taken place whilst he was sleeping off the effects of too much Buck's Fizz, my best chum demanded to know why I hadn't woken him up so that he could have joined in the fun!

'Surely you must have realized that I would have given anything to have been sucked off by either of those jolly girls,' he complained whilst we changed our clothes for dinner.

I shrugged my shoulders and replied: 'I'm sorry, Carl, but you were out like a light and even if I *had* succeeded in waking you up, I really don't believe you would have been in any fit state to participate in the orgy. Let's face it, you had drunk so much that the odds, are you wouldn't have been able to get a hard-on – which would have been terribly frustrating both for you and the girls!'

Nevertheless, I could quite appreciate why Carl was still feeling aggrieved when we went downstairs for dinner, though I permitted myself a smile when I noticed that he refused his father's offer of a glass of wine with the excellent roast chicken which Frieda had cooked for us!

After dinner, Doctor Hildebrand played the piano for our entertainment and, whilst looking through a pile of his sheet music, I picked out the little Piano Sonata in C major by Mozart. Frau Hildebrand noticed my scanning the music and said: 'Johann, can you play this sonata? It is one of my favourite pieces out of all Mozart's music for the piano.'

'I learned it this year,' I admitted but shyly added: 'But I am sure that Doctor Hildebrand would play the sonata far better than I.'

'Nonsense!' rumbled her husband as he strode across and peered over my shoulder to scan the sheet of music. 'Johann, only recently Herr Klein, your music master, told me how he wished Carl would practise as diligently as you. Now this piece is hardly the most difficult of Mozart's works. You are probably aware that it was written for one of his pupils, albeit by a master who knows how to make significant music easy.'

Clearly there was to be no escape! But, to be honest, since my first lessons at the age of seven with Herr Klein, I have always enjoyed playing to an audience and my poor parents had to suffer interminable hours of listening to me play those tiresome little tunes for beginners. Therefore it was with only a feigned reluctance that I allowed myself to be persuaded to perform the short little sonatina. False modesty is as foolish as overweening pride, so I shall not flinch from stating that I have been blessed with a certain ability as far as playing the piano is concerned and the company heartily applauded my rendition of the lilting melody.

However, I was quickly brought down to earth when Doctor Hildebrand, a genuinely gifted pianist who had performed Schubert's Fantasia in F Minor Piano Duet with Prince Kochanski at a charity concert in Vienna, took my place on the stool and with deceptive ease played Mozart's hauntingly beautiful Sonata in D Major for us.

It had been a long day and after a while Carl and I retired upstairs to bed. We were both extremely tired (Carl from drinking and me from fucking!) and in no time at all we both fell into a deep sleep.

As it turned out, music was to play an important role in my life early the next morning! I was the first to wake and after letting out a huge yawn, I sat up to stretch out my arms. I felt totally refreshed and it occurred to me that a brisk early morning walk would be a good way to start the day. My ankle had fully recovered and the bruises were now fading away so I threw back the covers and was about to shake Carl awake when I noticed the clock on my bedside table showed it was only twenty-five minutes past six, even though the rays of the sun were already shining through the curtains.

So I slipped on a vest and a pair of running shorts and quietly letting myself out of the back door, I decided to jog down to the spot where only the previous afternoon I had enjoyed such a thrilling time with Bibi and Lottie – but as I approached the stream I heard the sound of someone splashing about in the water and then, to the tune of an old Pomeranian ditty, a familiar female voice happily sang out:

'Come visit our pussies down here in the town,
You'll find some of them fair and some of them brown.
If you want a good fuck then at six o' the clock,
Go down to the meadow and show us your cock.
Our bums may be wide but our cunnies are strong
And can take any thick prick if you'll shove it along!'

I stopped short in my tracks and, from behind the cover of a tree, I saw that the voice belonged to Sonia, who was sitting naked in the water, soaping herself with a flannel.

Now what was I to do – announce my arrival or quietly retreat from the scene? For sure, no gentleman would be so impolite as to stay hidden in such circumstances, and in the case of a more modest girl, the latter course would have been the only one open to me. On the other hand, Sonia – admittedly with my eager connivance – had already amused herself in the lewdest fashion with my stiff prick, and I decided that I was justified in opting to make my presence known to her.

So I stepped forward and walked towards her as I called out: 'Hi there, Sonia! Having an early morning dip?'

She was startled by this interruption for a moment, but then she looked up at me with a smile and said: 'Hello, Master Johann, what brings you down here at half-past six? Couldn't you sleep? Well, now you're here you could do me a big favour by washing my back for me.'

'With pleasure,' I said. Sonia knelt up and said as she threw the flannel to me: 'It would be easier if you came into the water. Don't worry about drying yourself afterwards as I've a pile of towels here which are going to the laundry after breakfast.'

What a change had occurred in my attitude since the start of this astonishing vacation. Before setting out for Stettin, I would have been embarrassed even to take off my shirt in front of a girl. But now I didn't think twice about pulling off my clothes and exposing my naked body in front of Sonia – and I am not ashamed to state that I made no attempt to hide my erect cock from her gaze, for naturally it had begun thickening up at the first sight of her luscious nudity.

Sonia passed me the flannel cloth. I thoroughly soaped the creamy flawless skin of her back and then she dunked herself down in the water to wash off the foamy lather. Then she swung herself over and rose up on her knees to face me and I let out an involuntary gasp of sheer wonder as I drank in the voluptuous curves of her gorgeous soft body.

Gott in Himmel, I shall never forget how her bare breasts jiggled so enticingly as Sonia squeezed out the remaining soap from the flannel. The sensual girl giggled softly when she saw my eyes were riveted on her large tawny titties. With her forefinger she pointed at the knob of my upright shaft which was bobbing about in the water and remarked: 'I hardly need a police detective to tell me what you would like to do now.'

'No, I don't suppose you do,' I said huskily as I followed her out of the water onto the bank. She wrapped herself up in a bath towel and gave a smaller one to me. It didn't take long to dry ourselves in the warm morning air and then, with my fingers crossed, I watched Sonia spread out her large blue towel on the ground. She sat herself down upon it and invited me to sit next to her, saying: 'So how about joining me for ten minutes, Master Johann? I can see from the state of your stiffie that you're bursting to touch my titties!'

Sonia made a pillow of the remaining towels and stretched back languidly whilst I knelt down and massaged her lovely breasts as she purred with pleasure. Taking hold of my hand and pressing it against her taut nipples, she said encouragingly: 'Well, go on, Johann, suck my stalky nips!'

I could scarcely believe my luck but I took all the liberties I desired with her, kissing her pretty breasts, frigging her wet pussy with my fingers. In the meantime, she stroked my cock and pulled me over her. Thinking she wanted me to fuck her I moved myself downwards to insert my knob into her juicy crack, but she shook her head and said with obvious regret: 'Sorry, my dear, it's the wrong time of the month for that, but you can fuck my titties instead.'

With that she tugged my chopper forwards between her delectable breasts and I rubbed my shaft between the perfectly rounded globes whilst she cupped my balls in her hand. This was quite delicious, but before I spent, she moved my cock further upwards and brought the tip of my ruby helmet to her waiting lips. Now, as any red-blooded man will agree, having one's cock sucked can never be anything but a delightful experience. As my old English friend Lord Laurie of Islington commented to me only recently: 'Sucking his penis is the deepest, most sensitive way in which a woman can pay tribute to her lover's masculinity.'

Be that as it may, Sonia gave me the most exquisite tonguing, working her lips around my shaft, licking and lapping all the while as she traced long, lasciviously wet kisses on my quivering cock. The tip of her magic tongue now encircled my helmet, tickling and working its way round the tiny 'eye' on the top of the bulbous dome and her teeth scraped the tender skin so deliciously as she drew me in between her luscious lips.

'H-a-a-r-g-h!' I panted when she lowered her head and ran her tongue along the sensitive underside of my throbbing tool, sending almost unbearable waves of ecstasy sweeping through my entire frame. But every time the wicked minx sensed I was on the verge of a cum she stopped her sensual sucking, thus prolonging our mutual enjoyment which was for me was reaching new, previously unscaled heights of intensity.

Her head bobbed up and down over my twitching tool until a huge shudder of pleasure shot through me and a fountain of spunk shot out of my cock and slithered down Sonia's throat. The voluptuous young miss milked my prick with expert ease, sucking out every drop of my copious emission until my cock began to deflate.

I pulled my flaccid chopper out of her mouth and, as I rolled off her heaving torso, she smacked her lips and remarked: 'Well, I must say, Master Johann, your spunk has a less salty taste than Doctor Hildebrand's – though, of course, his prick is bigger than yours.'

I gaped at her in amazement, but she gave me a knowing wink and continued: 'Oh come on, *I* know that *you* know that Doctor Hildebrand has been shagging me whenever he gets the opportunity. I've very good eyesight and the other morning I saw you watching us fuck whilst you were perched up a tree in the garden. Did Carl or Bertolt tip you off or was it just by accident that you happened to have your binoculars with you?'

My cheeks flared crimson as I stammered: 'Please believe me, it was purely by chance, there was never any intention on my part to spy on you.'

'Of course I believe you,' she grinned teasingly as she flipped my flaccid shaft over onto my thigh. 'I would have been surprised if the boys had known about us because we've both done our best to hide the fact that their father has been giving me a good poke at least twice a week since April.'

'How did your affair begin?' I enquired curiously. It had just crossed my mind to wonder whether my own father had ever indulged with Angela or Elsie, our two pretty house-maids.

'It was just one of those things,' she shrugged. 'One morning I heard George, Doctor Hildebrand that is, singing in the bath. The rest of the family had gone to Salzburg the previous day to visit Frau Hildebrand's sister, but the master had some work he wanted to finish before joining them there later in the week. Now, I promise you that, though I had always been attracted to George, I did not plan to seduce him, but when I saw that he had left the bathroom door ajar, I could not resist the temptation to peep inside.

'So I put my head round the door and saw him standing with his back to me under the shower, turning his muscular body slowly round under the water jet as he lathered his hairy chest and flat belly. And yes, I confess that I took a long hard look at George's big cock which was swinging between his thighs and my pussy began to moisten with excitement when he soaped his shaft and it swelled up in his hand into the stiffest, thickest love truncheon you could ever wish to see!

'I leaned against the door and slipped my hand inside my blouse to rub my titties which had started to tingle as I watched George play with his prick, totally unaware that my eager eyes were watching his every move!'

My own shaft began to stir as Sonia gave a little chuckle and went on: 'Then and there I knew that I wanted him to fuck me, so I rushed back to my room, tore off all my clothes except for my tight white knickers and then ran back to the bathroom. I opened the door and there was George, standing on the bathmat stark naked and holding a towel with which he was wiping his face.

' "Sonia! What is the meaning of this?" he gasped, hastily draping the towel around his waist, though I had already noted with satisfaction how his cock still looked so meaty that he could not have brought himself off in the shower and would therefore be primed for action.

' "Do I *really* have to answer that question, Herr Doctor?" I said boldly, stepping forward and pushing my body up against him. I could feel his shaft rising when I pulled down the towel. His thick tool jumped up and stood high against his belly as I lifted my face towards his and sighed as he pressed his lips against mine. We exchanged a long and passionate kiss.

'We tasted and nibbled and probed each other's mouths as our bodies moved closer together. George offered no resistance when I put my hands on his shoulders and pushed them downwards. We sank to the floor where I thrust my titties in his face as I leaned back against the bath. He sucked them up wonderfully as I clamped my hand around his massive member and slid my fist up and down the warm, smooth shaft.

'He worked his hand inside my white cotton briefs and I shivered with delight as he slid the palm of his hand against my pussy lips before pulling down my knickers. Then he leaned down and pushed my knickers over my feet and, screwing the underwear up in his hand, he rubbed the cotton bundle up and down against my fluffy bush.

' "Oooh, that's nice," I gasped as he made a sheath for his forefinger with the wet material and frigged my cunney with it, wiggling his finger inside my crack until my knickers were saturated with love juice and then he eased them off his hand and frigged me with his bare fingers.

'I wriggled myself down to bring my face level with his cock and popped my lips over his knob, curling my tongue round the wide helmet, licking away whilst I clutched hold of his big hairy ballsack. He groaned with pleasure, but I desperately wanted him to fuck me so I jerked my head up and laid myself down on the floor. Parting my legs, I murmured that I would prefer to have his hot cock inside my juicy cunt.

'George did not have to be asked twice! He slid his fat knob between my pussy lips and immediately I began to spend as his cock crashed through into my tingling quim. We were both so highly charged that, after only a short while, his tool began to twitch and he filled my crack with such a flood of creamy spunk that his jism trickled out of my cunt and made a tiny sticky pool on the bathroom floor.

'We would both have loved to continue this glorious fuck, but George was already late for an appointment so we had to wait till later that evening when he returned from the surgery before we could enjoy another bout.'

By now my prick was once more standing as stiff as a poker but, *tempus fugit*, it was fast approaching seven o'clock and there was not enough time for Sonia even to bring me off with her hand. So we hurriedly pulled on our clothes and, with a painfully stiff cock, I walked back with her to the house. Luckily, our absence had not been noticed and of course I said nothing about Sonia's confession to Carl or Bertolt.

However, I must say that I looked on Doctor Hildebrand in a different light after this conversation with Sonia. It might not have been any of my business how he conducted his affairs, but even at this tender age, when I had only just begun the first of what were to be many excursions into bedrooms and boudoirs all over the world, I realised how foolish it was of Doctor Hildebrand to fuck one of his own housemaids. Moreover, it was somewhat *infra dig.* for him to poke her in his marital bed. Perhaps this sounds a trifle sanctimonious but, as several of my friends have found out to their cost, a wise man never fouls his own doorstep because infidelity often turns marriage into a powder keg with a short fuse!

Anyhow, this put me in a thoughtful mood as I tucked in to a hearty breakfast of boiled eggs and crusty bread rolls on which I slathered a generous helping of Frieda's tasty cherry jam and as I sipped my cup of coffee, Carl said to me: 'Johann, you're very quiet this morning. Have you anything on your mind?'

Well, it would have been most unkind to tell him what I had really been thinking about! So, thinking quickly, I blurted out how interesting I had found a recent article in the newspaper by Magda Seeler, a famous young actress and the daughter of the deputy mayor of Vienna, who wrote that it was time to change the role of women in society.

'I read that article, too,' said Frau Hildebrand. 'What she says is true enough, it's no wonder that there have been so few women writers, artists or political leaders. Throughout history women have been confined to unskilled roles. Why, it's only recently that women have been admitted to the medical faculty at the University!'

Doctor Hildebrand gave me a wink and grunted: 'Huh! You may call that progress, Katharine, but I'm damned if I do! There's enough competition as it is without hordes of female doctors coming onto the market.'

But before his wife could open her mouth to protest, he raised his arms in surrender and chuckled: 'Only joking, my love, only joking! Seriously, though, if Fräulein Seeler is demanding that women should be given the same opportunities as men, then naturally no sensible person could disagree with her. However, I think it would be wrong to disparage their work in the house. I'm not sure that I believe there would be a flowering of talent if women did not take charge of domestic affairs. Housework did not prevent those Englishwomen, the Brontë sisters, from producing their wonderful novels, and child-care is not a form of slavery which prevents women from sitting down to paint a picture or write a poem. Surely it is patronizing to women to say that our social patterns must be changed to accommodate their needs.'

He turned to his sons and ended: 'Well, don't you agree with me, lads?'

Now Bertolt and Carl had no hesitation in giving their support, but when the doctor put the same question to me, it was only because I didn't want him to think me impolite that I followed suit, even though I didn't fully concur with his line of argument.

Quite frankly, I couldn't see how having to undertake domestic chores – from having responsibility for running a complete household to undertaking simple tasks like washing clothes or polishing silver – gave any great scope for the mind to wander in a productive way, though I suppose that masculine poets, painters and writers have always had to shoulder the burden of how to make a living whilst pursuing their art.

On the other hand, I must say here that one of the reasons why women do not realize their full potential is the jealousy of other women. Too often, women who have found fame in the arts, sciences or what-have-you are wary of others of their sex. Perhaps this is because they have succeeded in a man's world and they want to keep it that way.

For example, I have heard that the chanteuse Babette, one of the most beautiful women in Paris who has earned an enormous sum during her season at the Moulin Rouge in addition to the expensive gifts lavished upon her by such wealthy admirers as King Edward VII of Great Britain, is supposed to be a veritable fiend to her female colleagues.

So maybe it was as well that Frau Hildebrand did not feel strongly enough about her husband's views to carry on with this discussion and she changed the course of the conversation by reminding the doctor that the coach he had ordered to take him to Stettin this morning would soon be at the door.

'Are you staying long in town, Father? I would like to come with you as I need to buy some more Collodian mixture.' *[A syrupy liquid of a solution of pyroxylin in ether and alcohol needed to coat the glass plate of the early cameras – Editor.]*

'Well, I promised to see old Dahrf, the rich shipowner we met last year at the Seligsohns',' replied Doctor Hildebrand, pulling out his watch from his waistcoat pocket. 'He has his own doctor, of course, but he wants me to examine someone in his family who has a medical problem about which he wants a second opinion. Well, I might be on my vacation, but it would be foolish to turn away a nice fat fee, especially as he has also invited me to luncheon at the best restaurant in Stettin!

'So I won't be able to give you a lift back till about three o'clock, Bertolt, though you can always hire a coachman at Hoffman's Livery Stables if you don't want to hang about waiting for me,' he concluded.

'Father, can Johann and I also come along?' asked Carl, and he turned to me and said: 'There's lots to see in Stettin. We can stroll around the harbour and look at the new Atlantic liner which will be launched by the Duchess of Hesse *[this lady was Alice, Queen Victoria's daughter, who married the Grand Duke of Hesse in 1864 – Editor]* next Thursday.'

'I don't see why not,' said Doctor Hildebrand who, unlike many high-class Viennese, made little attempt to bring up his sons in accordance with their station, although he did add that we should steer clear of the area where a number of low taverns had sprung up to cater for the dockers and shipyard workers and at lunch-time we should take some refreshment at a respectable inn away from the harbour.

'Don't take too much money with you, for the gypsies are in town and they are well-known for their skill as pickpockets,' he warned us. 'Carl, Herr Dahrf lives at number eleven Wollweberstrasse *[Woolweaver Street – Editor]*. I would like you and Johann to meet me there at three o'clock and we will go home together in my coach.'

When we arrived in the city, Bertolt alighted from the coach at Professor Zwaig's photographic store on the Kaiserstrasse and then Doctor Hildebrand dropped us off near the yard from where the huge new trans-Atlantic liner would soon be setting out for her maiden voyage. There were so many workers milling around – carpenters, joiners, riveters, *et cetera* – yet no one challenged us when we strolled through the gates of the shipyard and sat on the jetty watching all the activity around us.

Carl passed me an apple from the bag of fruit his mother had insisted we take with us to stave off the pangs of hunger and said thoughtfully: 'You know something, Johann, I've never really understood how iron ships keep afloat. After all, everyone knows that wood floats and metal sinks! So how do iron ships keep above water?'

My grasp of science was too shaky to answer his question, so I nudged him and pointed to our right where, some twenty metres away, an easel had been set up although there was no sign of an artist in the vicinity.

'He'll be back soon but let's see what the guy's put down on the canvas,' I suggested as I heaved myself to my feet. 'I suppose he's been commissioned to paint the new ship.'

Then I almost jumped out of my skin as a voice boomed from behind me: 'Absolutely right, young Johann, and I have to finish the picture so that Herr Dahrf can present it to the Duchess next Thursday.'

I swung round and there with a wide grin on his face was none other than Ludwig Gottlieb, the son of our neighbourhood friends back in Vienna! He was now in his early twenties and we had not seen each other since Ludwig left home to study at the University of Berlin eighteen months ago, but we recognized each other immediately and he clapped me on the shoulder and asked me how I came to be wandering around a shipyard in Stettin instead of going to Italy with my parents.

'I seem to remember they always spend this time of the year in Tuscany with the Marquis of Alba,' said Ludwig and so I introduced Carl and explained that I was on holiday with his family who owned a summer villa in the lovely countryside just outside the city.

'But what brings *you* here, Ludwig?' I enquired and he explained how, thanks to an uncle's friendship with the chairman of the Baltic Lloyd company for which the liner had been built, he had been invited to paint a commemorative picture of the launch of the S.S. *Alice*. 'That's the name of the ship, by the way, in honour of the Duchess.'

'You must come out and visit us,' said Carl, but Ludwig said: 'That's very kind of you, but I must finish this picture on time. I've only finished the preliminary sketches and I'm going to start work in earnest today. Truthfully, I'd rather you didn't stay and look over my shoulder when I begin, but I tell you what, why don't the pair of you take a walk round the harbour and meet me back here at one o'clock? It would be my pleasure to take you to lunch at an excellent café near here which serves the most delicious baked fish.'

We chorused our thanks and as we wandered off for a stroll I remarked to Carl: 'I'm rather surprised that your parents haven't mentioned anything about the Duchess coming to Stettin.'

He nodded his head in agreement and replied: 'You're right, it's very puzzling because they wouldn't want to miss an event like the launch of a new liner, it's always a big affair with a march by the local regiment of hussars *[elegantly dressed light cavalry – Editor]* and the town bands playing in the street.'

About half an hour later we came across Bertolt who was setting down his tripod in front of a battered old cargo-steamer flying the British flag and told him our news.

'How odd,' he frowned and then he snapped his fingers and went on: 'Wait a moment, I have it! Papa said he had an appointment with Herr Dahrf this morning about some medical matter. I bet he is trying to get seats in the directors' box for us next Thursday but isn't going to tell anyone until the last minute because he wants to give us all a big surprise.'

'Yes, that sounds just like Papa,' said Carl excitedly and I chipped in: 'Then we must be careful not to mention anything about the event as that would spoil the fun.'

After Bertolt had taken his photographs, I told him of our meeting with Ludwig Gottlieb and said that he was very welcome to join us, but Bertolt said somewhat mysteriously: 'Thank you, but I have to meet a friend at Professor Zwaig's shop. But I'll come home with you, so I'll see you at three o'clock outside Herr Dahrf's house on the Wollweberstrasse.'

So Carl and I left Bertolt to his private assignation and, after taking a pleasant walk during which we took in the sights and sounds of the bustling port, we returned to Ludwig who was bending down to slide his canvas away in a large leather case. As we approached he looked up and called out: 'Good timing, boys, I hope you're hungry because Frau Kuster is used to serving the longshoremen and after a hard morning's work, you can imagine that they pack away a big meal at lunch-time.'

The café was only a few minutes' walk away and, although quite a large establishment, it was almost full with workers from the shipyard and the only table Frau Kuster could offer us was right next to the kitchen door.

'I'm sorry I can't give you a better seat, Herr Ludwig, but we've been very busy today,' she apologized as we pulled out the roughly carved chairs. 'Still, you know the old saying, the nearer you are sitting to the pot, the better you'll eat!'

An attractive girl with a mass of light blonde hair served us a delicious meal of baked sea bass which we washed down with foaming jugs of beer. Then she served us plates of delicious apple pie and Ludwig smiled when he saw my eyes follow the waitress back to the kitchen. Giving me a gentle poke with his elbow, he chuckled: 'Rosa's a lovely girl, isn't she, Johann? I can see that you are growing up fast, but she is nineteen and take my word for it, she is too old for you in more ways than one.'

I wrinkled my brow and was about to ask Ludwig the meaning of this cryptic remark when Carl and I were startled to hear a loud yell coming from the kitchen above the noisy hubbub in the crowded café.

'Did you hear that?' I gasped as I began to rise from my seat, but Ludwig put his hand on my arm and smiled: 'Don't be alarmed, there is nothing to worry about. I should have warned you that sitting so close to the kitchen we might well hear such noises at around two o'clock.'

A second piercing shriek rent the air which surely must have been heard by other diners, yet to my astonishment no one except Carl and myself appeared to take the slightest bit of notice of the noise. I shook my head in disbelief and gasped: 'Is everyone here deaf? For heaven's sake, who is responsible for that dreadful racket?'

'Are you sure there's nothing to worry about?' asked Carl with an apprehensive look on his face, thinking no doubt of his father's warning to stay away from the inns around the docks as the sound of a third high-pitched screech floated through from the kitchen. 'It sounds to me as if some girl is being assaulted.'

'I don't see what's so funny about that,' he added indignantly when Ludwig threw back his head and burst out into peals of laughter. 'Oh, I'm sorry, I really am, but believe me, no one is getting assaulted, at least not in the way that you mean. No, what you can hear is Rosa enjoying her regular after-lunch fuck with the new young chef. She's quite a screamer, is Rosa, but the regulars here are used to it by now and nobody's really bothered by the sounds of a lusty young couple enjoying themselves.'

I looked at him in amazement and exclaimed: 'But doesn't Rosa know that everybody can hear her?'

Ludwig shrugged his shoulders. 'Oh yes, but she doesn't mind in the slightest,' he said carelessly. 'Nor does it bother Alfred who rather enjoys having people pop down and watch him on the job. Would you care to take a look for yourselves?'

'Yes, please,' said Carl eagerly and we rose quickly to our feet and followed Ludwig through the kitchen door and down a short flight of steps into the kitchen where Rosa was standing naked in front of a long wooden table, bending slightly forward with her arms outstretched and her fingers curled round the table edges. The quivering white globes of her bottom stuck out saucily and almost at once my cock started to thicken as I watched a slim young man pistoning his stiff shaft in and out of the cleft between the cheeks of Rosa's luscious backside. With every vigorous thrust he buried his glistening boner to the hilt, his heavy balls crashing against her wobbly rounded bum cheeks.

Rosa's plump backside slapped nicely against the chef's thighs as she fitted into the rhythm of his fucking and again she cried out with joy as his shaft see-sawed in and out of her crack. Reaching behind her, she caressed his wrinkled pink ballsack as she rocked to and fro, her head thrown back and her hair whipping from side to side as she called out: 'Yes! Yes! Yes! That's it, Alfred! I'm almost there!'

This spurred him on even more and, gripping Rosa's hips, he pulled her towards him with every inward thrust and pushed her away with each outward one. She wriggled her arse in a wild frenzy, rotating her hips to allow the young man's cock to ream out the inner nooks of her cunney. Then she threw back her head in total abandon and let out a final uninhibited whoop of passion as she achieved her orgasm and collapsed down onto the table. Alfred's climax followed only seconds later and his wiry torso stiffened perceptibly as, with an anguished hoarse cry, he made one final thrust forward and then pulled out his prick, spurting jet after jet of creamy jism over her luscious bottom.

'Note how Alfred made sure that he didn't spend inside her cunt because it's not the best time of the month for fucking without a French letter,' commented Ludwig whilst we watched Rosa hand Alfred a dishcloth to wipe his spunk from her bum cheeks.

In the meantime Frau Kuster came down the stairs carrying a large tray heaped up with plates which Ludwig gallantly insisted on taking from her, walking over to deposit the tray by the sink.

She gave him a grateful smile and said: 'Thank you, Herr Ludwig, there isn't any more that needs to be brought down right now. Well, I'm going back upstairs to have a cognac with a friend so would you be kind enough to tell Rosa that she must start clearing away in ten minutes?'

'With the greatest of pleasure,' he replied and with some surprise I noticed that Rosa was now sitting on the table, making no attempt to dress herself although Alfred was busily pulling on his clothes. When he had finished, he kissed her thighs and, after acknowledging our presence with a cheery wave of his hand, Alfred also took his leave through a back door into the courtyard.

'Where's he gone?' muttered Carl. Ludwig explained that Alfred now had to poke Frau Kuster's sister whose husband had been killed in a train accident in Leipzig three years before. The widow was greatly comforted by a weekly visit from the virile young man.

Then Ludwig turned to Rosa and gave her an affectionate kiss on her lips as he gently squeezed her lovely bare breasts which jiggled so invitingly in front of him.

She squealed in mock anger: 'Oooh, Ludwig Gottlieb,

you naughty man! How would you like it if I squeezed your cock?'

'I wouldn't mind at all,' he replied promptly and he took hold of her hand and rubbed it against the bulge between his thighs. Rosa giggled and proceeded to unbutton his trousers and pull out his swollen shaft which she cradled in her hands as she said: 'My word, your cock seems to get thicker every time I hold it.'

'That's because it can't wait to slide into your juicy notch,' growled Ludwig as he pulled down his trousers and underpants, but Rosa put a warning finger to his lips and said: 'Oh Ludwig, I'd love to feel your throbbing tool inside me, but you can't spend inside my cunney today. Let's wait till Friday when you can fuck me properly. But if you like, I'll suck you off.'

Ludwig cleared his throat and replied in a husky voice: 'Rosa, I'm sure that would be absolutely fabulous.'

Still holding his twitching truncheon in her hand, the sultry girl slowly slid off the table and went down on her knees in front of him, wrapping her free arm around his waist as she ran her wet tongue slowly under his hairy ballsack. This made Ludwig shiver all over as the beautiful girl kissed his bollocks whilst she gently rubbed her soft hand up and down his palpitating prick.

'H-a-a-r-g-h!' he groaned as with one hand Rosa grabbed his bottom and with the other held his cock and eased the crown between her generous red lips.

Then Ludwig gave a second deep groan as she sucked with uninhibited vigour on his mushroomed helmet which was now firmly jammed in her mouth. I could see Rosa teasing his rubicund knob, running the tip of her tongue around the ridge of the springy cap whilst she tenderly manipulated his balls through the wrinkled pink skin of his scrotum.

She purred with satisfaction when Ludwig began to jerk his hips and thrust his glistening wet chopper in and out of her mouth. She slurped away with unabashed delight on his cock and this exquisite sensation soon proved too much for Ludwig: he let out a moan of both frustration and delight as he felt himself being swept inexorably up to the pinnacle of pleasure.

'I'm going to shoot off,' he panted and when his blue-veined shaft began to tremble inside her mouth, Rosa realized that the moment of truth was only seconds away.

So she jammed her lips tightly over his cock as the first spurts of salty spunk splashed into her mouth and Ludwig's prick bucked uncontrollably as she held his shaft lightly between her teeth. His face contorted with effort as further gouts of jism hurtled out of his knob and Rosa smacked her lips as she swallowed his copious emission until he leaned back against the wall, exhausted from this invigorating exercise.

'Ooooh! You've made me so randy, you naughty boy!' she scolded him as she jumped back onto the table and rolled over onto her tummy to present us with a delicious view of her delectable rounded buttocks. 'As soon as you can, I want you to fuck my bottom – if the fancy takes you.'

Ludwig grinned and said: 'I'd love to, Rosa, but I'll need a little help to make my cock stiff again. Will you give me a helping hand?'

'Of course I will, dear,' she answered and then, turning her head towards the stairs where Carl and I were standing transfixed, she called out: 'Perhaps one of you young gentlemen will be good enough to give Ludwig the butterdish which you will find on the dresser.'

Carl almost tripped up over his feet in his haste to obey,

but he was rewarded with a smile from Rosa who lightly ran her hand across the tenting bulge in his trousers and a grateful pat on the back from Ludwig as he passed him the glass-lined dish. My chum was now so fired up that when he resumed his place next to me he tore open his fly buttons and started to frig his throbbing stiffie whilst we watched Ludwig dip his finger into the butter and smear it liberally into the crevice between Rosa's jiggling bum cheeks. Meanwhile, she took hold of his limp cock and flipped the flaccid organ up and down on her palm.

'H'm, this sad little cock looks like a suitable case for treatment,' she declared as she curled her long fingers around the shrunken shaft and began to fist her hand up and down it, rubbing Ludwig's prick at an ever brisker pace as she muttered lewdly: 'Come on, my dear, I'm sure you can rise to the occasion if you put your mind to it. Hurry up now, I want to feel your nice round helmet pushing its way between my bottom cheeks and then shooting a nice thick pressing of cock juice up my bum!'

This lascivious frigging soon produced the desired effect and my own tool began to throb wildly as I watched Ludwig's cock gradually rise up and swell into its former sturdy state, jutting out like an arrow ready to fly. Rosa gave his shaft a final squeeze and then took up a new position on the table, laying her arms flat and resting her head in her hands as she pushed her bottom up high in the air.

Ludwig stroked his pulsating prick and then coated it with butter before jumping up onto the table behind Rosa. He proceeded to guide his glowing knob firmly into the cleft between her voluptuous bum cheeks, the opening which was waiting to be invaded by his big cock.

'Oooh yes, go on,' she panted when she felt his knob-helmet pushing against her puckered arsehole and Ludwig pulled her buttocks outwards as he pushed his prick forward. He seemed to have little difficulty in easing his knob directly into the tight sheath of her back passage.

Once his cock was fully ensconced inside her bottom, Ludwig began to work his tool in and out of the tightly clinging orifice, heaving his whole body backwards and forwards, making Rosa's buttocks slap sensuously against his belly as the lascivious pair started to move in a quickening rhythm. As their motions became ever more frenzied, it seemed as though even Ludwig's swinging balls were being sucked into the luscious depths of the nubile girl's delicious *derrière*.

'Ahhh!' Carl gasped as a fountain of jism arced out of his knob and spattered on Ludwig's heaving backside and though up till now I had managed to keep my hands off my cock, I felt the seed rising unstoppably from my balls and I jerked open my flies just in time as the spunk hurtled out of my knob and gave Ludwig's arse a second spermy drenching.

Fortunately he was too far involved with Rosa to care overmuch about his wet bottom and I grabbed the dish-cloth that Alfred had used to wipe his spunk off Rosa's bum cheeks to dry my cock before passing it to Carl to mop his own shrinking shaft.

In front of us the lusty pair were working themselves up to the summit of erotic delight and Rosa was shrieking out her delight in a series of ear-piercing yells similar to those we had heard earlier on whilst Alfred had been fucking her doggie-style.

'Fuck my bum, you big-cocked boy! Yes, that's right, don't stop thrusting! Faster, faster, I know you have a gallon of spunk boiling up in your balls for me!' shouted out the lusty girl as she wriggled to and fro, opening and closing her bum-hole as she clenched and unclenched her snowy-white buttocks. Ludwig now leaned over her and fondled her lush breasts and firm titty-tips and from the way Rosa was waggling her bottom there was no doubt that she was thoroughly enjoying the experience of having his stiff shaft slewing in and out of the tight sheath of her back passage.

Ludwig continued to piston his prick in and out of her arse until, with a hoarse choking cry of fulfilment, he flooded her rear dimple with a flood of sticky spunk and Rosa squealed with happiness as they shuddered to a glorious mutual climax, falling forwards in a heap of tangled limbs.

The kitchen door opened and Frau Kuster returned clucking her tongue with annoyance. 'Rosa, must you really make such a noise when you're being fucked? Herr Beckenbauer and I can hardly hear ourselves speak. Anyhow, you must now get dressed because it's high time you started tackling the washing-up.'

Clearly the appearance of naked cocks in Frau Kuster's kitchen was not an unusual occurrence because she only threw us the briefest of glances before she continued: 'If you asked them nicely, perhaps these young gentlemen would assist you.'

Well, of course all three of us were only too pleased to help Rosa. Carl and I donned aprons and washed dishes whilst Rosa and Ludwig dried the plates and stacked them away. But after twenty minutes we had to take our leave in order to meet up with Doctor Hildebrand and Bertolt so, after thanking Ludwig for our delicious luncheon and Rosa for her all-embracing hospitality, we left the café and walked briskly back to the Wollweberstrasse as it was already almost three o'clock.

Ten minutes later we arrived at our rendezvous where Bertolt was standing at the side of the carriage. 'Oh, that's all right, I've only been here a couple of minutes myself,' he said mildly when we apologized for keeping him waiting. 'Papa left a note with the coachman for us to say that he has been unavoidably detained so we should go home by ourselves and tell Mama not to expect him back until dinner-time.'

'You two look a bit tired,' remarked Bertolt as we piled into the landaulet. 'Didn't Johann's friend take you somewhere nearby for lunch?'

'Yes, and you should have come with us as we had a smashing meal at Frau Kuster's café just off Danzig-strasse,' replied Carl. 'Did you find somewhere nice to eat?'

Bertolt shook his head and said: 'Not really, I only managed to grab a sausage and a glass of beer off one of the market stalls near the camera shop where something unexpected happened to me which turned out to be a damned sight better than a slap-up lunch!'

Carl and I looked at him curiously as he leaned back in his seat and chuckled happily to himself. Then he looked up at us and said: 'I'm dying to tell you about my lucky break but you chaps must swear that you won't let out a word to anyone about it.'

'You can trust us, Johann and I can keep a secret,' Carl assured his brother. 'Spill the beans, Bertolt: it sounds as if you had some very exciting adventure whilst we were feeding our faces.'

'I certainly did,' grinned Bertolt as he mopped his brow. 'And I enjoyed it so much that I'm no longer cross with you about filching that French magazine from my bedroom! Oh, come on, don't bother to deny it, no one else would rummage through my desk and all hell would have broken loose if by some fluke Mama or Papa had come across it! Anyhow, did you bring the magazine with you? I would rather like it back this evening because tomorrow afternoon I want to show the magazine to someone I think will enjoy looking at the photographs.'

'Okay, I'll give it to you as soon as we get home,' muttered Carl. To his relief the usually combative Bertolt did not harangue him further about the theft but continued to recount what had happened after he had alighted from the coach that morning.

He went on: 'As I told you, all I had in mind was to buy some collodian mixture at Professor Zwaig's shop and then take some pictures down at the harbour – but when I got to the shop, the Professor was just about to put up the shutters for the day. However, he opened up to let me make my purchase and then he informed me that he was closing the shop because he was giving a talk at a small hall nearby to members of the Stettin Camera Club and then spending the afternoon giving a seminar on various matters to more advanced students.

' "You may come and listen to my lecture if you like," said the Professor kindly. "I shall be talking about how best one can make photographs of classical studies which you might find of interest."

'I hesitated for a moment because, however interesting his discourse might be, the thought of spending a bright summer day cooped up indoors didn't really appeal. But gosh! Am I glad that I decided to accept his invitation!'

Now, although he had said that he had forgiven Carl for borrowing his erotic magazine without first asking permission, I thought it wise to keep Bertolt in a good mood, so I said flatteringly: 'Well, you're clearly very pleased that you took up the Professor's suggestion, so you can give yourself a pat on the back for taking the right decision. Frankly, most chaps wouldn't dream of spending any of their summer holidays listening to a lecture.'

'Thanks, but I don't deserve any plaudits for wanting to hear Professor Zwaig speak even though he warned me that there was a one mark entrance fee because he is one of the foremost photographic experts in the whole of Europe.

'Mind you, I will take *some* credit for taking advantage of the situation which arose after the Professor's talk,' he added with a gleam in his eye. 'But to return to my story: when we arrived at the hall there were already about one hundred gentlemen already seated and several more were standing at the back of the auditorium. For some reason, the Professor must have taken a shine to me, for he told me that I could take the empty seat at the side of the stage at the end of the front row which had been reserved for the Deputy Mayor who for some reason had been unable to come along. I was thinking how many keen photographers there must be in Stettin when Professor Zwaig started his lecture – but as soon as the lights dimmed and he began to screen a selection of his photographs on lantern slides, it quickly became apparent how he had attracted such a large audience and managed to keep their attention whilst he talked about the finer points of the art of photography.'

'Was he a witty speaker?' asked Carl and Bertolt smiled as he shook his head and replied: 'Not especially so, but to illustrate his lecture, the Professor showed hand-coloured studies of a beautiful girl whose pretty face was familiar to me. Now where had I seen her before? I thought to myself. Then I remembered that her name was Marguerite and that she had served me in the Professor's shop.

'At first, we were shown pictures of her dressed in all kinds of finery but then we were treated to a selection of slides of the girl in a series of classical poses, wearing little except some carefully placed muslin draperies, displayed as a nymph being ravished by Zeus or as *Diana Surprised by Actaeon*.

'I guessed correctly that Marguerite would soon remove even these wisps of material and, sure enough, the Professor illustrated the next section of his lecture on photographing the human form with pictures of Marguerite in the nude.'

'Gosh! Was she absolutely naked?' chortled Carl. 'Crikey, I bet you got a hard-on!'

Bertolt nodded and continued: 'I should say, and I'm damned sure every man in the audience did as well when the Professor put on the screen a nude pose of Marguerite looking at the camera with her back against the wall. Her pretty face was complemented by long strands of dark hair which fell over her shoulders and spilled over her breasts. She had her arms at her sides, making no attempt to hide the thatch of curly hair between her legs.

'There was dead silence in the hall whilst the Professor droned on about the importance of lighting to bring out skin tones, but he must have heard the collective sharp intake of breath when his assistant screened the next slide. It showed Marguerite facing the wall, bending slightly forward and pushing her gorgeous bum out at the camera!

'The chap next to me muttered: "*Mein Gott*, what a magnificent arse! I would give a hundred marks to slide my cock between those cheeks and bury it in her juicy cunt!"

'Well, I must say that I never thought for a moment that anyone, let alone myself, would have the opportunity to fuck this gorgeous girl, but at the end of the lecture (which was greeted by a storm of applause) the Professor answered a few questions and then the audience began to file out. However, I stayed and climbed onto the stage where the Professor had moved his lectern to one side and was now busying himself setting up a Liebermann Whole Plate Studio Camera.

'I asked if he was going to take any more photographs of Marguerite and he laughed: "No, Herman my lantern-slide projectionist and I are off to Graf von Frishschaur's house to repeat my lecture and give him and his friends a private view of my slides."

' "So why are you setting up a camera here?" I asked and he replied: "That is because Marguerite, the girl who posed for those slides, is a keen photographer herself and I promised her that she could use this camera until I return this afternoon. Ah, here she is now. Marguerite, my dear, come and meet Herr Bertolt Hildebrand."

'I turned round and there stood the ravishing girl dressed in an open-necked white linen blouse and a navy blue skirt. She had pinned up her tresses of silky dark hair and the sight of her twinkling brown eyes and pouting lips set my heart pounding at a fair old rate of knots.

' "Actually, we've met before at the shop," I said shyly and two delicious dimples appeared on her cheeks when she smiled and said: "Oh yes, I remember you, Herr Hildebrand. Don't you have a Zeiss Double Quarter Plate camera?'

' "That's right, and you commented on what a fine machine it was and I told you that it was a sixteenth birthday present from my Uncle Max," I said shyly, blushing furiously with nervousness.

'The Professor consulted his pocket-watch and said: 'My dears, I must be off. Marguerite, what time is young Richard supposed to meet you here?"

' "He should have been here by now," she replied with a hint of irritation. "I had the devil of a job persuading him to sit for me and I'm crossing my fingers that he isn't going to let me down."

' "Oh dear, I do hope that he won't," said the Professor as he walked away, leaving Marguerite and I alone in the hall. I looked at her enquiringly and she told me how she also enjoyed standing behind the camera as well as in front of it. Then the lovely girl went on: "You see, I wanted to take a series of photographs of a young man and after a lot of persuasion, I finally got Richard, Professor Zwaig's nephew, to promise that he would sit for me this morning. However, he wasn't very keen and it looks as if he isn't going to turn up which is such a bother because, on a sunny day like this, the light coming through the windows is perfect to take pictures and it isn't very often that I have the opportunity to use the Liebermann, the Professor's best camera."

'I was so keen to continue keeping company with Marguerite that at once I said that, though I had never done this sort of thing before, if she considered me to be a suitable substitute, I would be only too happy to take this chap's place. I swelled with pride when she clapped her hands and said joyfully: "Would you really, Bertolt? Oh, you *are* a kind boy. You do realize that I can't afford to pay you for your trouble?"

' "Oh, that doesn't matter," I said airily. "I've an idea, though. You can pay me by having lunch with me instead." She smiled and said: "Thank you, but I'm afraid that we won't have time to go out. We won't starve, though, as I've brought some sandwiches and two bottles of beer for when we take a break. Will that do?"

' "I should say so," I grinned, and I helped her bring up onto the stage a small piece of carpet and an elegant *chaise longue*. Now I know that after seeing the slides of Marguerite *au naturel*, it should have been crystal clear why Professor Zwaig's nephew had reneged on his promise! But I had failed to pick up on the full nature of the snap-happy beauty's requirements nonetheless. So it was with genuine shock that my face went white when Marguerite enthusiastically continued: "Right, I can hardly wait to begin. Bertolt, would you like to get undressed whilst I go round and lock the door to make sure that we aren't disturbed?"

'I could scarcely believe what I heard and looked at her in astonishment. "What on earth do you mean, Marguerite? Why should I take off my clothes?"

'She looked at me with a faint trace of impatience and said: "Well, how *else* would I be able to photograph you in the nude, you silly boy?"

'Now the penny finally dropped and it became blindingly obvious even to me why Richard Zwaig had failed to materialize and why Marguerite had been so eager to take up my offer. I took a deep breath whilst I considered my options – there was nothing to stop me simply walking out, but I had given my word and I could not bear to appear bashful in front of this gorgeous girl who would probably never speak to me again if I backed away from this challenge. So I gritted my teeth and said: "*All* my clothes, Marguerite?"

' "Of course," she said steadily. "Otherwise I would be unable to do either of us justice. I'll just adjust the lens and then I'll show you where to stand.

' "Don't worry, I won't bite you," she added with a smile, sensing my modesty. She went on: "Look, if it will make you feel any easier, I'll take off my blouse and skirt. It's so warm in here that I'll feel far more comfortable just wearing my chemise."

'I let out a small gulp as I sat on the *chaise longue* and pulled off my shoes, for it occurred to me that just a fleeting glance at the swell of Marguerite's creamy breasts would be bound to make my prick swell up. So as I undressed I tried to conjure up the most unarousing images in my mind. I settled finally on a blackboard on which was chalked up a row of English words we had had to learn last term.

'Closing my eyes, I softly chanted some of these words as I turned my back to Marguerite and pulled down my drawers, standing with just my vest covering my back. Then I hooked my thumbs under the garment and, raising my arms above my head, I yanked it off. Resisting the temptation to cover my cock and balls with my hand, I turned round to face the girl who, true to her word, had slipped off her blouse and skirt and was standing behind the camera clad only in a short pink chemise, the hem of which barely covered her knees.

'To her credit, Marguerite appeared quite unconcerned at the sight of my naked body. "Bertolt, would you please stand facing the auditorium? Good, now swing yourself slightly towards me, lay your hands on your thighs and raise your head. No, not too much. That's fine, now are you comfortable in that position? Yes? Excellent, now please keep as still as you can."

'Still concentrating on memorizing my English vocabulary, I complied with her request and, surprisingly soon, the fact that I was standing bollock-naked in front of Marguerite faded in importance. I actually began to enjoy taking up the poses she suggested and felt very proud when she walked up to me and said: "Your body is well suited to nude studies, Bertolt. You have a fine physique and I'm sure that I've captured that splendid look of determination stamped upon your brow."

'Her praise made me relax and though at first this allowed her to take some first-class photographs, I became all too conscious of my unclothed state when Marguerite placed her hands on my chest to move me round to the position she wanted.

'She stepped back a foot and looked me up and down critically. "Are you happy standing like that?" she asked and, acutely conscious of the fact that my prick was slowly but perceptibly stirring itself into a stand, I managed to stammer out: "Yes, I'm all right, thank you."

'However, Marguerite did not stroll back to take her place behind the camera. Instead, she stroked my chest and I gasped as I felt the cool touch of her slender fingers upon my skin. She chuckled softly as she traced a circular pattern around my nipple and murmured: "Yes indeed, you really are a very well-proportioned young man.

' "*Extremely* well-proportioned," she added huskily, looking directly down at my tool which was swelling up inexorably between my thighs. Desperately, I tried to prevent it rising up any further, but I had passed the point of no return and my face turned bright red as my shaft rose higher and higher, uncapping the taut knob as it swelled up to its full extent, standing smartly to attention up against my belly.

'I was convinced that Marguerite would toss her head in disgust and either upbraid me for my rudeness or pretend to ignore my stiffstander and simply walk briskly back to the camera. But in fact she just smiled and to my delight she reached out and clasped my tumescent todger in her hand. She began to frig my rampant tool, rubbing it inside her fist so arousingly that I became quite giddy with delight and was forced to hold on to the *chaise longue* for support.

' "Oh, I'm so sorry," I panted, but she was anything but offended by my prick's response and she whispered: "Bertolt, you don't have to apologize for having such a lovely big cock. I'm the one who should apologize for not resisting the temptation to wank it.

' "I really am very naughty," she muttered to herself as with her free hand she unbuttoned her chemise and freed the uptilted bouncy knockers to my excited view. Of course, I had just seen Professor Zwaig's lantern slides of Marguerite's bare breasts but how much more exciting were the soft creamy spheres in the flesh! She could see from my lustful gaze how affected I was by the sight of her proud beauties and she said invitingly: "Don't be shy, my dear. If you like, you can touch my titties."

'The sweet girl groaned with unslaked desire when I plucked up enough courage to move my trembling hands up and gingerly tweak her erect nipples between my fingers. Well, you won't be surprised when I tell you that moments later this sent me over the top and a tremendous spout of spunk shot out of my cock and splattered all over Marguerite's chemise.

'But this did not bother her too much because she shrugged her shoulders and said lightly: "Oh dear, I'd best take off this chemise and wash it as soon as we've finished here. Come to think of it, I'll have to do the same with my knickers as they're already wet with cunney juice."

'With that, Marguerite pulled off her chemise and wiggled out of her knickers. Seeing the wanton girl stripped to the buff kept my prick in a beefy semi-erect state as she now took hold of my arms and wrapped them around her, crushing us sweetly together. She lifted up her own arms to cradle my neck and pulled my face downwards. We kissed and she instantly slid her tongue between my teeth. My cock stiffened up again till it was as hard as iron as she moved my hands to her breasts and I thrilled to the touch of her rubbery nipples which rose up like hard little red pellets against my palms.'

'Gosh, you lucky beggar,' gasped Carl, leaning forward excitedly as he tugged at his trousers to try and make more room for his own throbbing erection. 'Fancy Marguerite giving you a hand job just for posing for her.'

Bertolt beamed: 'Ah, but the best was yet to come. She laid herself down on the *chaise longue*, placing a cushion underneath her bum. I fixed my eyes on her hairy pussy as she ran her finger all down its length. My heart began to pound – and I started to tremble all over when I realized that at last the time had come for me to enjoy my very first fuck!

'I laid myself across her and pushed my helmet against her puffy love lips but in my frenzy could not find the way into her sopping slit. So Marguerite kindly took hold of my cock and guided it home herself. I let out a blissful sigh as she inserted my knob between the outer lips of her cunt. I relished the feel of the flesh-grip around my glans before plunging my whole shaft deep into the wet folds of her joxy. She wriggled away happily as I pumped my rampant rod in and out of her juicy love channel. It felt like a soft hand frigging my shaft when the muscles of Marguerite's cunt caressed my chopper as I pistoned in and out of her clingy sheath. She bucked and twisted under my pounding, urging me to thrust even deeper as she raised her legs and wrapped her feet around my shoulders, allowing her cunney to clasp itself round my cock as her love juices dripped down onto my bollocks when they slapped against her arse. Then I cupped her warm bum cheeks in my hands and they rotated in my palms as my shaft slid in and out of her tight, wet little quim.

'My God, it felt like Paradise and I tried to make the fuck last as long as possible but soon I felt that tingling sensation in my balls and I knew there was no way that I could hold back. I cried out: "I'm going to spend! I can't stop it!"

' "It's all right, I've cum already," gasped Marguerite and she flexed her legs before reaching out and squeezing my balls as I arched myself upwards and then plunged deep down into her.

' "Aaaah!" I moaned in delight as my cock jetted a stream of jism inside her cunt. She quickly squeezed her thighs together and milked every last drop from my spurting shaft until it began to shrink and I pulled it out of her dripping pussy.'

'Was fucking as good as you had thought it would be?' asked his young brother and Bertolt's voice quivered with emotion as he replied: 'Believe me, Carl, it was simply magnificent! I didn't think anything could give me as much pleasure as the sucking-off that lovely Swedish girl Bibi gave me the other afternoon when you fell asleep after drinking too much champagne, but fucking Marguerite was an even more delicious experience.

'Honestly, I really hope that you two lads don't have to wait too long for your own first fucks,' he said sincerely and I smiled to myself but resisted the temptation to tell Bertolt that a few days ago I had already crossed that particular Rubicon with Christa, the tightrope artiste from the circus, because that would have made poor Carl jealous. As it was, Bertolt's tale of how he lost his virginity aroused my chum to such a pitch that he could hardly wait for us to arrive back at the house where he rushed upstairs to the bedroom and relieved himself with his trusty right hand!

As I remarked when recounting my own joyous rite of passage, the first experience of love-making can colour a young person's lifelong attitude to the opposite sex, especially if a disastrous introduction to the delights of the bedroom is not quickly countered by a more pleasurable joust between the sheets. An inability to enjoy to the utmost those sensual joys which set *homo sapiens* apart from the rest of the animal kingdom can often afflict both men and women with an incurable suspicion of the opposite sex.

For example, my father is convinced that this is the basis of the misogyny of such men as Nietzche, Strindberg and Weininger and why on the other hand Goethe's female characters are more true to life and more interesting than his male ones (if we except Gotz and Mephisto).

However, I am content to leave such matters to professional pundits such as Doctor Schleich of Berlin, Professor William Bucknall of London and other learned gentlemen and continue these recollections with the story of my next lesson in *l'art de faire l'amour* which I learned from a dark-eyed gypsy girl only a few days after hearing Bertolt's raunchy tale.

That particular morning did not begin propitiously for Carl who woke up with a raging toothache. Despite his protests, Doctor Hildebrand insisted on taking my poor chum into town to be examined by his old friend Herr Danziger, the best dentist in Stettin.

His brother's misfortune gave Bertolt the chance to cadge a lift into town where he hoped he might enjoy a second torrid love-making session with Marguerite. Frau Hildebrand was busy supervising the preparations for a dinner party that evening in honour of our neighbours the Seligsohns and the shipbuilder Herr Albert Dahrf and his good lady.

Thus I was left to my own devices and I decided to take my drawing-pad and pencils and wander through the countryside. Freida made me a packed lunch and I set off towards Jascnitz where I thought I might sketch a picture of the sixteenth-century houses in the village square.

The previous days had been cloudy and cool, but the sun had reappeared and I thoroughly enjoyed my walk through the unspoilt wild countryside. I hummed to myself the tuneful little nonsense ditty still popular in the area even though it dated from the French invasion of Pomerania some seventy-five years ago:

Lembolo, lemboli,
Sanfte Mode tipperi
Ong, dong, dreo, katt,
Katt mokt sich de Naf' nich natt,
Juckt dat Fell und juckt de Leber,
Kummt Napoleon und Lefebre!

Interestingly enough, although I haven't been back to Stettin for more than twenty years and so perhaps such folk memories have now died out, certainly in the 1880s in Lower Pomerania a favourite if baffling drinking toast was: "Prost! General Knusemoing!"

Doctor Hildebrand explained the origin of this strange custom to me by saying that it came from the people hearing the French soldiers saluting their commanding officer with the words: "Mon général! Ce que nous aimons!" *[This explanation is confirmed in* A History of German Folk Songs *by Bernhard Durken, Columbia University Press, 1978 – Editor]*

Be that as it may, as I strolled along the path through a dense clump of woodland, I thought I heard the noise of footsteps behind me. Twice I stopped, turned round and looked behind me but on neither occasion did I see anyone there and I decided that I must have imagined it. So I walked on. Yet there was no shaking off the frightening feeling that someone was keeping pace for pace behind me. I became somewhat apprehensive because I had not forgotten Doctor Hildebrand's warning about the gypsies and I began to wonder whether some vagabond was trailing me, waiting his moment to pounce and rob me of my purse.

However, no cut-throat appeared as I quickened my pace and, although I still could not rid myself of the notion that I was being followed, I finally decided that I was probably being tracked for fun by some boy from Jascnitz which was now only about two kilometres away. So it was without undue trepidation that when I reached a mossy hillock of earth in a clearing I slipped my rucksack off my back and sat down upon it to wait for my mysterious follower to show himself.

The puzzle was solved a few minutes later when I heard a quickening patter of light footsteps approach me and I tensed myself to run off if indeed they were those of a ne'er-do-well tramp.

However, to my relief the figure rounding the curve into the clearing was none other than that of a lissome young gypsy girl dressed for the heat of summer in a low-cut white top and a black skirt which barely reached below the knees of her bare legs. She really was stunningly attractive with a pretty face blessed with an unblemished sun-tanned complexion and there was a gay twinkle in her flashing dark eyes as she came up to me and said: 'Good morning, sir. Do you mind if I rest here for a while?'

'Of course not,' I replied, courteously doffing my beret to her. 'This is common land and you have as much right as me to sit wherever you like.'

'Thank you kindly,' she said with a wry smile as she sat down beside me. 'However common the land might be, some people try to keep gypsies off it. We do have some thieves and scoundrels amongst us but no more than any other group of people.'

I could not keep myself from studying her saucy little face and then my eyes dropped lower to take in the clearly visible heaving of her proudly jutting breasts as she recovered from her exertions. Whilst I gazed at the girl, I chided myself for being so worried about being followed to Jascnitz by such a lovely lissome creature.

Nevertheless, anyone would have been disturbed by being tracked in that way and I said to her: 'Have you been running to catch up with me? I thought I heard someone behind me but you must have hidden yourself every time I looked around to see who it was.'

She immediately apologized and said: 'I'm so sorry, I didn't mean to startle you, but until I came close to you, I couldn't see exactly who you were and I was worried that you might be Mikhail. He's a young man from our camp who wants me to marry him but though he's a nice enough fellow, I'm only seventeen and I don't want to be tied down to him or anyone else just yet.'

This sounded like one of those romantic adventures which my mother loves to read and I asked: 'Is he pestering you to change your mind? Is that why you were running away?'

'Not really,' she said, shaking her mane of shiny black hair. 'Oh, Mikhail has certainly begged me to change my mind, but it's my father who is driving me crazy. He has threatened to throw me out if I don't accept Mikhail who is quite well-off and has promised my father goodness knows what if he can make me marry him.'

Strengthened by the gigantic egotism of youth, I said recklessly: 'Well, if either of them comes chasing after you, they'll have me to deal with.'

Although I was tall for my age and possessed a reasonably well-built physique, the girl must have realized that I was at least two years younger than her. But she did not mock me. Instead, she entered the spirit of the conversation and, holding out her hand, she said: 'My name is Natasha and I thank you for your offer of help, although I don't believe I shall be harassed again by anybody until I return to our encampment on the other side of Jaschnitz.'

I took her hand and, having read several of my mother's romantic novels, I followed the fashion of the heroes in these tales of derring-do when they were introduced to damsels in distress and pressed her fingers to my lips, declaiming: 'My name is Johann Gewirtz and you must allow me to protect you from anyone who wishes to do you harm.'

Looking back on what happened during the next few hours, I very much doubt if the feisty girl was ever in any real danger. In all probability, Natasha allowed me to assume this protective role simply to puff up my own ego. Nevertheless, she accepted my offer to share my lunch with her and I have good reason to think there was a genuine attraction between us.

Putting the matter on the most basic level, there was more than fifty marks in my purse which would represent a fortune to a poor gypsy girl like Natasha. Later that afternoon it would have been extremely easy for her to filch all of that money, but she did not attempt to avail herself of any of these many opportunities.

However, she *was* very hungry and it was just as well that Freida had packed half a cold chicken as well as a small loaf of bread and some fruit. 'There's only water in my flask, I'm afraid,' I said sadly for the gallant young men in my mother's books always seemed to be able to serve glasses of wine at the drop of a hat.

'That doesn't matter a bit, Johann,' she said, brushing off the crumbs from her skirt. 'Thank you for a lovely lunch. I just wish I had something to give you in return.'

I could have suggested something to her! But whilst I insisted that all I wanted in return was the pleasure of her company, her eyes fell on the drawing-pad which I had taken out of my rucksack.

'Johann, are you an art student?' asked Natasha. When she flipped open the pad and looked at the sketch I had made the previous day of Sonia's head, she smiled: 'And who might this pretty girl be? Is she your sweetheart?'

Here I must digress for a moment to say that when I decided to pen this autobiographical narrative, I resolved not to write a mere apologia for my actions, and so at this point I must not flinch from recording that my answers to Natasha's questions were, to say the least, somewhat economical with the truth!

The fact of the matter is that I nodded my head and replied: 'Yes, I am a student at the Sorbonne in Paris and Sonia, the girl in the picture, is one of my close friends.'

Well, in my defence, I could claim that art was a subject in which I excelled at the high-class gymnasium *[The equivalent of a British public school – editor]* Bertolt, Carl and I attended back in Vienna and that Sonia and I enjoyed a relationship which was on intimate enough terms for her to suck my cock! And looking back on the affair, I would be surprised if Natasha really believed me for surely no one could take me for being any more than sixteen years old.

However, Natasha appeared to accept my reply without demur and she said: 'Would you like to sketch me, Johann? Or might this make Sonia jealous?'

'Oh yes, I would love to,' I answered promptly. 'And Sonia wouldn't mind in the slightest. Anyhow, it's none of her business who models for me.'

The sultry-eyed girl smoothed back the strands of shiny black hair which partially covered her face and said: 'Then let's begin. Now, where would you like me to sit?'

I positioned Natasha on top of the hillock whilst I knelt on my haunches on the ground in front of her. Now, I had placed myself in the shade of a large beech tree but the bright afternoon sun was beaming directly down upon Natasha. She made no complaint although the heat must have made it rather uncomfortable for her to keep stock still whilst I sketched away.

Perhaps she was more used to being outdoors than me, but after about a quarter of an hour I needed a break from my work even though I had the benefit of being shielded from the sun by the leafy branches of the beech tree. We had emptied the flask of water and I rummaged in the rucksack to see if Freida had packed anything else to drink. Thankfully there was a small bottle swathed in brown paper in a side pocket of the rucksack and I began to unwrap it as I called out to Natasha: 'Let's take a rest for a bit. Now I wonder what's inside this bottle I've just found in my bag. Let's hope there's something nice in it because you must be even more thirsty than me, sitting in the glare of the sunlight.'

'Yes, I am rather thirsty,' she agreed and the lissome gypsy girl gracefully slid down on her knees beside me whilst to my surprise I pulled out an envelope from the folds of thick brown paper rolled round what I could now see was a small bottle of colourless liquid. A quick glance at the label was enough to inform me that it was Russian vodka.

'Oooh, that's my favourite drink,' announced Natasha and picking up the envelope and opening the unsealed flap she took out the folded sheets of thin opaque paper. She handed them to me as she continued: 'Johann, you had better read this letter, there might be something important in it.'

'Well, I'm not so sure we should read someone's private correspondence,' I said doubtfully. 'This rucksack belongs to the father of the chum I'm staying with for the summer holidays. Is there any name on the envelope?'

A few years later I would have known better than to ask this of her, but alas I made poor Natasha blush with shame as she lowered her eyes and replied: 'I don't know because I can't read or write. I've always wanted to learn but it's almost impossible for any gypsy children to attend school as we're always on the move.'

I nodded my head and looked down at the envelope which was simply addressed to 'George'. As careful readers will recall, this was Doctor Hildebrand's forename and I know I should have only scanned the first page of the letter which the doctor had clearly not realized had been left with the bottle of vodka. I assumed it had been given to him as a present, perhaps by a grateful patient.

One glance was enough to tell me that this letter had been penned by a feminine hand, and it very soon became obvious that this was not just a thank-you letter, but a fully fledged *billet-doux* from Princess Juliet Rostov of St Petersburg.

'Well, what does it say?' enquired Natasha when she saw my eyebrows arch sharply as I read the steamy contents of the first page.

'Um, actually it's a love letter to a gentleman with whom I am acquainted,' I gulped as she snuggled up next to me and purred: 'Oh, I would love to be able to write a love letter, Johann. Do read it to me.'

I wrinkled my brow whilst I considered whether to agree to Natasha's request. I reasoned that it would be safe to do so if I did not reveal Doctor Hildebrand's surname (not that it would mean anything to her) and, to be honest, my curiosity had been aroused. I rather wanted to see for myself what Princess Juliet Rostov had written to Doctor Hildebrand.

So I cleared my throat and said: 'Very well, Natasha, I'll read the letter to you. It is from a Russian princess named Juliet to her lover and begins:

Darling George,

My dearest, it is long past midnight but I find it impossible to sleep, for my mind is still filled with images from our all too short romantic tryst in Budapest. Ah, what thrills of sensual feeling sweep through my body as I recall the passion of our nights at the Hotel Europa, of lying naked on crushed and rumpled sheets and watching the early morning sunlight caress your body as you lay sleeping whilst I listened to the muted sounds of the birds welcoming the dawn.

Georgie, perhaps I should not tell you this in case you become conceited, but just thinking of your rugged face, your broad hairy chest and, of course, your majestic prick makes me tingle all over and I do so wish you could be miraculously transported to my lonely bed!

I can only console myself by remembering some of the wonderful moments we shared together. One that readily comes to mind is how we fell into each other's arms when the train from Vienna steamed into the railway station. I had arrived earlier in the day, but your train was late and I had been waiting impatiently on the platform to greet you. Sweetheart, I shall treasure the memory of the way your eyes lit up and you rushed towards me and buried me in an enormous bear-hug.

'Oh George, how wonderful to see you again, I've missed you so much,' I breathed and my lips spread into a wide smile as I felt the stiff pressure of your cock against my belly.

"And I've missed you, Juliet!" you whispered in my ear. "I can hardly wait to get to the hotel where I'll gather you in my arms, throw you down on the bed and make mad passionate love to you."

Do you recall what I did next? I pressed myself up against you whilst I slid my hand up the inside of your thigh and gently squeezed your erection. "Darling, don't do that here!" you panted as your eyes darted round the crowded concourse."

'Why not? I want you to fuck me here and now!" I replied and began to giggle when over your shoulder I caught the shocked stare of a fat middle-aged lady standing behind you. Your cheeks turned bright red when you turned your head and saw her spin on her heels and march off.

When you had regained your composure, you wagged a reproving finger at me and sighed: "Juliet, you really mustn't be so naughty! Remember, we mustn't draw attention to ourselves. Just think about how the balloon would go up if someone recognized us and told my wife or your fiancé they had seen us canoodling together."

"I'm sorry, darling, it's just that I want your cock inside my pussy so much that I get carried away when I see you," I said contritely and you gave a throaty little growl of delight and kissed me on the lips before pulling out of our embrace and shepherding me towards a luggage trolley onto which a porter was piling your cases.

"Follow me, I have a fiacre [a small carriage with a folding roof – Editor] *waiting outside the station," I said to the porter and giggled again when I saw the bulge in the front of your trousers.*

Once the cases had been safely stowed onto the back of the carriage, we clambered in and I snuggled up against you and said softly: "George, I want to tell you something – it's been such a warm day here that I didn't put on any knickers this morning."

How I chuckled when I saw your jaw drop and when I added that in fact I wasn't wearing any underclothes, you hissed: "No underclothes! You mean you were standing on the platform in just a thin cotton dress!

"What am I going to do with you?" you asked rhetorically and then you gulped and your eyes dropped down when I took hold of your hand and trapped it between my thighs, feeling your fingertips move against my warm crotch as I replied: "Oh Georgie, do I really need to answer that question?"

"But the driver might turn round and see us," you frowned, although this possibility did not prevent your fingers tracing the outline of my pussy lips! Anyhow, I shook my head and murmured: "He won't notice anything, darling. Come on, you can't stop now."

To encourage you further, I pulled my skirt up over my thighs and you slid your hand underneath the thin cotton fabric. Then I sighed with pleasure as you parted my pussy lips with your finger and teased the hooded nub of my clitty. My breathing became ragged and my head tossed from side to side whilst I impaled myself on your stabbing finger.

Do you remember how excited I became and how I clutched at your arm and beseeched you to fuck me without further delay?

"No, no, not here, we've stopped in a narrow street and someone might look in whilst we're waiting to get through," you pleaded, but your defences began to crumble as soon as my hand stole across to your lap, squeezing and rubbing the straining bulge between your legs. I couldn't resist laughing softly whilst I watched

your face contort with excitement and then as I hoped, you threw caution to the winds and suddenly you were tearing off your trousers, pulling them down your legs as you muttered: "This is sheer madness, we could be arrested and thrown in jail if we're caught . . ."

You rolled across me and I sank back and spread my thighs whilst I reached up and yanked down your drawers, catching my breath at the sight of your massive prick as it sprang into view.

"Move up me," I commanded in an urgent whisper and when you did, I grasped your hot throbbing shaft and drew it down and forward until the swollen purple knob was rubbing against my yielding pussy lips.

"Yes! Yes! Yes!" I panted as I felt your width stretch my tight wet love channel. Then with a low growl you started to drive your thick cock into my cunt, jerking me against the seat and lifting my bottom from the leather with the fierceness of your thrusts. Your arms slid underneath me and you scooped up my bum cheeks in your hands and then you gasped: "Oh God, I have to cum, I can't stop!"

"That's all right, Georgie! Shoot your load, I want it all!" I wailed as your jism drenched my cunney and my cunt convulsed into a series of pulsing spasms until I was too exhausted to cum any more.

There was just time for us to adjust our clothes before the coachman pulled up in front of the Hotel Europa and a smartly dressed concierge opened the door of the carriage for us. You pulled out your wallet to pay our driver but I put my hand on your arm and said: "George, don't worry, I've already paid him."

"Oh, you paid in advance, did you?" you said as we walked into the hotel. "Well, I insist on reimbursing you."

I gave you a knowing wink and said: "You don't have to give me any money, darling. We paid the driver en route. Didn't you see the grin on his face when we got out of the carriage?"

"What do you mean, we paid en route?" you frowned and when the penny dropped, you slapped your cheek and gasped: "My God, Juliet, surely you didn't arrange for—"

Well, I had planned to let you believe I had made a bargain with the driver to let him watch us fuck instead of giving him his fare at least till we were upstairs in your bedroom, but I simply couldn't keep a straight face and burst out laughing as I shook my head and assured you that I had only been guilty of a wicked tease!

You're a real sport, Georgie, because as soon as you realized how you had been fooled, you also began to laugh and then with a gleam in your eye you murmured: "Wait till we get upstairs, my girl. I'll pay you back for playing such a rotten trick on me."

"Promises, promises," I said softly as we walked through the foyer to the reception desk and I made you draw in your breath sharply when I pinched your bottom whilst you signed the hotel guest book.

However, you were as good as your word when we arrived in your suite and the porter had retired after bringing up your cases. "How charming of the hotel manager to greet you with a bottle of chilled champagne," I said as you uncorked the bottle with a "pop" and poured out two glasses of the fizzy wine. "He must think of you as a very important guest."

"Yes, I'm sure he does, although that's not because he likes the colour of my eyes," you explained with a sardonic grin. "It's simply that Herr Reis knows that I make all the hotel arrangements for the Viennese Medical

Association and naturally he wants us to return to Budapest next year for our diamond jubilee conference."

I helped to unpack your clothes and then you announced that you were going to take a warm bath to refresh yourself after your journey before changing for dinner.

"This evening I am hosting a reception for the famous English surgeon Sir Jonathan Elstree who is giving a paper on the latest developments in anaesthesia at our opening meeting tomorrow morning," you added and I groaned: "Oh dear, don't sit me beside him, I'll wager he can't speak German or Russian and knows only a smattering of French from his schooldays. You know what these Britishers are like, they believe that everyone else in the world should learn English!"

"It so happens that Sir Jonathan is fluent in German and French," you said reprovingly as you sat on the bed and untied your shoe-laces. Then you gave me a severe look and commented: "But I'm not too sure whether I should invite you to dine with us after nearly giving me a heart attack just now over that business with the wretched cab driver!"

"Oh, don't be like that, Georgie," I pouted as I sat down next to you. "I'm sure you can find better ways to punish me."

How your eyes gleamed as you stroked your chin and said: "M'm, I suppose so. But let's undress whilst I decide what your punishment should be."

"Now that sounds more promising!" I said brightly as I unhooked my skirt and began to unbutton my dress.

Well, Georgie, I'm sure I don't have to remind you what happened next! When we were both naked, I gave a little squeal as you pulled me over your knees and I deliberately wriggled my bottom in anticipation as you pinched my bum and said sternly: "You've been a naughty girl, haven't you, Juliet?"

"Yes, I cannot deny it," I replied in a low voice and you went on: "And you know what happens to naughty girls, don't you?"

"They get their bottoms smacked," I said and you grunted: "Quite right! So brace yourself, I'm going to give you a good sound spanking!"

And with those words, you parted my bum cheeks and inserted the tip of the little finger of your right hand inside my pussy and slid it in and out for a few moments until my quim was dripping wet before pulling it out and beginning my punishment in earnest. You started to slap my bum in a series of light, rapid strokes which made me wince as my bottom began to tingle.

"Oooh! Oooh! OOOH!" I cried out as I entered into the spirit of the game and you snapped: "Quiet now, Juliet! Your punishment isn't finished yet. I'm not letting you up till I see your bum cheeks turn pink!"

Nevertheless, you didn't really hurt me, of course, and I felt so raunchy when you finished smacking me and began to massage my wriggling backside and I could hardly wait to be fucked when you hauled me up and threw me down on the bed. I parted my legs as you plunged your big stiff cock inside my soaking cunt and my hips moved with yours, picking up the rhythm as I wrapped my legs around your back whilst our lips met and my mouth was immediately filled by your tongue . . .

Oh Georgie, wouldn't you love to be in bed with me now, pistoning your thick prick into my sopping slit and watching me lie back with a blissful smile on my face as you fondle my breasts and tweak up my perky red nipples between your fingers?

Darling, I do so wish you were here for my body is aching for you. Alas, I am all alone and can only play with my own pussy, sliding my thumb inside my cunney whilst I finish this letter and dream about your powerful veiny shaft dipping in and out of my juicy quim.

What a glorious time we had in Budapest, Georgie, and I can hardly wait till October when we will meet again in Salzburg. Till then I shall try and fill the days by remembering those ecstatic hours – and by thinking about the wonderful nights of passion we shall soon be enjoying together.

All my love,
Juliet

My voice thickened as I looked up from the sheet of paper and saw that Natasha was lying back on the hillock of earth, sensually rubbing her pussy through the thin material of her skirt with one hand whilst with the other she pressed her heaving breasts together.

Neither of us said a word as we stared at each other whilst I tried to think of what I should do next, but fortunately the decision was taken out of my hands when Natasha reached out and slid her fingers around the throbbing bulge which had appeared in my trousers whilst I was reading Princess Juliet's raunchy letter. Clearly, Natasha had also been aroused because she whispered throatily: 'What a big boy you are, Johann! How would you like to fuck me with that nice fat cock?'

Before I could reply, she pulled me to her and our mouths met in a deep, passionate kiss. I wrapped my arms tightly around her as our wet tongues tangled together and my hands roamed across her soft tits, squeezing and caressing her proud, uptilted breasts.

Suddenly Natasha pulled me away and I inwardly groaned, thinking that I had moved too quickly, but thankfully I was quite mistaken. She slid down to the ground as she quickly fumbled with my belt and fly buttons and then, with a sensual glitter in her eyes, the uninhibited girl pulled my trousers and pants down to the ground.

Released from its confines, my cock sprang up and bounced against the bridge of her nose as she clasped hold of my throbbing tool. My eyes closed when Natasha took hold of my shaft in her hand, gently stroking it whilst she licked my hairy bollocks. She pushed my shaft flush up against my belly whilst she tongued my scrotum, sucking on each ball in turn until her tickling tongue brought me to a fever pitch of excitement and I moaned with delight when she released my prick, lifted her head and ran her tongue up and down the sensitive underside of my shaft before her lips closed over my helmet and transported me into another world.

'H-a-r-g-h!' I gurgled and opened my eyes to see Natasha looking up at me, a wicked twinkle playing around her pretty, sun-tanned features. She swirled her tongue over my knob, her tongue gently playing with the tiny hole from which pre-cum was already starting to ooze out.

The lusty minx bobbed her head to and fro, taking almost all my length inside her mouth and I pushed gently back and forth, enjoying to the full the way my rock-hard chopper snaked down Natasha's gullet with each slippery stroke. I rotated my hips to increase the pressure of her soft lips on my shaft as she sucked greedily on her fleshy sweetmeat and I could feel my fleshy truncheon tremble as I continued to fuck her mouth.

Then I reached round to the back of Natasha's head and

pulled her closer to me so that my entire pulsating prick was buried in her throat. Beads of sweat now glistened on my forehead as I felt her finger slide along the crack of my backside. I had no idea what was coming and my whole body shuddered involuntarily when I felt her fingertip insert itself into the tight, puckered entrance to my anus and push relentlessly inwards until it had gained entrance up to her first knuckle.

At first it was painful as her fingernail rasped against the tender flesh, but then the pain subsided into an incredibly erotic experience as she kept her finger jammed inside my arse, rocking it slightly back and forth whilst she continued to suck my cock. The sensations were so strong that very soon my balls tightened and I spurted a massive torrent of sticky hot spunk into Natasha's mouth. She swallowed every last drop of my copious emission until my shaft started to soften and I removed my limp tool from between her lips.

I thought this would be the finish of this delicious joust, but not a bit of it! Natasha undressed and for a while I rested my head against her soft bare breasts. However, I was not allowed to take it easy for very long and she soon scrambled to her feet and began to dance sensually in front of me, slowly sliding her finger between her pouting pussy lips.

The gypsy girl's luxuriant tresses of black hair fell over her shoulders as she capered towards me and then she sat herself down so that her lithe bronzed body was now next to mine. My cock began to thicken as, raising her head, she slipped her arms around my neck, gripping me tightly as we exchanged a passionate kiss. Her tongue shot out and slithered into my mouth as she writhed in lascivious delight as my hands cupped her proudly jutting breasts.

'Fuck me, Johann, fuck me,' Natasha gasped, pulling

me across her as she parted her thighs to give me a fair view of her puffy pink love lips and the red chink of her cunney which stood out in the dark curly muff surrounding her dripping honeypot.

I wiggled myself between her legs and Natasha took hold of my palpitating prick and guided my knob between her yielding quim lips until her clingy sheath had totally enveloped my shaft and the hairs of our pubic bushes matted together. Next she drummed the heels of her feet against my bottom whilst my chopper slid in and out of her juicy ooze. A tidal wave of the most exquisite ecstasy washed over me and my eager young cock stretched the walls of Natasha's cunt to their limits. She reached round my sides to grab my bum cheeks and our movements became faster and faster. Soon I began to shiver as I felt my orgasm boiling up in my balls. I slowed the pace of my thrusts until Natasha's moans grew higher and higher and I judged that she also was ready to spend.

Then I speeded up the fuck again, plunging my shaft in and out of her soft, wet crack until she arched her back up from the mossy bank. Then, with a cry, she fell back as I shot a tremendous jet of jism inside her love funnel as we shuddered to a glorious simultaneous climax.

When we had recovered we dressed ourselves and I insisted on accompanying Natasha to the gypsy encampment. As we walked along I said to her: 'When I was younger, I always dreamed about what fun it would be if I were a gypsy living in a caravan, dancing round the camp fire at night with no worries about having to go to school the next day. So do you enjoy the wanderer's life, Natasha, or have you ever thought about settling down?'

'Oh Johann, I've thought of nothing else for years now,' she replied fervently. 'I would do anything to live in a house and learn how to read and write. Honestly, the only thing I enjoy these days is listening to the stories and the songs of the old people.'

'I adore gypsy music. Do you know any gypsy songs?' I remarked and Natasha nodded her head and said with a smile: 'Yes, I love them, too. I'll sing one of my favourites to you, if you like. It's rather a sad song but the words express exactly how I feel about my present way of life. Would you like to hear it, Johann?'

'Very much,' I said as we stopped and to a slow, melancholy tune, she sang:

'A song, a joyous wanderer's song
I followed by the sound,
Sped the mighty stream along
O'er mead and marshy ground;
Many a place to which I'd come
I left ere night was over,
For that it was more than home
I never could discover.'

From the heartfelt sincerity in her voice it was clear that Natasha was genuinely unhappy at not being able to live a normal, settled life. This saddened me until I had a brainwave and I realized that I was able, like the knights of old in my childhood storybooks, to rescue this beautiful damsel in distress and, if not marry her and live happily ever after, at least carry her off to my castle!

I took a deep breath and blurted out: 'Natasha, I've had a great idea. If the idea appeals to you, I can help you obtain a position with my family as a scullery maid. It won't be the most exciting job in the world, but I know my mother would have no objection to my sisters and I teaching you how to read and write.'

The sultry girl stared at me and then replied in a

rembling voice: 'Do you really think you can? Oh, I ould like nothing better and I've never been afraid of rd work.'

She clapped her hands with excitement, but then suddenly her face fell and she said gloomily: 'It's kind of you to try and help me, Johann, but would your parents take in a gypsy into their household? I swear to you that I'm an honest girl but people say such terrible things about us and—'

'My parents would never listen to such tosh,' I said stoutly. 'Why, they are rather like gypsies themselves, always travelling somewhere or other. They were in America earlier this year to see some relatives of my father and they have only just come home from a holiday in Russia.'

'But I am a total stranger to them,' cried Natasha. 'They would need a letter of introduction from some adult whose word they trust before taking me in – and with respect, my dear, I don't think your word would be enough.'

I waved aside her objection though in my heart I knew that she was right. But seconds later I snapped my fingers and said: 'Maybe you have a point, but I know just the right person to write such a letter on your behalf. Can't you guess who I mean?'

'No, I can't think of anyone at all,' she answered and I burst out laughing and said: 'Well, it's the owner of my rucksack, of course!'

'The owner of your rucksack?' she repeated in a puzzled voice. 'But I've never met him before in my life.'

'Maybe not,' I chuckled as I squeezed her hand. 'On the other hand, we both know something about Georgie, the gentleman who received that passionate letter from Princess Juliet which I read out to you a few minutes ago.

Well, his full name is Doctor George Alfred Hildebrand and he owns the rucksack!'

Natasha did not catch my drift and she smiled: 'Is [illegible] now? So why should this Doctor Hildebrand, whoever he is, want to help me?'

'Well, if for no other reason, I'm sure he would like to get back that letter and extract a solemn promise from us both never to breathe a word about it to a living soul!'

She may have been only a poor gypsy girl, but Natasha showed she possessed a truly noble character because she immediately shook her head and said: 'No, Johann, you could get into serious trouble if you tried to blackmail him. And anyhow, it wouldn't be right for him to recommend me for a post without us having even met!'

'It's hardly blackmail,' I protested weakly. 'After all, I'm not asking Doctor Hildebrand for any money and we'll keep our word not to tell anyone about his naughty little jaunt in Budapest.'

We argued about the idea for a while and we finally reached a compromise agreement which was that I would give the letter back to Doctor Hildebrand telling him I had found it in the rucksack and, if asked, would say with indignation that I would never open a letter which was not addressed to me. Only then would I go on to say how I had met an unhappy gypsy girl and explain to him why she would be so grateful if he would spare five minutes to talk to her.

She agreed to this plan of action only with reluctance for she correctly assumed that, although I would keep my solemn promise not to blackmail Doctor Hildebrand, from the tone of my voice and the words I would use, he would suspect that I knew more about the contents of Princess Juliet's letter that I was prepared to admit!

However, we sealed this agreement with a loving kiss

and I said to Natasha: 'Can you meet me here at noon tomorrow? I'll try and bring the doctor with me and you can tell him yourself how he can help you.'

'Yes, the men are all going to a fair in Stettin so it will be easy for me to slip away,' she replied. Then she smiled and went on: 'And thank you for everything, Johann. Even if this scheme doesn't work and we never see each other again, I'll never forget your kindness.'

'Oh, it'll work, all right,' I said confidently. 'And never mind about not forgetting my kindness, I'd far rather you didn't forget my love truncheon!'

She giggled and, giving me another quick kiss on the lips, she ran across the field towards the gypsy encampment.

CHAPTER THREE

Later that day I confronted Doctor Hildebrand in his study and put my plan into action. The good doctor said nothing but he pursed his lips and gave me a quizzical look when I handed over the letter to him. However, he wisely decided – as the British saying puts it – to let sleeping dogs lie and refrained from commenting further upon the matter as he slipped the envelope back into his pocket.

Then he listened with courteous attention whilst I explained Natasha's plight to him and readily agreed to meet her the next day. 'I make no promises, you understand, Johann,' he said as I walked to the door. 'If her story is true, this girl appears to deserve all the help that we can give her to better herself.'

'Thank you, sir,' I said and I was just going to open the door when he added: 'Just one final question, my boy, before you go. In the strictest confidence, has Natasha offered you any inducements to speak on her behalf? I would appreciate your word that you will answer truthfully.'

Well, I had already fucked Natasha and whilst I don't deny that the thought of further raunchy sessions of rumpy-pumpy with the lusty girl hadn't entered my mind, I could answer this question in all honesty. Now it was my turn to effect a studied air as I replied disingenuously: 'Inducements? Of course not, sir, Natasha doesn't have a groschen to her name.'

'I wasn't thinking about money,' said Doctor Hildebrand drily. 'When I was your age I well recall an evening when my parents had gone out to dine and a certain young kitchen-maid came into the drawing room and asked if I minded if she entertained one of her followers in her bedroom. "Not at all," I said and she said that if I promised not to tell my parents about it, she would give me a lovely treat the next day. This was, um, my first introduction to, um, sexual practices and, quite frankly, it crossed my mind that you had found yourself in a similar position.'

'No, Natasha has offered me nothing in return except her gratitude,' I said firmly and, to his credit, he did not attempt to press me further. I went upstairs to change for dinner. My mind was still preoccupied with Natasha when I opened the door and I don't know who was more startled, Carl, Sonia or myself when our eyes met, for Carl was lying naked on his bed and the randy housemaid was kneeling beside him fisting her hand up and down his quivering stiff erection.

'Carl, if you're determined to be found out, you may as well get Sonia to toss you off in the dining room,' I grumbled as I closed the door behind me. Sonia frowned as she looked down at Carl and said accusingly: 'Well, what have you to say? I distinctly remember you went across to lock the door before you undressed.'

'Oooh, don't stop, Sonia,' panted my chum as she released his twitching tool from her grasp. 'I'm sorry, I was so fired up by the prospect of what you were going to do that I could only think about how quickly I could pull off my trousers and pants.'

'That's all very well, but think of what would have happened if your father or mother had walked in!' she scolded him. 'Just for that I'm going to make you cum straightaway.'

Nevertheless, Sonia ignored my pal's prick and extended the thumb and index finger of her right hand to pinch the wrinkled pink skin of his scrotum. She raised the low dangling bag high by its own loose skin and then she used the fingertips of her left hand to tease his testicles as they slid about within his raised ballsack.

It was clear from his gasps of passion that Carl adored this stimulation and a dribble of pre-cum now oozed out of his knob. Then Sonia grabbed hold of his cock and her experienced fist slid slowly up and down Carl's thick shaft, the firm movement of her hand regularly covering and revealing the ruby blush of his helmet whilst she continued to massage his balls. Carl gasped as she began to pump his prick faster and faster, her fist a flying blur and only moments later a veritable fountain of creamy spunk squirted out from his knob as his cock reared and plunged inside Sonia's working fist whilst it sprayed a copious emission of sticky jism onto his belly and into his curly thatch of pubic hair.

'H-a-a-r!' groaned Carl as Sonia looked up at me with a twinkle in her eye and beckoned me over to the bed. She swiftly undid the buttons of her blouse and shrugged the garment off her shoulders and my shaft immediately swelled up when she tugged her chemise over her head and exposed her luscious bare breasts to my excited gaze. Then she licked her lips and sensually cupped the magnificent snowy globes in her hands and pushed them almost into my face as she whispered: 'How would you like to suck my titties, Master Johann?'

'Very much,' I said thickly as I reached out and rubbed my fingertips against the inviting rubbery red berries. I licked each one in turn like a sommelier tasting a new wine and my tongue swirled around first one nipple and then the other as Sonia threw back her head, her hands steadying herself on my shoulders.

'Take off your clothes,' she said to me in a husky voice and then she turned to Carl and ordered him to lock the door.

'Make sure you do it properly this time and then you can come and watch Johann fuck me,' she added before turning back to me – and by this time I was naked and we embraced as we rolled together on the bed, writhing around in each other's arms as Sonia's tongue and lips hungrily sought my body. I put my hand down between her legs and discovered that her knickers were already soaking wet. I pulled them off and ran my forefinger along the slippery groove of her sex and she moaned softly and spread her legs as my fingertip delicately explored the sensitive folds and my knuckle brushed against her erect clitty.

'Oh yes, yes!' she squealed as I rolled on top of her and my cock started to leap and dance about between her thighs, seeking an entrance in the glistening bush of hair through which her puffy pussy lips pouted out so enticingly. My hands roved across her gorgeous breasts and I fingered her engorged thrusting titties whilst Sonia clasped her hand around my pulsating prick and guided my knob into her dripping cunt.

Sliding my cock in and out of her wet, warm cunney was quite heavenly and I moaned in sheer ecstasy as I jerked my hips to and fro, fucking the eager girl with unalloyed delight. Our movements rapidly became more heated when I thrust forward hard, sending my shaft plunging deep into her squelchy slit.

By God, how I enjoyed this magnificent fuck, slewing my willing shaft in and out of her juicy love channel. Sonia yelped as she felt the tip of my knob touch the innermost walls of her cunt and she wrapped her legs around my waist to hold me firmly inside her as I continued to pound away, my prick driving in and out of the tender folds of her cunt from which her juices were liberally flowing. She began to buck to and fro, her bum cheeks lifting themselves off the sheet as she closed her legs around me like a vice whilst I continued to pump in and out of her sopping sheath.

'Oooh! Oooh! Oooh!' yelled Sonia as she shuddered her way to a delicious orgasm and when she had calmed down I set up another rhythm, fucking her with short, sharp jabs and she climaxed again whilst I panted out a warning that my own spend was near. The young vixen massaged the underside of my ballsack and immediately this extra stimulation brought on my final surge. With a hoarse cry I emptied myself into her, flooding her cunney with tremendous spurts of hot, sticky sperm. She screamed with delight as the spunky gush sent shock after shock of erotic energy coursing through our veins. Then she expertly milked my cock with repeated squeezes of her cunt muscles until I pulled out my deflated shaft and heaved myself off her.

Not surprisingly, when I looked to my left, I saw that the sensual spectacle of our fucking had stiffened Carl's cock up again. I said to Sonia with a grin: 'Poor Carl! I know you're cross with him because he forgot to lock the door, but it would be rather cruel to deny him his first fuck. How about it, or is your pussy now a bit sore?'

My best chum was lucky, for Sonia's blood was up and she replied: 'No, come on, Carl, I'm game for another go.'

'Can I really?' cried Carl and Sonia smiled as she pulled him on top of her. Frantically he tried to insert his knob into her cunt but his inexperience showed for he was unable to find his way to his desired haven through the hirsute forest of her pussy hair and I said to him: 'Wait a second, old boy, may I help you?'

'Yes, please, Johann,' he panted and so I told him to lift himself up for a moment and I inserted my hand between their bellies and took hold of Carl's rock-hard battering ram and directed the purple domed knob towards Sonia's pouting pussy lips.

'Now slide your cock forward and you will see that the key will fit the lock,' I said as I removed my hand. Hey presto! With his first thrust he pushed forward into her welcoming sheath, with the second he was half-way home and with the third his entire pulsating prick was entirely ensconced inside her juicy honeypot.

Carl's tight little arse cheeks trembled with excitement and I was pleased to see that, after my initial instruction, he seemed to have a natural understanding of what was required of his cock. He did his best to prolong the ecstatic experience and forced himself to push in and out as slowly as he could and this was most pleasing to Sonia who responded with her own upward heaves to her partner's downward thrusts. Her bottom rolled violently as she clawed at his back and now he grasped her shoulders and began to ride her like a Wild West cowboy atop a bucking bronco. Her legs straightened out and her heels drummed against the mattress as she arched her back, working her cunney muscles back and forth along the velvety length of Carl's twitching tool.

With a hoarse cry of rapture he sheathed his shaft so fully inside Sonia's cunt that his balls fairly cracked against the top of her thighs. This so aroused the lascivious minx that she rotated her hips wildly, lifting her lovely bottom to obtain the maximum contact with his cock. He groaned with lust as Sonia's fingernails raked across his back and she panted: 'Y-e-s-s! Y-e-s-s! Y-e-s-s! That's so delicious!

Now shoot your spunk and make me come, you young rascal!'

A primordial sound spilled out from deep within the gorgeous girl as an all-enveloping orgasm shivered through her body and, to their mutual delight, Sonia reached her peak of pleasure just as the first convulsive shudders rippled through Carl's body and his cock squirted out his tribute of sticky warm jism into her flooded love funnel.

Carl slumped down upon Sonia's lush curves in a state of blissful exhaustion, but when she turned her head she saw that my cock was now standing up again and ready for another bout. She gently rolled Carl from on top of her and said with a voluptuous smile: 'Master Johann, your nice thick cock looks very tempting but my pussy will get sore if you fuck me again. So I'll just suck you off if that's all right with you.'

'Of course it is, please help yourself,' I said, returning her smile as I dropped to my knees and wriggled my way up the bed until Sonia could pull my aching shaft towards her rich red lips. She raised her head and made me gasp when she slid those lips over my knob and took my cock into her soft, mobile mouth, swirling her tongue over the smooth mushroom dome of my bell-end and sending shockwaves of pleasure shooting through my entire body.

'Woooh!' I gasped as I placed my hands on Sonia's head and she quickened the movements of her tongue, washing my helmet whilst her right hand snaked down and began to frig her still-juicy cunt. I closed my eyes and lost myself in the sheer ecstasy of the delicious sensation as Sonia licked and lapped away, stroking her wicked tongue up and down the slippery length of my shaft and pitching me into fresh paroxyms of delight. Then she squeezed her free hand around the base of my cock, sucking the sensitive underside harder and harder until I could feel the tingling power of the spunk rushing up to my cock from my tightened ballsack.

Sonia sensed that I would soon be spending because she pulled my prick out of her mouth and muttered: 'I'm going to swallow some of your spunk and then I want you to let the rest splash on my titties because I want to feel your cum as well as taste it.'

With that she rubbed her hand up and down my glistening wet shaft and the first gush of spunk spurted into her mouth. Then she swung my prick downwards and aimed my knob at her titties. I covered them with little white puddles of jism which Sonia massaged into her skin with one hand whilst with the other she diddled herself up to a second delicious spend.

The three of us lay sated on the bed until Carl noticed the time and with much giggling we dressed hastily. Before she left, Sonia promised that, if possible, she would come back and continue the fun and games after Doctor and Frau Hildebrand had retired to bed.

Meanwhile Carl and I spruced ourselves up for dinner and as we walked out onto the landing we met Bertolt who greeted us with a cheery smile.

'You look happy tonight,' observed Carl and Bertolt chuckled: 'I certainly am, and so would you have been if you had also spent an afternoon fucking the lovely Marguerite! Oh, I'm sorry, Carl, I don't want to make you envious but don't fret too much. After all, you're only just fifteen and your time will come soon enough. With any luck, you might get the chance to dip your wick next summer.'

No doubt it was on the tip of Carl's tongue to inform his older brother that less than an hour before he had already enjoyed his first fuck, but wisely my chum kept silence and simply winked at me as he said: 'Well, I very much hope you're right. Anyhow, who are the people dining with us this evening? I've never heard of Herr and Frau von Langen.'

'I hadn't either till Mama told me about them. Not that she knows very much for they have only met once before, at the Seligsohns',' said Bertolt as we walked down the stairs. 'But it seems that Herr von Langen owns one of the largest shipyards in Stettin and Frau von Langen is an accomplished amateur pianist and often gives recitals for charity.

'Anyway, the good news is that Carola, their sixteen-year-old daughter has also been invited and Mama says that she's a real beauty! Too old for you boys, I'm afraid, but *I'm* looking forward to meeting her.'

The von Langens arrived as we reached the hall. When my eyes fell upon Carola von Langen, I had to agree with Frau Hildebrand's assessment of her physical attractions for the young lady in question was indeed a strikingly pretty girl with sparkling blue eyes and a mane of strawberry blonde hair which she wore in silky ringletted tresses. My eyes wandered shamelessly up and down her dress which was of the same azure hue as her eyes and fashionably nipped in at the waist, accentuating the glorious spheres of her proud young breasts.

As well as being a wealthy shipowner, Herr von Langen took an active interest in politics and though I could say nothing – for it was hardly my place to argue with such a distinguished guest – I listened with increasing impatience whilst he argued the case against democracy, saying that if you took two men, one from a low and another from a high class of society, who would be best to judge the merits of any political question?

'It's simple logic,' he went on, wagging his finger to

emphasize his point. 'A man from the upper echelons has had the education, the means to fully acquaint himself with all the pros and cons of any political question whilst an illiterate working man is obliged to take his opinions at second hand and whether he will vote one way or the other in an election depends on which hands he may chance to fall. His teacher may be ignorant or, worse still, he could be one of those damned Socialist agitators who have reasons of their own for working on the working man's passions and credulity.'

He gulped down the wine in his goblet and then turned to Doctor Hildebrand and, with the kind of smugness in his voice we all tend to show when we confidently expect acquiescence from the person who is being invited to agree with our opinions, he concluded: 'So may I assume that I have you in my corner on this matter, George?'

The good doctor gave a wan smile and replied: 'Well, there can be no doubt that freedom used foolishly can only be a force for chaos and the voting powers of our people should be based upon sound judgement operating on sound knowledge. Certainly, I would not enjoy finding myself on a sailing ship where the voices of the cook and loblolly boys counted for as much as those of the officers or if the "great heart" of the crew was called upon to settle the ship's course!

'However, I would prefer to live in a country where great decisions are taken by the majority of citizens rather than by a despotic few. So I believe it is in all our interests to make sure that the most humble in our society are given a chance to learn basic skills of reading and writing. For this would mean they would be less likely to fall prey to the trickeries of agitators.'

'Come now, doctor,' said Herr von Langen with a frown. 'Surely you are not suggesting that I should be taxed so that another man's family can be educated at my expense?'

Doctor Hildebrand nodded: 'I'm afraid I am, my dear Fritz, for I truly believe that we must limit individual freedom for the greater good. Look, at night many streets in Stettin are lit by lamp posts, h'mm? Well, I am sure that there are a great many streets through which you have never passed and are unlikely ever to do so. Yet you would not cavil that you are being taxed merely to lighten the darkness for other people. The authorities would not let you off if you made such a plea and, to be quite candid, I do not see why they should.

'We all benefit from living in an ordered society and if its preservation means contributing to teaching other people's children, not only would I be ashamed to say no – for none of us came into this world with a gold spoon in our mouth – but I believe it would not be in my own interest to do so.'

Herr von Langen was unable to counter the force and lucidity of his host's reply and he merely muttered something about the doctor not having enough practical business experience to make a true judgement. But he was more than happy when Frau Hildebrand changed the conversation to a discussion of the exhibition of paintings by the Spanish artist Ignacio Murtinho Braga at the city's art gallery.

Meanwhile, it had been only with great difficulty that I had managed to restrain myself from applauding our host's fine words, although the shining look of approval I gave Doctor Hildebrand would have been clear to anyone who had happened to throw a glance in my direction at the time. However, I was not to know that no one except Carola van Langen had seen me . . .

I discovered this after dinner when the ladies retired to

the drawing room and Bertolt decided to stay with his father and Herr von Langen who, whilst disagreeing on political affairs, found they had much in common with their mutual love of good wine, good music (and, as I knew, in the case of the good doctor, a good fuck!)

So Carl and I sauntered out into the garden where the gorgeous Carola was standing on the patio, gazing out intently towards the greenhouse.

'Hallo there,' I said as we approached her, but instead of replying she simply smiled at us and silently pointed in the direction in which she had been looking so earnestly. We walked up to her and my eyes widened when I saw a young man in a coachman's uniform with his trousers round his ankles standing by Sonia who was sitting on a low stone wall clutching his thick, stiff cock in her hand.

She began to frig the youth's massive shaft slowly, rubbing her hand up and down the swollen love truncheon until it looked fit to burst and then she leaned forward and took the ruby coloured uncapped helmet between her lips, sucking almost half his length into her mouth. Her wet lips strained to encircle it but finally she made herself comfortable and started to bob her head up and down his pulsating prick until she had taken every morsel of cock deep into her throat.

Then I saw her slide her hands underneath his hanging ballsack and I guessed that she must have tickled his arsehole with the tip of her finger because within seconds we heard the coachman groan: 'I'm cumming, Sonia, I'm cumming, I can't stop!'

Sonia began to swallow in anticipation as he fucked her mouth, jerking his cock to and fro and, as he had warned, he soon shot his load and a trickle of spunk must have dripped down onto Sonia's skirt as he withdrew his still semi-erect tool because he now said anxiously: 'Oh God! I'm sorry, Sonia, but it looks like I've stained your dress.'

'No matter, Jurgen,' said Sonia reassuringly. 'In any case, it's my fault, I shouldn't have frigged your bum and made you spend so quickly. Anyhow, spunk washes out easily enough with the special new soap powder we've brought with us from Vienna.'

[The first detergents using surface-active chemicals such as an alkyl sulphonate were starting to be widely used at this time – Editor].

Sonia giggled and continued: 'I tell you what though, if you're quick, you can fuck me doggie-style to make up for it! Can you get another hard-on?'

'I should say,' answered Jurgen hoarsely, taking his cock in his hand and frigging his prick whilst Sonia whipped up her skirt and pulled down her knickers. She moved to the side of the greenhouse and turned her back to us as she put her hands against the glass and the fair-haired young coachman shuffled towards her, still sliding his hand up and down his throbbing stiffstander until he was positioned behind her. Then he lifted her skirt and slid his cock into the crevice between her peachy dimpled buttocks and into her sopping slit.

Jurgen was an athletic fucker and it was a real treat to see him slide his cock in and out of Sonia's juicy crack in a steady, fast-paced rhythm, achieving maximum penetration of her pussy by bending forward and rubbing his hands against her titties as he pumped merrily away.

Unfortunately, in his haste to secure a better view Carl knocked his foot against a loose stone and the sound made Jurgen turn his head. When he saw that there were three spectators watching his every move, he froze with fright with Sonia's bum cheeks pressed against his belly and his cock ensheathed inside her cunt.

'Carry on, my man,' I called out in an easy, friendly fashion. 'It wouldn't be right to leave poor Sonia unsatisfied.'

He still stood transfixed but when Sonia heard my voice she urged Jurgen to continue, saying: 'You heard what Master Johann said, Jurgen: you can't stop till you've flooded my quim with love juice.'

She wiggled her backside and he began again to fuck Sonia's cunney, this time in a series of powerful slamming thrusts. I heard Carola take a sharp intake of breath and, when I glanced quickly at the beautiful girl, it was clear from the flush of colour in her cheeks and the heaving of her bosom that she was relishing the sight of her coachman's cock see-sawing in and out of Sonia's cunt whilst the tiny rosebud of her arsehole quivered and winked with each stroke from Jurgen's blue-veined chopper.

As the lewd pair rocked in unison, Sonia threw back her head and let out a delighted little yelp as she reached behind her and squeezed her partner's ballsack. Sensing the time had come for him to spend, Jurgen gritted his teeth and his torso went rigid as he spilled out his injection of frothy white spunk inside Sonia's clinging slit. She cried again with glee as her climax swept through her body and Jurgen gave one last final thrust before pulling out his wet, deflated cock from the crevice of Sonia's bottom.

Jurgen then mumbled his apologies to us whilst he swiftly pulled up his trousers, but Sonia wiped her face with a towel she had brought out from the kitchen and said to Carola: 'I'm also sorry if we shocked you, my dear. Still, I can't believe that a pretty girl like you hasn't ever enjoyed a bit of rumpy-pumpy yourself.'

Carola did not reply to this slightly impudent observation, but she acknowledged Sonia's remark with a short smile before turning on her heel and making her way back to the drawing room with Carl and myself in tow.

I was pleased to discover the cloud of disagreement over politics between Doctor Hildebrand and Herr von Langen had not sullied the atmosphere and the company settled down to play some jolly parlour games. The evening's entertainment was continued by Bertolt giving us a fine rendition of Mozart's Sonata in B Flat Major with Doctor Hildebrand taking the violin part which was added by an unknown musician in 1793, and then I was persuaded to play my party piece, Chopin's Nocturne in E Flat Major, being rewarded by an enthusiastic reception from the listeners and especially Carola who told me how she adored the music of the half-Polish composer.

'I would love to hear you play the Étude in E Major,' she remarked and I gave a tiny chuckle and said: 'So would I, but I'm afraid that I haven't learned it. But if you can allow me some time to practise the piece, I would be delighted to play the Ballade Number Four in F Minor for you.'

However, I found myself hoist with my own petard for Carola gave me a dazzling smile and said: 'Do you mean it, Johann? Then can you practise the Ballade tomorrow morning and come round to our house afterwards to play it for me?'

The prospect of spending a couple of hours brushing up my knowledge of the admittedly beautiful music did not greatly appeal, but I could hardly go back on my word, especially when Frau Hildebrand, who was sitting near us and had heard the conversation, chimed in: 'You're in luck, Johann, I know for a fact that we have the sheet music of the Ballade inside the piano stool.'

'How wonderful,' I exclaimed as I did my best to look pleased at hearing this news. 'But unfortunately I will have a problem in getting to and from Stettin tomorrow.'

'Oh, that's easily solved,' said Carola happily. 'Papa will be at work all day and Jurgen will be free to take you and bring you back here.'

'Jolly good,' I said with as much sincerity as I could muster in the circumstances and we continued to chat about music until the time came for the von Langens to leave. However, my spirits were raised as we made our farewells and I was sure that Carola had deliberately squeezed my fingers just a mite more than was necessary when we shook hands and she said: 'Johann, I look forward to seeing you again tomorrow afternoon. Shall I instruct Jurgen to be here at half-past two?'

'Yes, that will be perfect,' I replied and when Carl and I retired to our room and I told him of what I had arranged with the lovely Carola, he declared: 'Well, well, you never know your luck. Mind you, I wouldn't like to spend a morning of my summer holiday practising at the piano. Still, we didn't have anything arranged for tomorrow. If the weather holds up I think I'll walk up to Jascnitz and take a look at the gypsy camp.'

This reminded me that I had not told Carl the story about my adventure with Natasha, but naturally I did not mention a word about his father's letter from Princess Juliet! Nevertheless, I did tell him about Natasha's desire to leave the Romany way of life and how Doctor Hildebrand had agreed to meet her to judge for himself whether she could be given a letter of recommendation to my parents or any future employer.

'You lucky beggar,' commented Carl as he pulled on his nightshirt. 'If this Natasha does join your household, I can imagine how she'll show her gratitude to you!'

This thought clearly aroused him for when I came back from the bathroom I could see that Carl was slowly frigging himself under the bedclothes.

'Don't forget that Sonia might come in,' I observed as I slipped into my own bed, but Carl grunted that the randy housemaid had told him that she would be too tired to visit us again tonight, but that she would try and make some time for us one evening later in the week.

'She loves a good fuck and I wouldn't be surprised if Bertolt is poking her,' Carl sighed as he pulled his hand away from his cock and rolled over to his side. 'Still, it's late and I am a bit tired myself so perhaps it's for the best. Goodnight, Johann.'

'Goodnight, Carl,' I answered and probably it was the excitement of all the strenuous fucking I had enjoyed with Natasha and Sonia, but I scarcely had time to think about whether the meeting of the gypsy girl and Doctor Hildebrand would go as well as I hoped before I fell fast asleep.

The next morning we woke to the patter of rain upon the bedroom window, but by the time we finished breakfast the sun was making a valiant effort to break through the clouds.

'Don't fret, I'm sure we've seen the last of the showers for today,' said Doctor Hildebrand comfortingly to his oldest son who was looking miserably out of the drawing-room window.

Bertolt gave a heavy sigh and remarked: 'I do hope you're right, Father. It's so annoying, though, because I had planned to ask Lottie Seligsohn if she would like to come out with me for a ramble this afternoon.'

'Well, at least it's stopped raining,' said Doctor Hildebrand, looking at his pocket watch as he added: 'I have one or two letters to write before I go out. Bertolt, my boy, you've nothing else to do today so, rather than mope around here, why don't you take a walk over to the Seligsohns' villa and see if Lottie is free? Even if the weather doesn't clear up enough to go swimming, at least you could ask her to come back here for luncheon.'

Bertolt perked up at this suggestion and said: 'Good idea, father, I'll just have a word with Freida before I go.' Then he heaved himself off his chair and walked towards the door.

'See you later, everybody,' he called out brightly, but after the door had closed behind him Doctor Hildebrand gave a gentle chuckle and said: 'I think poor old Bertolt is smitten by Lottie. But I believe that she and her blonde Swedish friend, um, what's her name now—'

'Bibi,' I said helpfully and he nodded his thanks and went on: 'Ah, yes, Bibi, quite a stunning girl, don't you agree? Anyway, I happened to see Frau Seligsohn yesterday and she told me that the girls went out last night to the theatre with Simon, Herr von Langen's eldest son, and a Polish friend of his from Warsaw, so I just hope that poor old Bertolt won't find himself *de trop* this morning.'

'Well, at least he doesn't have to spend the morning practising Chopin,' I commented as I pulled up the lid of the piano stool and searched for the sheet music that I needed.

'Come, come, Johann,' said Doctor Hildebrand, wagging a reproving finger as he delivered a genial reprimand. 'I heard your conversation with Carola von Langen last night. No one had a gun at your head when you offered to play the Ballade in F Minor for her.'

'True enough, sir,' I admitted with a grimace and when I found the music, I set it up on the stand and, scanning the first page with a worried look on my face, I groaned: 'This is one of the longest works I've ever learned and it's far from easy to play.'

'Well, I'm going to leave you to it,' said Carl hastily. 'Good luck, Johann, have a nice time with Carola. You must tell me all about your little concert this evening.'

He left the room and Doctor Hildebrand came across to the piano and, putting his hand on my shoulder, he said: 'I quite agree with you, my boy. Chopin was a pianist himself, of course, and always showed a great interest in keyboard technique. Still, we want you to put on a good show this afternoon. Now I have half an hour or so to spare, would you like me to go through the music with you?'

'Yes, please,' I said with relief and, under the guidance of Doctor Hildebrand, I struggled through the entire piece and then turned to him and said: 'What do you think, sir? Please give me your honest opinion.'

He thought for a moment or two and then said tactfully: 'Well, my honest opinion is that it's obvious you haven't played the Ballade for some time and so naturally you are somewhat rusty. So I suggest you practise only the first two pages.

'I'm sure that the lovely Fräulein von Langen will be suitably impressed by a flawless performance of the first eight minutes of the piece,' he added with a twinkle in his eye. 'The best of luck to you, Johann, but I'm afraid I can't stay any longer. There are some important letters which I must write before I meet up with your gypsy girl.'

Dear reader, my mother often told me that the Dutch have a saying about how false modesty is as bad as overweaning pride, so I make no apology for stating that I am fortunate enough to possess more than a modicum of natural musical ability. *[If anything, our author is being unduly modest for, beyond question, he was one of the most gifted amateur pianists in Europe by the turn of the century. In April 1908, at the express invitation of Franz Ferdinand, the Archduke of Austria, he accompanied Enrico Caruso when the world-famous tenor made a series of private gramophone recordings in Vienna. Alas the masters were tragically destroyed in a fire at the Imperial Palace four years later and no copies are now thought to have survived – Editor]* Be that as it may, I mastered the first ten minutes or so of the music by luncheon and I was quietly confident of my ability to perform satisfactorily for Carola by the time Jurgen the coachman arrived to take me back to the von Langens' home in the smartest suburb of Stettin.

As Doctor Hildebrand had forecast, the weather had greatly improved and I sat up next to Jurgen on the driving seat of the small carriage. He shook the reins and the horse trotted down the path, but the young coachman was clearly still ill at ease over what had happened last night for before we had travelled more than a hundred metres he had already started to apologize once more for his part in the incident.

I stopped him and said with a grin: 'For goodness' sake, Jurgen, as far as Carl and I are concerned the matter is closed. Quite frankly, we enjoyed watching you poke Sonia and for what it's worth I don't think Fräulein Carola was too troubled or she would have reported what she saw to her parents by now.'

'I suppose you're right, Master Johann,' he said as he guided our horse onto the road into Stettin. 'It's just that I would be dreadfully sorry to lose this job because Herr von Langen is a good employer.'

'Is he now? You surprise me,' I said drily and, though it was wrong of me to gossip to a servant about his employer, I went on: 'To be frank, from his conversation at the dinner table last night I wouldn't have thought Herr von Langen cared very much about the people who work for him.'

'He's not that bad, though he likes you to show respect,'

answer Jurgen with a brief smile, but from the tone of his voice I deduced there was something more he wanted to tell me, so I said: 'Look here, Jurgen, I really did enjoy the little show you and Sonia provided last night and far from you feeling that you need to apologize – if anything, I owe you a favour! So, if I can be of assistance with any problem which is troubling you, just say the word. Even if I can't help, you have my promise that I won't mention the matter to anybody, not even Fräulein Carola.'

Jurgen had listened very carefully to this little speech and clearly I had gained his confidence, for he pulled the horse over to the side of the road and blurted out: 'Well, if you put it like that, there *is* something I'd welcome your advice about, Master Johann. You see, last night was the second time this week I've been in trouble exercising my John Thomas.'

He paused and bit his lip. 'Oh, what's the use! Forget I spoke, young sir, I should have kept my mouth shut.'

'Don't be foolish,' I exclaimed, for Jurgen's secret story sounded very interesting. 'As I just said, I owe you a favour and, as my father always says, it's often much easier for someone not involved in a particular situation to find a way out of any difficulties.'

Jurgen pondered on this for a moment and then slowly nodded his head. 'That makes good sense and I won't beat about the bush. What's bothering me happened last Friday. Herr von Langen's sister, Frau Beatrice Schroeder, has been staying at the house whilst her husband is away on business in America. She is about thirty-five but has kept her figure and is still a very attractive woman.

'Now do you remember what a warm day it was on Friday? Well, her sister-in-law and Fräulein Carola were engaged elsewhere and so Frau Schroeder spent the afternoon by herself in the garden drinking cooled white wine. I was polishing the landaulet when one of the maids came running into the stable-yard with a message that Frau Schroeder was asking for me. Naturally, I wiped my hands and went to see her to find out what she wanted of me. I thought she might want to be driven somewhere, but when I approached her I could see from the way she was slumped in her chair that she had been hitting the bottle though she was only slightly tipsy as opposed to being completely sozzled.

' "Ah, there you are, Jurgen," she said, beckoning me to come closer. "So are you ready to perform a service for me, my man?"

' "Yes, of course, Frau Schroeder," I replied nervously and she laughed out loud when I went on: "Is there somewhere you wish to be taken to?"

' "There certainly is," she agreed as she grabbed hold of my arm and heaved herself upright. "I told Eva to call you because I must have sat out here in the heat for too long and I feel rather giddy. So I need a strapping young chap like you to help me into the house and you may have to carry me to my room if I don't have enough strength to tackle the stairs." '

'Oh dear, what a terribly embarrassing business,' I said sympathetically and Jurgen groaned: 'You can say that again, Master Johann! And worse was to come! Frau Schroeder was swaying so much as we walked into the house it was obvious that the only way she could get to her room would indeed be if I carried her up the stairs. In fact, she suggested this herself again and giggled like a schoolgirl as she threw her arm around my neck.

' "Well done, Jurgen! It's as well that you're such a muscular young chap," she said as she pointed to her room. I carried her across the landing and, still in my arms, she reached out and opened the door. I staggered in and on her instructions laid her gently down on the bed.

' "Now close the door and come back here. I have another job for you," said Frau Schroeder and, though I was feeling scared, what could I do but obey? Anyway, she sat up and went on: "You won't find this task so difficult. Just fetch me that black leather travelling case by the side of the wardrobe, there's a good boy."

'I picked the case up and gave it to her and she opened it and brought out a small bottle of brandy and two glasses. Then she winked at me and put her hand on my arm as she said in a husky voice: "I just adore a good brandy, don't you? But it's no fun drinking alone, so I want you to join me. There, that isn't such a dreadful imposition, is it?"

' "No, of course not, *gnadige frau*, but I'm not allowed to drink on duty," I stammered, but she waved away this objection and laughed: "Oh, to hell with all that, no one will ever know! Anyhow, you won't have to take out the horses again today. Neither Frau von Langen nor Carola will be going out again after they return home this evening."

'She poured generous measures of brandy into the glasses and then handed one to me. "Your good health!" she smiled as we clinked them together and I took a hesitant sip. It really was an excellent brandy and soon I began to feel more relaxed and sat on the bed whilst Frau Schroeder gaily chatted away, saying how much she was enjoying her vacation but how she was also missing the company of her husband, Ernst.

'I was wearing only a short-sleeved shirt on my upper body and I felt a warm shiver all through my torso when she grazed her fingertips along my arm and whispered softly: "Especially at night, if you follow me, Jurgen. Not that Ernst is any great shakes between the sheets. Between you and me, he always cums much too quickly. Why, no sooner has he slid his shaft into my pussy than he shoots off. I can't tell you how unsatisfactory this situation is for me – and to be fair, for poor Ernst as well." '

The coachman stopped and exhaled a deep breath, but my cock had already begun to stir for it was crystal clear that Jurgen was going to be invited to take part in some rumpy-pumpy. Naturally enough, this was the first time I had heard about this problem during the subsequent years I have known of at least three close friends who have been treated – thankfully with great success – for this distressing condition.

Ah well, as the French say: *Si jeunesse savait; si vieillesse pouvait!** These days I am well qualified to give good advice to any gentleman afflicted by this malady, but of course as a callow fifteen-year-old, I knew nothing about this distressing condition. Ironically enough, it was the lads who were the first to spend who were declared the winners of our masturbatory games at school, although even if I knew then what I know today, I would hardly have been in a position to offer any comfort to Frau Schroeder!

However, Jurgen was now ready to continue and he went on: 'I was now really enjoying myself and I didn't even attempt to refuse when Beatrice (for by now she insisted I stopped being so formal when addressing her) poured me out a large refill and I didn't feel uncomfortable any more when she steered the conversation back to her unfortunate husband and said: "Of course, I get dreadfully frustrated. After all, can you imagine how upsetting it is for a lady if her partner spunks before her cunney has hardly had time to become nice and juicy?"

* If only youth knew; if only old age could.

'She bit her lower lip and giggled: "Oh dear, I've been rather free with my words, but you know what brandy is supposed to make you feel."

'I also began to feel merry and I chuckled: "A double brandy makes you randy, is that what was in your mind?"

' "Exactly so," she said as she drew me closer to her and threw her arms around me. She rubbed her knee sensually up and down between my legs and, when she felt my prick swelling against her shin, she flashed me a wide smile and breathed: "It certainly makes me randy and now, dear Jurgen, I'll show you how pleased I am that it's had the same effect on you."

'We sank down on the bed, entwined in each other's arms and, as we kissed, Beatrice unbuttoned my trousers and pulled out my straining shaft. She grabbed hold of my cock in her hand and planted a passionate wet kiss on the top of my bell-end, holding my balls in one hand whilst with the other she eased down my foreskin and slid her tongue along the underside of my pulsating prick.

' "My God! I didn't lock the door! Suppose someone comes in!" I gasped wildly but she looked up and giggled: "No one will come in, Jurgen, and even if one of the girls did knock at the door, I don't know whether I would send her away or ask her if she wanted to make up a threesome. Now wouldn't that be exciting? Oh, don't look so bashful. Why, I'll wager a hundred marks that you've had your eye on Rosamund, that pretty little redhead who works in the kitchen, ever since she started here."

'I didn't attempt to deny that I was keen on Rosamund, but I would have preferred to have got up for a moment and bolted the bloody door! However, I didn't have a chance because I became nothing more than mere putty in Beatrice's hands when she began to unbutton her blouse and whispered: "Now you must undress me, my young fellow-me-lad."

'So I yanked off her shoes and helped her shrug out of her blouse and skirt. Then she pulled off her chemise and as she lay there naked except for a frilly pair of French knickers, she said with a smile: "Go on, feel my titties! I'm a real live woman, not a nude statue in a museum."

'Believe me, Master Johann, for a moment or two I thought I was dreaming as I slowly smoothed my hands over her lovely bare breasts, but Beatrice was so impatient to be fucked that she lifted her bum off the bed and tugged off her knickers herself!

' "Stand by to repel boarders!" she called out throatily as she climbed on top of me with her knees against my ribs and rubbed her pussy against my knob before guiding my helmet between her love lips. She gave a huge moan of delight when my cock entered her and I must admit my head started to spin like a top as I felt her cunney muscles contract and relax whilst she rocked from side to side with my tool embedded inside her and I cupped my hands around her big round breasts and rubbed her strawberry-red nipples till they stood out between my fingers.

' "Oooh! How delicious! I've waited so long to have a thick stiff cock throbbing away inside my cunt!" she purred contentedly as she bounced up and down on my tool. She ground her hips and then leaned right back so my shaft almost fell right out before she leaned forward again and panted with pleasure as I filled her sopping sheath.

' "H-a-r! What a lovely spend! You can cum now, Jurgen!" she panted as she speared herself again on my cock. Each of her spasms tightened her cunney and I started to jerk my hips upwards to meet her pushes and she shuddered through a second climax as I pumped jets of jism into her juicy crack.

'Beatrice was in the seventh heaven of delight and could hardly wait for me to recover and poke her again. She sucked my cock till it stiffened up again and, after licking my balls, Beatrice wiggled round, thrust out her bum cheeks at me and, as she pulled them apart, told me to smear some cold cream on my cock and stick my prick in her bottom.'

'And did you?' I asked. Jurgen silently nodded and then let out a long despairing sigh which I found difficult to understand. I exclaimed: 'Good grief! For the life of me I can't think why you should look so down in the dumps! I would have thought that most coachmen would have paid good money to be in your shoes, for so far it all sounds as though you had a damned good time obliging your boss's sister. Or did someone come in and spoil the party whilst you were giving her one up the bum?'

He shook his head and replied: 'No, we weren't interrupted, but after we finished she made me promise to come to her room that night and she would drain my balls again. Well, to cut a long story short, I've had to go to her room every night this week and, not to put too fine a point on it, I'm absolutely knackered! Now you may laugh, Master Johann, but I have to be up at half-past six every morning to get the carriage ready to take Herr von Langen to the shipyard and come the afternoon I can hardly keep my eyes open! I was so tired the other day I nearly drove this small landaulet off the road and into the river!'

'Dear me, I see what you mean,' I said, trying my best not to smile, although I must confess that I found it rather amusing to think of poor Jurgen staggering out of Beatrice's bed totally exhausted after yet another session of wild fucking.

'On the other hand, I noticed you had enough energy to shag Sonia last night, so Frau Schroeder can't be *that* demanding,' I continued. But he looked up at me and said in a hollow voice: 'That was only because Beatrice had spent the night with some friends and I'd had the first good night's sleep since last Thursday!'

Jurgen pulled at the reins and the horse began to amble down the road as he groaned. 'I've heard it said that you can tire of caviare and champagne. I've never believed that before, but I do now! Honestly, Master Johann, I'm at my wit's end.'

I scratched my head and observed: 'Oh, come on, Jurgen, surely there's a very simple solution to this problem – all you have to do is to tell Frau Schroeder the plain, unvarnished truth: that you need your beauty sleep! Say to her that, whilst you very much enjoy making love to her, she must give you an occasional night off!'

'Don't you think I've tried that?' he replied with a frown. 'But she just laughed in my face when I said as much to her. "You're just tired of screwing me," she said accusingly and she reached out and gently squeezed my balls as she added with a touch of scorn: "Tough luck, Jurgen! You'll just have to ask for some time off during the day because I have to go back to ten-second Ernst in two weeks' time and till then I'm damned if I'm going to miss out on one single night of fucking!" '

'Did she say what would happen if you didn't show up?' I asked and he gave me a rueful smile and said: 'Beatrice didn't beat about the bush. She warned me that if I didn't make an appearance every night she would tell her brother that I had been extremely insolent towards her and demand that I be dismissed.'

'Wow! She's a very determined lady, isn't she?' I exclaimed and then said with a shrug: 'Oh dear, it looks to me as if you're lumbered with her for the next two weeks – unless your overworked cock drops off before then!'

Jurgen rubbed his chin and said slowly: 'Yes, I'm afraid you're probably right, though this morning I suddenly had a thought of one way I could sneak off duty for at least one night.'

He paused and I looked at him enquiringly and asked: 'Well, what's your idea? Go on, Jurgen, spit it out.'

'If I could find Beatrice a substitute, I'm sure that would do the trick,' he said eagerly. 'And I was thinking of *you*, Master Johann. She's a grand fuck and could probably teach a young gentleman like you some naughty things you haven't even read about before. Please say you'll help out. You're my only hope. I swear to you, if I don't get at least eight solid hours of sleep tonight I think I'll just collapse on the job.'

'Which one? Whilst you're shagging Beatrice or whilst you're driving Herr von Langen to his office?' I chuckled as I considered Jurgen's heartfelt plea. Now, though my head told me bluntly how idiotic it would be to get involved with Frau Schroeder, my throbbing tool was almost bursting out of my trousers and, as the old Viennese maxim puts it, when the prick stiffens up, common sense flies out of the window . . .

God knows how I am going to explain things to Carola, I thought to myself, but I shrugged my shoulders and said: 'Very well then, Jurgen, you can ask Beatrice if she fancies trying out a fresh cock later this afternoon, but you must make sure that someone will be available to drive me back to Doctor Hildebrand's by six o'clock this evening.'

'I will! I will!' the coachman assured me eagerly. 'Oh, thank you, Master Johann, I can't tell you how grateful I am. If I can ever repay you—'

'All right, all right,' I said somewhat testily. 'I can't see myself ever calling upon you to poke one of *my* girl friends but, if such an unlikely event ever arises, I won't hesitate to contact you.'

He thanked me again as he manoeuvred our steed through the gates and into the driveway of the von Langens' palatial residence. When we pulled up outside the front door, Jurgen muttered: 'I'll speak to Frau Schroeder right away and find out if she's willing to go along with the idea of swopping cocks just for one day.'

'Let me know how you get on as soon as possible,' I said as I jumped off the seat onto the gravel path. Carola must have been looking out of the window waiting for our arrival, for as the butler opened the door, she rushed past him and came out onto the path to greet me.

'Johann! How nice to see you again!' said the gorgeous girl, giving me a friendly peck on the cheek and then slipping her arm in mine, she led me into the house. 'I expected you about fifteen minutes ago, did Jurgen have to wait whilst you had one final practise?'

'Not really,' I answered with a tiny smile. 'And I owe you an apology, Carola. Despite my boast to you last night, I'm afraid that I shan't be able to play the complete Ballade today. I must be honest with you – Doctor Hildebrand kindly listened to me play this morning and he tactfully suggested that I concentrate my efforts into trying to perfect the first five minutes or so rather than stumbling through the entire piece and making Chopin turn in his grave.'

'Oh, you poor boy,' she exclaimed as I followed her into the music room. 'If I had realized how difficult a task you had set yourself, I would never have let you go through with it. After all, it is holiday time!'

I replied: 'Thanks for saying so, but it's my own silly fault. Anyhow, I hope that you and your mother won't be too critical of my performance.'

'Don't be silly, Johann, but in any case Mama is out this afternoon on her fortnightly excursion to visit sick members of our employees' families,' said Carola mischievously. 'She goes armed with one of our footmen and a huge tureen of nourishing soup. I'm sure she finds that many people have been miraculously restored to health when she calls round, because if I were feeling ill and had taken to my bed, I can't think of anything worse than being visited by Mama and having a bowl of soup thrust down my throat!

'Her visits are probably the reason why Papa's workers so rarely fall ill for no invalid ever escapes her attention: at the first whisper of illness, they know that in just a few hours Mama will be knocking on the front door!'

'You wicked girl,' I grinned, though of course I was far from displeased to learn that Frau von Langen was not at home. Then with a studied carelessness I added: 'However, I understand from Jurgen that your Aunt is staying with you for a holiday. Is she interested in music? If she is, please *don't* invite her to listen to me play!'

Carola tapped me on the arm and said: 'I'm sure you are being too modest, Johann. Nevertheless, I won't seek out Aunt Beatrice because now that the coachman has returned she will almost certainly call him to her room. Perhaps you noticed how pale Jurgen looked? Well, I don't suppose he mentioned this to you, but my aunt has taken a great shine to him. He was probably very flattered because she's only in her early thirties and is a most attractive woman. Yesterday Aunt Beatrice confided in me that since last Friday she had managed to get him to poke her at least five times a night every night so poor Jurgen must be feeling quite shagged out.'

This last remark put me squarely on the spot – should I

or should I not inform Carola that I was already in possession of this information?

Now, I have always held that it is better to follow a positive course and throughout my life I have found that one usually does better by choosing to do something rather than by deciding to do nothing. So I followed my instinct and told Carola that I was aware of Jurgen's liaison with Frau Schroeder, but took care to add that the exhausted coachman was not guilty of merely passing the time in retailing juicy tit-bits of gossip about the sexual peccadilloes of a lady of quality. At first Carola looked at me with a grave expression on her pretty face whilst I gave her chapter and verse about Jurgen's predicament, but when I told her of his suggestion that I offer my cock as a substitute to Frau Schroeder, she burst out into fits of laughter.

'Well, I'm glad you find it funny,' I commented sourly, but Carola nudged me in the ribs with her elbow and said: 'Now then, Johann, there's no need to get on your high horse. I'd wager the Koh-i-noor Diamond that you agreed to let Jurgen ask Aunt Beatrice if she would go along with his proposal. You men are all the same, you'd do anything for a—'

She was interrupted by a knock on the door and Jurgen came in to ask if I could come outside for a moment as he had a message for me.

'It's all right, Jurgen, I know all about your plan so you and Johann don't have to sneak away in secret, grinned Carola. 'So did Aunt Beatrice say yes or no?'

Jurgen glanced at me and, when I gave a little nod, he gulped: 'Frau Schroeder said she would consider the idea and if Master Johann is agreeable, she wants him to go up to her bedroom in about an hour and, um—' His voice faltered and so I said encouragingly: 'Go on, Jurgen, spit it out!'

He gave me the ghost of a smile and went on: 'Well, it's all up to you, Master Johann, because she gave me her word that I can have the night off but only if your performance is up to standard!'

'What an awesome responsibility lies on your shoulders – or rather on a more private part of your anatomy,' observed Carola who was finding this situation very amusing. 'Johann, I trust you'll do your bit to help poor Jurgen out of his difficulties.'

'You wouldn't mind?' I asked and she shook her head and then she asked Jurgen to step outside for a moment before continuing: 'Johann, I'm going to let you in on another little von Langen family secret – I'm no ice maiden, that's for sure, but I am still a virgin and although I'll readily admit that I'm very attracted to you, I'm not ready yet to go all the way with you or anyone else in bed.'

'What has that to do with anything?' I asked in some bewilderment and she went on patiently: 'Only that I don't want you to think me a spoilsport. I hope that we will become close friends and will continue to correspond with each other after you leave Stettin. So when I decide to take the plunge, it may well be that, assuming you are ready, willing and able to comply with my request, I shall call upon the services of your sturdy shaft. But, in the meantime, please feel free to fuck my aunt. For to answer your question, I should not mind at all if you accept the offer for it would be most impolite to refuse such an invitation from a lady.'

Carola paused and then flashed me a wide grin as she concluded: 'Anyhow, shagging Aunt Beatrice should be great fun. She is a sensual woman who will probably teach you some interesting refinements in *l'art de faire l'amour* which perhaps you will pass on to me one day.'

Clearly, the die was cast! As Carola rightly said, fucking

her aunt was hardly an imposition. Nevertheless, I was still more than a little nervous at the idea of being summoned into Frau Schroeder's bedroom. Suppose my prick refused to play? Male readers will need little reminding of how treacherous a teenage tool can be. Only a few days before this incident, I was sitting quietly in the garden reading a newspaper article on the political situation in the Balkans when for no reason my shaft suddenly stiffened and refused to go down for at least five minutes. On the other hand (although this had not yet happened to me), I had heard several scary stories from older boys at school about how, after having finally persuaded their *amorata* to part their legs, their cocks simply refused to swell up.

So I felt I needed some time to pluck up my courage and I gulped: 'Very well, I shall attend to Aunt Beatrice after I've played you the opening of Chopin's Ballade. I practised the music for at least an hour this morning and I will feel I wasted my time if—'

'You can play it to me afterwards,' Carola interrupted with a gentle smile as she pushed me out into the corridor and directed me to her aunt's bedroom. 'I'm sure you won't have forgotten the piece in an hour's time. Go on, my dear, do your duty, Auntie Bea won't bite you. Well, not *too* hard!'

In spite of my anxiety, I let out a chuckle and made my way upstairs. Outside Frau Schroeder's bedroom I took a deep breath which I slowly exhaled as I knocked on the door.

'Come in,' called out a friendly female voice and I opened the door. Then I stood stock still as my gaze fixed upon Frau Beatrice Schroeder who was reclining naked on her bed, joyfully frigging herself. She had one hand cupping a large rounded breast whilst the other was clamped in the hairy brown bush between her thighs and her fingers were sliding up and down the crack of her cunney.

Fortunately, my worries proved unfounded and my cock had sprang up to its full length even before she passed her tongue sensually over her top lip and said to me: 'Ah, you must be Johann Gewirtz. Run me a warm bath, there's a good boy.'

'Very well, Frau Schroeder,' I said meekly and, as if in a dream, I walked slowly to the bathroom – but when I passed by the side of the bed, she went on: 'Wait a moment! You're late, young man and as you see, I've been forced to begin without you. However, I can see from the bulge in your trousers that you're primed for action so let's not waste any more time. Sit down here and take off your clothes – I'll have my bath later! Oh, and do let's start as we mean to go on. There's no need to be formal, Johann. You must call me Beatrice.'

This command brought back my previous nervousness and my shaft softened as I pulled off my clothes. But Frau Schroeder was wise enough to say nothing when I turned my back to her as I tugged down my undershorts except to praise my figure and say: 'What a lovely tight pair of bum cheeks! Now let's have a look at your cock! M'm, that looks like a fine, beefy specimen. Let's see if a little kiss will make him stand to attention.'

At her bidding I climbed into bed and lay on my back as she raised herself up on her knees and bent over me, taking my bashful tool into her hand and then popping it into her mouth where she swirled her wet tongue over my knob. In a matter of moments matters took their natural turn and my cock regained all its strength and throbbed like a stiff bar of steel between her lips and Beatrice whispered huskily: 'There, that's better, isn't it? Now, just lie there. I'm going to sit on your lovely thick tool. Don't be frightened, Johann, you'll love the feel of your cock gliding juicily into my moist little cunt.'

'I'm sure I will,' I said as she positioned herself on top of me, leaving the lips of her pussy just a millimetre or two from the tip of my straining shaft. Then she placed my hands on her big firm titties and I moved my palms over them which seemed to excite her even more.

'Close your eyes and relax, dear boy, I have a feeling that this is going to be a fantastic fuck,' Beatrice murmured as she took my chopper in her hand and guided it firmly into her well-lubricated love channel.

She sighed with delight as she speared herself upon my cock, trapping the entire length inside her clinging quim. How she wriggled with pleasure as she bounced up and down on my twitching tool, leaning forward to let her heavy breasts dangle in front of my face!

There was no doubt as to who was orchestrating this salacious love-play. I was mere putty in Beatrice's hands as she slid up and down my rampant rod although I can't say I didn't enjoy it immensely. Automatically my hips pushed up to meet her downward thrusts.

After a while she increased the speed of her fucking rhythm. My cock began to throb uncontrollably and I panted out that my spend was near. With one last push upwards I gushed out a fierce jet of spunk inside Beatrice's cunt and this finished her off very nicely. We whimpered together with every spasm as our juices mingled together in a flood of mutual jism.

Well, Jurgen and Carola had both warned me that Beatrice Schroeder was a voluptuous hot-blooded lady and, sure enough, as soon as she had tongued my cock back to a rock-hard stiffness, she suggested that we move into a *soixante-neuf* position. This worried me, for although I knew what was in her mind, this would be my first experience of kissing a lady's cunt. I was somewhat apprehensive about the idea, not so much because I wouldn't relish the experience but because the fumblings of my untrained tongue might cause Beatrice to comment adversely on my performance.

Now, of course I should not have been concerned, for a sensible woman like Beatrice would not have wanted to crush my ego by insensitive criticism – to be frank, not just out of kindness but for reasons of self-interest because an adverse remark would not improve matters and would probably end my interest in continuing the romp.

However, she was not put to the test for readers blessed with a good memory will recall that at the beginning of these memoirs I noted the fact that on my thirteenth birthday my father gave me a copy of Professor Louis Baum's *A Young Person's Guide To Human Procreation* (or *Fucking for Beginners* as the book was jokingly called by my friends when I showed it to them at school). So I had at least some theoretical knowledge of what was expected of me as we made ourselves comfortable with Beatrice astride me on her knees with her lovely bottom pressed against my face whilst she bent down and sucked my cock in between her lips. Then she lowered herself down on me till her spunk-coated pussy lips were pressed against my mouth and immediately I began to lap up the morsels of our previous repast. I felt Beatrice shudder all over when I gingerly slurped around the folds of her pussy. When I inserted the tip of my tongue inside her cunt, she responded by swirling her own tongue up and down that so-sensitive area between my arsehole and my balls, a stimulation that sent me into a state of sheer ecstasy.

Not only did this lascivious tonguing drive me wild:

more importantly, it gave me greater confidence to lick out Beatrice's juicy love funnel and for the first time I inhaled the pungent feminine aroma of an aroused cunney. To be absolutely honest, at first I found the odour slightly overpowering but I gradually became accustomed to it and soon had no qualms about swallowing down Beatrice's cuntal juice.

Then she transferred her tongue to my knob, washing the dome expertly until my cock was yearning to be placed back in her squishy honeypot. I gasped out as much to Beatrice who swiftly moved herself off me and lay on her back with her legs open and her puffy pink pussy lips jutting through the silky bush of brown curls which covered her mound. I sank my rigid rod deep into its welcoming wet softness and felt the walls of her cunney clamp themselves around my cock which made me immediately start to pump hard in and out of her juicy quim, sliding deeper and deeper. She cried out in delight as my chopper ground against the erect button of her clitty.

On this second ride on the roundabout of love Beatrice was the first to spend, shivering and trembling all over when she reached the pinnacle of pleasure. She cried out with joy as she entered the delicious throes of orgasm and her cunney gripped my prick even tighter as one delicious spasm after another shook through her entire body.

'Ooooh! Oooooh! Come on, Johann, shoot your spunky fuck juice, you naughty big-cocked boy!' she groaned lewdly whilst she gripped my bum cheeks and pulled me even deeper inside her.

I found myself thrusting in and out of her sopping snatch at breakneck speed and very soon my seed boiled up inside my tightened balls. I exploded inside her, filling her sated pussy with copious splashes of spunk as I grunted loudly in the frenzy of emission until my trembling tool had been milked dry and I slumped exhausted upon her.

We were both in need of a rest and I laid my head down upon Beatrice's beautiful soft breasts whilst she gently played with my glistening limp shaft, purring like a kitten as her fingers wandered all over it. She looked up at me and sighed: 'You're a natural fucker, young Gewirtz. However, am I correct in assuming that a third fuck is out of the question?'

'I'm afraid so,' I answered and, remembering my mother's instruction when I was a child about what to say to my hostess after a party, I grinned: 'But I had a wonderful time, Beatrice. Thank you for having me.'

Beatrice burst into laughter and said: 'Well said, Johann, I couldn't have put it better myself. I'm so glad you enjoyed yourself as much as me. I know that many women say that sex is not the most vital factor in their lives but I find that impossible to believe because for me it *is* the most important. I am not over-difficult to please but I do so love to be fucked by a stiff thick cock like yours. There is nothing in the world that can compare with that exquisite feeling – I adore it!'

'Can I be of further service?' I enquired and she kissed my cheek and said: 'Thank you, my dear, I would be obliged if you would now run a nice warm bath for me.'

I padded out into the bathroom and turned on the taps before wiping myself down with one of the towels and returning to the bed to pick up my clothes where I began to dress. Beatrice slid her legs out of the bed and reached up to unpin her hair which made her glossy brown locks tumble down on to her shoulders. Her luscious large breasts, each topped by a strawberry-coloured nipple, jutted out proudly and below, at the base of her smooth flat tummy, lay a curly bush of hair through which I could see the outline of her pussy lips. Then she hauled herself up and I caught my breath when she walked to where her bathrobe was hanging on a hook on the wall. Despite its previous exertions, my cock stirred as I was given a view of her perfectly rounded pair of bum cheeks.

'Oh ho, I see my fine friend still has some life in him,' she murmured hopefully, but I shook my head quickly and said: 'Just a final salute, I'm afraid, because I really don't have time for anything more.'

Beatrice looked disappointed as I pulled on my trousers but, though it has always been a lifelong maxim of mine never to turn down the chance of a good fuck, I muttered something about how it would have been most impolite to keep Carola waiting for me any longer. When I finished dressing Beatrice threw her arms around me and gave me a big hug as she kissed me on the lips and said firmly: 'We must do this again before I leave for home.'

'I would like that very much,' I said sincerely and then before I left I asked Beatrice if she would keep her promise to let Jurgen rest from his labours last night.

'Yes, I suppose so,' she sighed and added with a twinkle in her eyes. 'Though you had better warn him that I'll be especially frisky tomorrow!'

Carola was most amused when I recounted this last remark to her over a steaming cup of coffee. 'Nevertheless, Jurgen's balls will be relieved to have the opportunity to replenish themselves although he has a wandering eye and I know he fancies Rosamund, a pretty young red-haired girl who has just joined our household staff.'

'So his cock will be in action again this evening,' I commented wryly, but Carola shook her head and went on: 'I'm not so sure about that for I have a strong fancy that Rosamund may be of the tribadic persuasion.

'Well, to be quite candid, I *know* she is because she made that very clear this very afternoon when I decided to change my clothes after luncheon. I went upstairs to my room and took off the dress I was wearing and was about to change into a lightweight silk frock when I saw that a button was missing from the garment I wished to put on. I pressed the bell for my maid, and a minute later there was a respectful tap on my door. But instead of my personal maidservant Minnie it was the pretty new girl, Rosamund, who came in and dropped me a curtsy.

' "You rang, ma'am?" she said and I replied: "Yes, I want somebody to sew a button onto this black silk shirt whilst I finish changing. But why did you answer my call, Rosamund? Where has Minnie got to?"

' "I'm afraid that Minnie isn't feeling very well, ma'am. This heat has given her a terrible headache so I told her that I could take on her responsibilities whilst she went and had a lie down for an hour or two as I had the afternoon off," she explained and I said: "Well, that's very kind of you, Rosamund. I'm sure Minnie will be very grateful – and so will I if you can sew on this button for me."

' "'Course I can, Miss Carola, I'm a dab hand with a needle and thread," she said as she took the skirt from me. "Good," I went on. "I've a needle and some fine dark cotton in the sewing basket on my dressing table."

'Then I pulled off my underclothes and walked naked into the bathroom where I dusted my body with some refreshing violet talcum powder. After I had finished, I wiped my hands on a towel and looked at myself in the mirror and cupped my hands around my breasts and squeezed them together. I was complimented on my figure by the other girls at my boarding school. My breasts were no means the biggest in our dormitory but they are well shaped and jiggle nicely above my snowy white belly when I move. *If only they were bigger*, I sighed to myself as I looked critically at my nude body in the long wall mirror.

'I began to play with my nipples, flicking them up to hardness whilst I recalled the scene last night in your garden when we saw Jurgen poking your servant, what was her name now—'

'Sonia,' I said helpfully and she nodded and continued: 'Yes, of course, Sonia. I couldn't help thinking that I wished that my breasts were as well developed as hers.'

'Your breasts aren't small,' I interjected truthfully. 'And in any case, it's quality, not quantity, that counts.'

'Many thanks for the compliment, Johann,' said Carola, blowing me a dainty little kiss. 'But we girls worry about our breasts just as you boys worry about the size of your cocks. Admit it now, don't most boys think that all their friends appear to be better endowed than themselves?'

'Not all of them,' I answered quickly. 'However, you are absolutely right in that there isn't a chap I know (myself included) who would say no to an extra few centimetres of cock.'

Carola chuckled throatily and said: 'Well, there you are, then, why should girls be any less foolish? Anyhow, there I was, idly day-dreaming when I suddenly realized that Rosamund was standing in the doorway looking closely at my naked figure. I turned to her and said: "Ah, have you finished sewing on that button already? You certainly didn't waste any time."

' "Thank you, Miss Carola," she said and she dropped a curtsy as I passed by her and picked up the skirt which was lying on the bed. "Will that be all or is there anything else I can do for you?"

' "No, that will be all, thank you, Rosamund," I

answered, but I noticed her eyes had wandered back towards the bathroom and I continued: "Tell me though, what did you find so interesting in my bathroom?"

' "Nothing except you, Miss Carola," the maid replied as she respectfully lowered her eyes to the carpet. Then she lifted her head and the words came tumbling out in a rush as she continued: "I'm not the only one who keeps your photograph under her pillow, you know. All the other maids do too and not only because you're such a kind lady to work for."

' "Goodness, if that is really true then I'm most flattered," I laughed as I laid down on my bed. "But I cannot think what else there can be which makes the girls want my photograph."

'Rosamund's cheeks flushed a charming shade of pink as she muttered: "Oh, Miss Carola, I can't tell you that. If I did, you might be so angry that you would give me notice."

'Naturally, this evasive remark aroused my curiosity and I eagerly urged the pretty redhead to explain herself. At first she refused but when I took her hand and squeezed her fingers and promised the girl that I wouldn't be annoyed with her whatever she said, Rosamund sat down on the bed and said: "All right, ma'am, I'll tell you, but I don't like to say it out loud. May I just whisper it in your ear?"

'Normally I would probably have refused such an impudent request, but I was so interested to find out what the girls thought about me that I gave a little giggle and said: "Very well then, Rosamund, come over here and tell me quietly if it embarrasses you so much to speak out properly."

'In a flash she was pressing herself against my nude body and placing the palm of one hand on my cheek and the other on my head behind my right ear, she whispered: "Miss Carola, the other reason that the girls below stairs adore you is because you are so beautiful. If you would ever like to kiss and cuddle any one of us, you only have to say the word."

'I was so shocked by her answer that I drew back my head and repeated blankly: "Kiss and cuddle me? Why should you want to do that?"

'Rosamund must have decided that she might as well be hanged for a sheep as for a lamb for she kissed my ear and murmured: "Because we would have such a sweet time together, that's why."

I gasped with surprise as she boldly squeezed one breast as she transferred her lips to the other, sucking in my erect nipple inside her mouth. Fired by her passion I responded by cradling her head in my hands and running my fingers through her glossy reddish-brown hair.

'She licked all round my stiffened nipple and muttered throatily: "Doesn't that feel good? Wait a moment and I'll do something even nicer."

'Rosamund sprang up and in only seconds off came her black maid's dress revealing that she was wearing only a pink vest, black stockings and a pair of tight white knickers on this hot afternoon. I could just about see her large breasts through the thin material of her vest and moments later she tugged the vest over her head and I watched them bounce free in all their naked glory, the raspberry nipples rigid in anticipation of an erotic romp. The girl sat down on the bed to pull down her stockings and then she stood up to wriggle out of her knickers. Then this lusty miss quite deliberately flaunted herself in front of me, turning slowly round on her long well-shaped legs to display her taut dimpled bum cheeks.

'I am not ashamed to admit that my excitement had

been whetted by Rosamund's sensual beauty and I am sure that by now your cock would have been bursting out of your trousers, Johann, at the sight of this pretty girl's delicious young body. Her breasts were full and firm, her tummy as flat as a pancake and her pussy was covered with a clipped thatch of tightly curled auburn hair which perfectly matched the silky tresses she had let down from her bun to cover her shoulders.

'She threw herself back on the bed and her lips met mine, first just brushing against them and then pressing more insistently. Our tongues slithered together as we kissed and I wrapped my arms around her neck, wanting her even closer. I was becoming unbelievably aroused by the feeling of her erect nipples rubbing against mine.

' "What a gorgeous pussy you have, Miss Carola, it looks good enough to eat! Such lovely big cunney lips, too!" she breathed softly and she smoothed her hand down over my belly until she cupped my cunney firmly in her palm and I lay back to savour this exquisite sensation as the clever minx then whispered: "Part your legs a little wider and bend your knees and then you can rub yourself off on my hand."

'I took up her suggestion and worked my furry pussy back and forth against the heel of her palm, increasing the speed of the movement as my excitement grew. The cunning little tribade added to the pleasure by raising her thumb and pressing it down onto my clitty so that with each forward bumping of my hips a thrilling wave of ecstasy crashed out of my quim and spread throughout every fibre of my body.

' "Ahhh! That feels divine," I gasped as my knees trembled with delight. The delicious feeling of the contact of her fingers on my now dripping crack was so enervating that I began to moan and work my bottom faster whilst dear Rosamund increased the circling action of her thumb.

'Then she slipped her forefinger into my cunt down to the second knuckle and kissed me passionately whilst she reamed out my juicy quim. I began grinding my hips in rhythm with her finger-fucking and I cried out: "Oh, my God, this is even better. Please don't stop!"

' "Don't worry, I won't stop till you cum," she panted and I threshed around from side to side as I felt my cunney muscles squeezing Rosamund's wicked finger in quick, hard contractions as together we rode the wind. Very soon this caused me to spend and my cuntal juices spurted out all over her hand as I shivered all over from the force of my climax.

' "Oh look, Miss Carola, you've made my hand all wet," Rosamund giggled happily as she climbed on top of me and pushed her ripe titties up in front of my face. I sucked and licked the rubbery little nipple-cherries. I pushed her soft breasts together with my hands and moved my mouth from one tittie to another until she too spent profusely and it occurred to me that we could carry on this delicious game with my dildo. But we had to stop there because, if she had stayed any longer, Rosamund would have been missed and one of the footmen might have come looking for her.'

Carola stopped and looked down at the huge tenting bulge in my lap with a lusty gleam in her eye and chuckled: 'Goodness gracious, Johann, it's quite clear that you enjoyed listening to my little story.'

'I should say I did!' I said boldly. 'But what I want to know is whether you would let a boy play with your pussy?'

'Of course I would,' she answered with a gay laugh. 'I am not by nature a tribade and would far rather pet with a boy than with a girl. But we don't even get a chance at my school to meet any young men and so we are forced to find feminine playmates to pleasure our bodies. Anyhow, I love having my cunney sucked so much that I don't really care a fig *who* does it!'

'I don't suppose you would allow me to—' I began, but Carola immediately interrupted me and two delightful dimples appeared on her cheeks as she wagged a warning finger at me and declared: 'Dearest Johann, I would like nothing better than for you to lick me out, but you must give me your solemn promise that you won't try to poke me. Remember, I am still – if only technically – *virgo intacta* and wish to remain so for the time being.'

'You have my word of honour,' I said without the slightest hesitation. This was the first of many times in my long history of dalliances with the fair sex that I swore to go no further than my partner desired, and I have never broken such a pledge of honour. There may be many reasons for a girl's reluctance to go all the way but, whatever they may be, a true gentleman always respects the fact that at any given time, a lady who may enjoy being sensually caressed does not necessarily wish to travel the full distance down love's path to a fully-fledged fuck.

One is entitled to attempt to woo her into taking the steps to a final delicious consummation. Indeed, a girl might rightly feel indignant if one did not plead with her to change her mind, for a failure to do this might make her believe one did not really care that much for her physical charms!

However, I have nothing but contempt for those miserable cowards who are not above using gross deception or, worse, physical force for their own nefarious ends. I have no wish to boast, but I have fucked a great number of women and I am convinced that my success is partly due to the fact that I have never tried to force a female to do anything that she genuinely did not want to do.

'Very well then, come upstairs with me,' said Carola and, with my cock now threatening to burst out of the prison of my trousers, I followed the lovely girl to her room. When we were safely inside she locked the door and we threw ourselves down on the bed, giggling happily away as we helped to undress each other.

Carola pulled open the buttons of my trousers and released my throbbing tool which saluted her by standing up erect as a guardsman on parade when she yanked down my drawers. At the same time I helped her shrug off her blouse and slip off her chemise. I licked my lips when I gazed at the superb swell of her bouncy bare breasts with their exquisite saucer-shaped areolae topped by the most mouth-wateringly pert nipples one could wish to see. Then my eyes were drawn downwards to the shiny strands of the wanton girl's pussy bush through which I could see her puffy pink love lips. In no time at all we had stripped ourselves naked and our tongues explored each other's mouths as we kissed with a fiery passion. Carola allowed me to roll her onto her back and smooth my fingertips into the rich profusion of silky hair which covered the entrance to her love channel.

'Kiss my cunney,' she breathed as she clamped her thighs around my hand. 'Oh Johann, finish me off as quickly as you can – I'm dying to spend!'

Without further ado I slid down the bed between Carola's parted legs and placed my lips upon her dripping crack. I inhaled her distinctive musky aroma which was rather less pungent than that of her aunt for Carola's cuntal juices were already beginning to flow when I ran my tongue down the length of her long crack. She shivered all over when (to be honest, more by accident than design) I stopped licking her quim to pay homage to her clitty which had hardened up like a tiny nut. I gave it my best attention, nibbling and tickling as she writhed from side to side making it quite difficult to keep my mouth glued to her sopping slit. I stretched out my arms to play with her pert titties as Carola bucked and twisted in a paroxysm of erotic fervour.

'Oh! Oh! Finish me off!' she cried and I thrust my tongue even deeper inside her juicy snatch, lapping up her juicy spend until she exploded into a climax and flooded my face with her love juice.

'Now it's your turn, my dear,' said Carola when she had recovered. As we changed places she grabbed hold of my cock and proceeded to wash her talented tongue all over my knob before closing her lips over my helmet and sliding my thick shaft down her throat in one fluid gulp. Then she eased back, licking the underside of my shaft until she reached my balls which she sucked into her mouth, swishing them around before releasing them to lick all the way up to my knob again.

A virgin she might be, but Carola was a superb cock-sucker and I spent quickly, jetting streams of sticky jism which filled her mouth while she milked every last drop from my sated prick until it began to soften.

Carola looked at the clock and said that we had better get dressed as her mother would soon be returning home. I had no desire to meet Frau von Langen on the landing or to be seen by her coming down the staircase, so I hastily pulled on my drawers and suggested that we put on our clothes in double-quick time and make our way back to the music room.

'I've yet to play the piano for you, though after such a wonderful sucking-off I don't know whether I now have the strength to do so,' I laughed as I buttoned up my shirt.

It was as well that we did dress ourselves quickly because I had only just sat down at the piano when Carola's mother came bustling in after a hard afternoon's work tending to the needs of some of her husband's sick workers and their families who had been struck down by a mysterious disease which was causing great distress.

At first, the doctors of Stettin were concerned that they might have to fight against another plague *[Hundreds of people died in a dreadful cholera epidemic which raged through Pomerania in 1866 – Editor]*, but thankfully this bout of disease turned out to be only a virulent form of influenza. Still, this was bad enough and a number of elderly people had already died, so there was a genuine demand for Frau von Langen and her nourishing soup.

'Have there been any new cases, Mama?' asked Carola. Frau von Langen answered: 'No, and thank the Lord we seem to be over the worst. I was rather worried about old Geischow who used to be your father's chief clerk but he polished off a whole bowl of stewed fruit this afternoon and I think he is on the mend.

'So have you done anything interesting this afternoon?' she asked as she sat herself down. I was hard put to keep a straight face when Carola answered sweetly: 'Not really, Mama, although the time passed very pleasantly – especially as we found we had a certain interest in common.'

'I presume you mean music, dear,' said her fond Mama who turned to me and said: 'Johann, were you going to play something for Carola?'

'Yes, Chopin's Ballade Number Four in F Minor,' I said, but I was saved from exposing my lack of ability by the butler who came into the room and announced that a message had been delivered from Herr von Langen who needed Jurgen to deliver a letter for him. This meant that the coachman could only get me back to Doctor Hildebrand's by six o'clock if I left straightaway.

'Then I'm afraid I must leave now,' I said and Carola sighed regretfully: 'Oh, do you really have to go? You're very welcome to stay the night, isn't he, Mama?'

'Certainly,' said Frau von Langen hospitably but, although I was tempted by the thought of another romp, I realised that my cock might be in demand not only by Carola but also by her insatiable aunt. Now I realized why Jurgen was in a state of such agitation! I decided that the situation was so complicated that it would probably end in tears so I shook my head and said: 'That's very kind of you but I really should be on my way.'

Carola walked out with me to the coach and, before I climbed into the vehicle, she pulled out her visiting card from her pocket and said; 'Now you will keep your promise to write to me, won't you?'

'Certainly, though only on condition that you answer all my letters,' I replied as she kissed me on the cheek and said: 'Of course I will, you silly boy. Goodbye, Johann, I'm sure we shall meet again – but where? I have a hunch it will be somewhere more exciting than Stettin.'

'I'm sure it will,' I said as I returned her kiss and boarded the landaulet. Jurgen cracked his whip and we pulled off at a smartish pace along the drive and out through the gates of the von Langen mansion.

Not surprisingly, I felt rather tired that night and by half-past nine I was ready to retire, leaving Carl to make up a fourth at whist with Bertolt and his parents.

I could hardly wait to get to bed, yet when I slid under the covers and closed my eyes I found that I could not doze off. Pictures of how I had fucked Frau Schroeder's juicy cunt and the salacious way Carola had sucked my cock ran through my mind like hand-coloured prints in a photographic album. A smug smile crept across my face as my hand strayed almost unconsciously to my crotch where I fondled my stirring shaft, running my hand up and down its burgeoning length.

As I remarked at the beginning of these memoirs, I have always held that masturbation is – unlike vices such as alcohol and tobacco – a free, enjoyable and completely harmless source of pleasure. Nevertheless, some friends of mine are quite coy about the so-called Sin of Onan. Yet for a red-blooded man there are only three ways to relieve sexual frustration, the best of which is, of course, fucking. The other two are emission through wet dreams or the far more reliable method of bringing oneself off.

For myself, I am not ashamed to admit how much I enjoy a good wank, especially when it is my own fingers that are clasped around my cock. In later years, after this particular evening, I often discovered that many women tend to rub too roughly, perhaps unconsciously imitating the unsubtlety of most men's most sexual attitudes. Indeed, one of the reasons I was so attracted to Carola was that she could caress my prick almost as well as I could, knowing exactly when to tease and cajole and when to be more forceful to bring me up to a spend.

I squeezed my knob when visions of Carola's head bobbing up and down on my stiff shaft floated into my brain and my fingers slid faster and faster along my twitching tool whilst I imagined that I was actually fucking the pretty, lithe-limbed girl. What bliss it would be to have Carola wrap her legs around me, urging me on to drive my sinewy shaft hard and deep into her wet little love funnel! I sighed with joy at the ecstatic thought but very soon I started to pant with lust. My heart began to pound as I arched my back and spent abundantly over my nightshirt.

Ah well, what a shame it was that Carola and I had no idea when we would meet again. I felt as deflated as my cock whilst I wiped myself on the small hand towel that I had purposely brought in from the bathroom.

Now I was becoming quite drowsy and I must have fallen asleep soon afterwards for I do not remember hearing the ten o'clock chimes of the grandfather clock. Neither do I recall Carl coming in and taking the towel off my eiderdown before he settled down for his own session of self-stimulation before being gathered into the arms of Morpheus.

Here I shall conclude my account of this magnificent summer holiday and my first full experience of the joys of *l'art de faire l'amour*, for nothing more worth recording occurred for the rest of the vacation.

Alas, I was unable to see Carola again because, only a few days later, Herr von Langen took his family off on a trip to Berlin. But I did receive a note from her before she left, reminding me again to keep in contact with her.

Finally, I must record the fact that Doctor Hildebrand's meeting with Natasha the gypsy girl went so well that, there and then, he offered to take her back with us to Vienna, telling her that she could stay with his family until she found a situation. The night before we left Stettin, the overjoyed girl packed her clothes and pitifully few possessions into a bag and, when her father went out to carouse with his friends, she informed her mother that she was leaving the camp at dawn the next day. This news was greeted with tears, but Natasha swore a solemn oath that in the following Spring she would journey to the great annual horse-fair in Lódź to see her mother again.

CHAPTER FOUR

As I had confidently expected, my father and mother were only too pleased to offer Natasha Slatakov a place in our household and she soon showed herself to be such an eager and conscientious worker that she quickly earned my parents' trust. So much so, in fact, that – ironically enough in view of Natasha's desire for a settled life – within a few weeks my father called her into the drawing room to tell her that, in a couple of days, he would be leaving for a short stay at our estate near Pinczow to check with the overseer that all was in order there.

'I would like you to come with me, Natasha,' my father informed her. 'There won't be too much housework as we'll stay for three days or so in the gamekeeper's cottage. I specially furnished it out for my trips when I managed to rent out the big manor house to some big-wig merchant from the town. Still, I'll be bound that the cottage will need a good clean.'

'Can I come with you, father?' I asked. He looked at me in some surprise and said: 'Do you really want to, Johann? You spent three weeks in that part of the world only a month or so ago.'

'But I've never been to Pinczow and I would like to see the place,' I answered. He looked up at my mother and said: 'I don't see why not, Johann, you aren't due back in school till the week after next, are you? Gertrude, I take it you have no objection?'

My mother smiled and said: 'Well, Johann would probably be better employed revising some schoolwork before the new term, but I suppose it would do him good to spend a few days with you, especially as we shall be spending so much time away this autumn.'

Two days later my father left alone for Pinczow because he wanted to break his journey in Berlin to spend an evening with two of his oldest English chums, Sir Michael and Lady Harper, who had been invited to the city by a mutual friend, the Duchess of Magdeburg, for a grand weekend party to celebrate her fiftieth birthday.

Despite my heated protest, my mother refused to let Natasha and I travel to Pinczow without an escort. 'When you reach Berlin, you not only have to change trains but travel across town to another station,' she said firmly. 'So you need a man to look after the luggage and make sure that you don't get lost in the big city.'

So our burly young footman Manfred was deputed to accompany us but, after gaining my father's support, I managed to wring the concession from my mother that Manfred should return to Vienna after he had seen Natasha and I aboard the Pinczow train to Berlin.

I must admit that Manfred proved to be a useful travelling companion, for as well as keeping an eagle eye on our cases as they were loaded onto the train (since the opening of the station, the *Hauptbahnhof* had been plagued by sneak thieves and pickpockets) during the long journey itself the footman was on hand to fetch drinks from the restaurant car.

He performed his duties so cheerfully that, as I scanned the pages of the newspaper I had purchased at the station bookstall, it crossed my mind that he might have been smitten by Natasha's feminine charms. I wondered whether these feelings were reciprocated by the sultry gypsy girl.

If they were, I had no objection for it was obviously very difficult for me to continue any intimate liaison with Natasha. It would be a breach of my parents' trust if I became entangled in an affair with her. And, frankly, even if the circumstances had been different and notwithstanding the fact that Natasha was a sensual girl and generous with her favours, I knew full well that I was much too young to be seriously thought of as a lover.

My father was a major shareholder in the railway company and, although the train was fairly crowded, we travelled in the luxury of our own private compartment. Therefore, as Manfred and Natasha were sitting opposite me, I was able to put down my newspaper and announce that I was going to put my feet up across the row of seats and have a little nap.

Now, to be honest, I had only planned to pretend to doze off so that, even if I kept my eyes closed, at least I could hear whether Manfred had anything of interest to say to his pretty workmate. However, my shameful plan to eavesdrop on their conversation was at first thwarted because the early start to the day coupled with the anticipatory excitement of the journey and the gentle rhythm of the wheels clicking along the track in fact made me really fall asleep.

I don't think I actually slept for more than about half an hour but, when I began to stir, I heard Natasha say: 'Manfred, don't do that, it's not fair. Can't you wait till I come back home and then we can spend the whole night making love?'

My forearm was shielding my face and they could not see that my eyes had fluttered open, giving me a grandstand view of the frisky pair. The footman had his arms around Natasha in a passionate embrace as he panted: 'But my darling girl, it's been more than a week since our last little cuddle. My cock's fairly bursting for you! Feel it for yourself!'

Recklessly he pulled open his trousers and his rampant throbbing shaft rose majestically out of his drawers to salute her. My head was level with his crotch so perhaps it was just the angle of vision, but nevertheless it seemed to me that Manfred was fortunate enough to have been blessed with the most enormous cock, at least twenty-five centimetres long and much thicker than my own adolescent prick.

'Here,' said the footman vehemently, placing her hand on the uncapped helmet. 'See how hard it is, dear! Please!'

Manfred clutched her in an even tighter embrace and their lips met in a clinging impassioned kiss as he pulled her hand down to his twitching tool.

'Don't do that, Mannie,' murmured Natasha, but she made no real attempt to move her hand away from his shaft and my own cock now began to thicken as I watched her clamp her fingers around his huge pulsing prick. She slid her hand up and down the blue-veined fleshy column and Manfred gurgled with delight when she suddenly lowered her head and planted a smacking wet kiss on his knob.

He groaned as Natasha pulled herself upwards and he whispered fervently: 'Oh darling, you can't leave me like this, it's just too much to bear. Bring me off, there's a love.'

She looked at him with a wicked little smile and then nodded her head and replied in a low voice: 'All right, but keep quiet whatever you do. We don't want to wake Master Johann.'

I bit my lip to keep myself from giggling and giving the game away as Manfred nodded his agreement. Natasha took his colossal cock in both hands and gave it a friendly rub before sliding down on her knees and beginning to lick and lap all around the ruby mushroom-shaped crown of the footman's gigantic chopper. He groaned with ecstasy as she circled the dome with the tip of her tongue and then sucked his bell-end into her mouth, slurping her lips over his meaty shaft. Manfred's eyes were screwed up tight and, despite his promise to remain silent, he gasped in rapture as Natasha gave his knob a long swirling lick before plunging her mouth down again and giving the ridge of his helmet a teasing brush with her teeth.

In one sinuous movement she opened her mouth as wide as possible and took in about half his tremendous boner between her lips, sucking strongly and rhythmically whilst her fingers stroked and tickled his balls.

Although he'd undertaken to keep quiet, Manfred still could not prevent a choking growl of release escaping from his throat as he pumped a stream of spunk into Natasha's mouth which she swallowed with relish, gulping down his copious emission until she had milked him dry. Then she hauled herself back to a sitting position and wiped her lips on her hand whilst Manfred stuffed his wilting cock back into his pants and buttoned up his trousers.

When I judged that they had regained their composure I let out a loud yawn and, after stretching out my arms, said: 'I'm rather thirsty, Manfred. Would you mind going to the restaurant car and bringing me back a glass of apple juice? And buy two more for yourself and Natasha whilst you're there.'

I gave the footman some money and he thanked me

before he stood up and opened the door of the compartment. Then he closed it behind him as he made his way down the corridor to the bar. I looked at Natasha and said to her in as innocent a voice as I could muster: 'I feel much better now. It's so refreshing to get your head down, isn't it, Natasha?'

It was impossible to tell whether the hot-blooded girl was aware of the significance of my question although she flashed a searching look across at me before answering coolly: 'Yes, very much so, Master Johann, although, of course, I don't often have the chance to do so during the day.'

Now, I knew that I was taking advantage of my position by teasing her in this way but I carried on anyway: 'Quite so, though for some reason this reminds me of a rather amusing story concerning my grand-uncle Wilhelm which I'm not supposed to know, but my sister Anna told me all about it last year.

'It appears that in 1862 Great-uncle Wilhelm was on a train journey in his private compartment smooching with a girl from the chorus of the new Opera House at Linz when the engine collided with a bull. His carriage was thrown off the rails and careered down an embankment. By good fortune neither of them were seriously injured, but when rescuers reached Wilhelm and his lady friend, they found them coupled together on the floor totally naked! He was lying on his back and crying out "Help! Help! Help!" whilst the girl was sitting astride him, bouncing up and down on his lap with his cock up her cunney screaming out: "Fuck! Fuck! Fuck! Oooh Wilhelm, that's really amazing, it feels like the earth has moved!"

'Afterwards, she explained to him that at first she had thought the sharp jolting of the carriage was in fact caused by Great-uncle Wilhelm's big cock – he was supposed to have been extremely well-endowed – and she was so dazed that she had not realized exactly what had happened.'

Natasha laughed out loud and said robustly: 'A likely story, Master Johann! I don't believe a word of it.'

'Well, it *does* sound far-fetched,' I admitted as I joined in her laughter. 'But even if the tale isn't actually true, it's one of those that should be!'

'That's for sure,' she agreed and she hauled herself off her seat and plumped herself down next to me as she asked: 'So Herr Wilhelm survived this crash – and did he live happily ever after to a ripe old age?'

'He did indeed, and there's another secret story about how he kicked the bucket,' I informed her. She gave my knee an encouraging little pat as I continued: 'He wasn't so lucky when a pretty ballet dancer accepted his invitation to dine with him at a discreet little supper room in Vienna to celebrate Wilhelm's eighty-second birthday.

'They went back to his apartment and, as I understand it, the girl had just finished sucking his cock and he was shooting his sperm down her throat when he suffered a massive heart attack. The doctor reckoned he probably died as his head fell back on the pillow.'

'What a shame! Still, at least he died happy,' observed Natasha brightly. Then she paused and, looking me straight in the eye, asked me: 'Be honest now, Master Johann, were you *really* asleep just before?'

'Yes, I was absolutely flat out,' I replied with a false look of puzzlement on my face and, strictly speaking, this answer was true enough although I had deliberately given her the impression that I had seen nothing of her canoodling with Manfred. Of course, I should have let sleeping dogs lie, but I just couldn't resist adding: 'What a strange question, Natasha. Did I miss anything interesting?'

Natasha shrugged her shoulders and said: 'Possibly, but you woke up at a very convenient time. I'll be honest with you, Manfred and I were having a cuddle and it would be very embarrassing to think that you had seen us petting.'

Inwardly I blushed with shame, but I blustered on: 'Natasha! What sort of chap do you take me for? Anyhow, surely you must realize that any gentleman worth his salt would turn his head away if he saw a girl sucking her boyfriend's cock.'

As the words left my lips I realized that I had fallen into the simplest of traps and I buried my head in my hands as Natasha said sharply: 'I don't believe I mentioned anything specific about what Manfred and I were up to. Admit it, Master Johann, you were spying on us!'

'No, I wasn't,' I said hotly, but the game was up and I added sulkily: 'It so happened that I finished my nap just as Manfred unbuttoned his trousers. I'm sorry, Natasha, I should have let you know I had woken up before you began to lick his prick, but you must also take some of the blame for letting yourself get carried away.'

'Yes, that's a fair point and I too apologize,' she said. Then she cocked her ear and said. 'Listen, I think that's Manfred coming back. We'll finish this conversation later.'

In fact, she was unable to do so for a while because Manfred never left our side until we had changed trains and had taken our seats on the Berlin-Warsaw express. Then, once we had waved goodbye to him as we pulled out of the station, Natasha and I settled back in our seats and she said: 'I can now tell you why I behaved so outrageously with Manfred. You know how much I love living in your house. Well, Manfred has a hold over me,

Master Johann, and I'm worried that if I don't do as he says I'll lose my job.'

'You mean he's blackmailing you? There's an easy way to deal with him, Natasha,' I said reassuringly. 'You must tell my father the whole story as soon as we get to Pinczow.'

She shook her head and cried out: 'But, Master Johann, suppose that he doesn't believe me?'

'Well, then you're no worse off, are you?' I rejoined. 'I don't know what you've done but, in the end, you'll have to face the music or you'll always be enslaved by Manfred or anyone else who finds out whatever it is that worries you so much. Anyhow, why should my father not accept your word as opposed to that of another servant?'

'Because Manfred has been in your family's service for three years now and there is no reason why he should not be believed, whereas your parents have only known me for less than three months,' she retorted. But from Natasha's tone I could see that my argument had struck a chord with her. So I said: 'Come on, tell me what has been happening and, if you like, I'll then tell my father all about it.'

'Oh, I don't think that would be a good idea,' she said doubtfully but I pressed home my point and went on: 'Of course it would, Natasha. How can I help you unless I know exactly what's been going on? Look, I've a good idea – tell me the full story and I promise you that I won't pass on anything to my father or anybody else without your agreement.'

She thought about this for a few moments and then nodded her head and said: 'All right, Master Johann – as you say, what have I got to lose? I can't let myself be bossed around by Manfred all the time or I might as well have stayed in the gypsy camp at Jascnitz.'

'Quite so,' I concurred and, although she was clearly embarrassed, the words soon came tumbling out as Natasha told her story. She began: 'Do you remember about a fortnight ago your parents invited a British gentleman to dine with us?'

'Oh yes, Lord Rodney Burbeck. He writes on European political affairs for an English newspaper called *The Times* and is an old friend of my father.' I could not stop myself giving a little chuckle at the thought of the debonair Milord (who unlike many of his countrymen spoke excellent German) being discovered by Manfred the footman in an amorous clinch with the sultry, black-haired gypsy girl.

However, it soon became clear that I was on the wrong track although Natasha continued: 'Yes, he seemed to be a very jolly gentleman. If you remember, the blonde scullery maid, Bella, helped to serve the meal and – please don't repeat this to your father, Master Johann, it has nothing to do with Manfred – she told me that the Milord had pinched her bottom as she leaned down to pick up his napkin which had fallen to the floor. Anyhow, after we had washed up the dishes, Frau Bickler said that Bella and I could go on up to bed.

'Now, as you can imagine, we didn't have any nightdresses in the gypsy camp and I still can't get to sleep wearing any clothes. So, after I had undressed and washed myself, giving a little shiver from the cool night breeze which was blowing through the open window, I walked across my little room in the nude and pulled down the blind.

'As I pulled it down there was a knock on my door and, before I could call out, Bella came in dressed in her cream nightrobe, with a bottle tucked under her arm and holding two small glasses in her hand. She smiled at me and said:

"Oh good, I'm glad you haven't gone to sleep yet because I'd like you to share this little present that Lord Rodney Burbeck gave me just now."

' "He gave you a present, Bella? Why should he do that?" I asked in all innocence and she burst out laughing and said: "Well, let's just say that he was so grateful for the relaxing massage I gave him in the downstairs loo whilst he was waiting for his cab that he gave me this bottle of Scottish malt whisky."

'I had never heard of this whisky and Bella explained to me that it is made from barley and tastes very nice. "Try it, Natasha," she said as she set down the bottle. "British doctors say it is good for you. Careful, though, it's just as powerful as vodka." '

'That's true enough,' I agreed with a smile. 'I've never tasted it myself but my father is very fond of whisky and Lord Rodney usually brings him a dozen bottles when he visits us.'

Natasha nodded and said: 'Well, of course, neither Bella nor I had tried it before either and I can tell you, Master Johann, that whisky has a kick like a mule! Anyhow, after we had drunk some, we both felt sleepy and I didn't feel I could really object when Bella yawned and asked: "Oh my, are you as tired as me? Would you mind if I slept in here? My bed is terribly uncomfortable. The Countess has ordered a new mattress for me but it won't be delivered till next Thursday."

'So I slipped between the sheets and, to my surprise, after Bella had taken out her hairpins and let her long blonde tresses fall down to her waist, she unbuttoned her nightshirt and pulled it over her head. Then she turned out the light and lay down next to me, snuggling up close as she said: "There, that's better. I prefer to be naked in bed but it's too cold sleeping by myself and my room gets stuffy if I close the window."

'There was still enough moonlight shining through the blinds for me to see Bella who is, as you know, a very attractive girl. As I watched her moisten her rich red lips with her tongue, it did cross my mind how well her light complexion and slim figure went with my own swarthy looks, even down to our pussies which contrasted so nicely, mine being covered with dark curls and hers with fluffy blonde hair.

' "Are you comfortable, Natasha?" she said softly. "Why don't you lay your head on my shoulder and close your eyes?"

'Yes, I'll admit I had more than an inkling of what Bella was up to, but I did as she asked and made only a token objection when she began to smooth her hands over my breasts, rubbing my nipples between her fingers.

' "Bella, you're being very naughty," I admonished her drowsily but I made no attempt to stop her as she continued to caress my breasts, cradling my tits in her hands. "Oh, what lovely large titties you have, darling – I'm quite envious as they're so much bigger than mine," she cooed and when I felt her lips close upon my nipple, swirling it around in her mouth, shivers of desire started to run up and down my spine.

'I relaxed and lay there passively as she moved her hands down the insides of my legs and I found myself getting more and more aroused as her knowing fingers inched towards my pussy. My hips jerked forward when she lightly ran her forefinger all along the length of my moistening slit and I let out a little moan when she slid her long fingers into my muff. As the heel of her hand rubbed my cunney, up popped my clitty and Bella whispered: "Ah ha, I've found your secret spot, haven't I?"

' "Yes! Yes! Yes!" I panted as she drew little circles

around my love bud until my entire body was squirming with pleasure. Without taking her fingers from my cunt, she brought across her other hand and dipped a long finger into my squishy love channel. The sensation was so electrifying that I sat bolt upright and squealed: "Oh, Bella, that feels wonderful."

' "Good, because it's wonderful for me too, you sweet girl," she murmured in my ear. "Finger fucking your juicy cunney makes me so wet. Feel my pussy, darling, it's positively dripping with love juice."

'Bella took my hand and placed it between her cool, firm thighs and my own cunney began to tingle again as I trailed my fingertips through her flaxen fluff. She pulled my head towards hers and we covered each others' mouths with kisses as we finger-fucked each others' cunnies until Bella moved herself down the bed, kissing my breasts, my tummy and my belly button before nuzzling her lips inside my sopping black bush. She kissed my pussy lips with great fervour and cooed: "M'mm, what a delicious little crack! And such a sweet perfume, too!"

'Without further words she started to tongue my quim, moving all along my sopping slit, exploring, tasting teasing – and then suddenly she stopped!

' "Ooooh! Go on, Bella, go on," I groaned, but she moved her head up and when I opened my eyes I nearly jumped out of my skin because a certain young man had heard our moans of passion and, whilst we had been pleasuring ourselves, had crept unseen into my room!'

'Manfred the footman, I presume,' I interrupted and Natasha nodded and said wryly: 'The very same. To be fair to him, when he first heard sighs and moans coming from my room, Manfred went to investigate because he was concerned that I had been taken ill. But there's no doubt in my mind that, once he had reached my door, he knew very well that what he was hearing was something very different.

'Anyhow, his eyes were out on stalks and I could see from the bulge in his trousers that he was enjoying the sight of two naked girls playing with each other! He mopped his brow and said hoarsely: "Let me join in, girls, three can play this game much better than two!"

'But Bella pouted: "No, Manfred, I'm not in the mood for cock, thank you very much. You've had a good look so now you can go back to your own room and toss yourself off, you rude boy."

'He looked at her angrily and growled: "All right, then, if that's what you want. But Herr Dachsmann wouldn't be exactly overjoyed if he knew what you two had been getting up to. He's been the butler here for fifteen years and he doesn't stand for any hanky-panky. One word from him to Grafin *[Countess – Editor]* Gewirtz and you would both be out on your ears first thing tomorrow morning."

'Now, I've only known Herr Dachsmann for a short time, but I was convinced that Manfred was not bluffing – especially as my sudden arrival had put Herr Dachsmann's nose out of joint because he is usually consulted about the employment of new staff. So I said: "Don't be so hasty, you two, there's no need to fly off the handle. Manfred, why don't you come here and let me give your cock a special twelve-lick sucking?"

' "Is that the way Romany girls pleasure their men?" he gasped as he wrenched off his trousers so quickly that one of his fly buttons came off and flew across the room.

' "Not really, but it's the way that I personally like to arouse my lovers," I answered as he pulled down his drawers and shuffled round to my side of the bed, holding his pulsating prick in his fist.

'Now, I know how proud men are of their cocks and a little flattery will always get them eating out of your hand, so I took hold of his hot shaft and said admiringly: "My, what a lovely big chopper! Bella, we could both have some grand fun with this monster lollipop."

' "No, he's all yours, dear, I really don't fancy cock tonight," Bella pouted as she sat up to watch me slide my hand along Manfred's stiff, throbbing shaft. "But don't let me stop you enjoying yourself."

' "I won't," I said simply as I delicately fingered the wide crown of Manfred's bulbous prick before I pulled it closer to my mouth so I could begin licking and lapping all around the ruby-coloured dome. He gave a throaty gurgle of delight as I circled my tongue all around his helmet and then he let out a heartfelt little yelp when I crammed as much of his thick tool as I could take into my mouth.

'I sucked his cock with relish, varying the intensity and the timing before I released it for a moment to look up to Manfred's face. His eyes were closed and he was breathing heavily as I returned to my sweet labours, giving his knob a long, swirling lick before plunging my mouth down to give the ridge a teasing nibble with my teeth.

'This drove Manfred so wild that, with a hoarse cry, he wrenched his cock out of my mouth and tore off the rest of his clothes before jumping into the bed. Bella kindly rolled to one side to give him enough room to lie on his back and I climbed over him. Facing his feet, I lowered myself gently upon him with my hairy pussy directly over his mouth as I leaned forward to resume gobbling his twitching shaft.

'I must say that Manfred was more than happy to repay the exquisite pleasure my twirling tongue was giving his cock, for he immediately parted my love lips and pressed his mouth firmly against my moist pussy. Now it was my turn to gasp with delight when warm waves of sheer ecstasy shimmied out from my crotch as Manfred rolled his tongue all around my cunt whilst I bent over him, working my mouth up and down his blue-veined boner. I ran my teeth gently along its sensitive underside and then sucked in his smooth fleshy helmet and flicked my tongue teasingly over its slitted end.

'Then he withdrew his mouth from my cunt and slipped two fingers into my open wetness, sliding them in and out and arousing me so much that I decided I could only get satisfaction from a fully-blown fuck. So I grasped his cock with both hands and rubbed it up to bursting point before leaping off his fingers and moving my soaking slit down over his sinewy shaft, sitting with my bum cheeks on his thighs whilst I rode up and down on his palpitating prick.

'Manfred grasped my buttocks in his hands and squeezed them whilst I slid up and down his luscious tool, contracting my cunney muscles with every downward thrust to our mutual ecstatic delight.

' "Oooh, that's too much, I'm going to cum!" he warned when I reached down with my hand and played with his balls. He began to force his strong shaft upwards in a fierce series of powerful jabs. Then I felt his prancing prick begin to tremble and, with one mighty heave upwards, he spurted a stream of sticky jism into my cunt. He shot so much spunk into my quim that my pussy overflowed and a rivulet of Manfred's jism and my own cuntal juices mixed together ran over his quivering cock and dribbled down my thigh.

'I rolled off him, enjoying to the full the delicious sensations of my climax which were now slowly fading away. Then I looked towards Bella and saw that our little exhibition had whetted her sensual appetite for she had recapped the whisky bottle and was using it as a dildo, sliding its neck in between the pink pussy lips that protruded out of the fluffy muff of flaxen hair between her thighs.

'Despite his copious ejaculation into my seething cunt, Manfred's cock swiftly thickened up again at the erotic sight of this pretty girl lewdly playing with her pussy. I slicked my fist up and down his swollen shaft until it was again as hard as an iron bar. Then I gently removed the whisky bottle from Bella's hands and, opening it up, I poured a generous amount into her blonde bush, rubbing my forefinger along her crack until – despite her previous reluctance to entertain a prick in her pussy – she was begging for Manfred to fuck her properly with his big stiff cock.

'I thought that Manfred would fuck the gorgeous girl directly, but he clearly enjoyed the taste of malt whisky because he carefully moved over to kneel in front of her. He then proceeded to bury his head between her thighs and nuzzle his lips around her pussy. I craned my head to see his tongue slip into her juicy quim and Bella writhed from side to side as he licked up the pungent mixture of whisky and love juice from her cunt.

'However, after he gulped down this potent liquid, Manfred gave a loud hiccup. I almost choked with laughter as Bella pretended to be shocked and wagged her finger in admonishment as she said: "Manfred, how *could* you! Surely you know that it is considered very bad form to hiccup into a girl's cunney even if she *is* only a lowly chambermaid."

' "I'm sorry, Bella," he muttered apologetically. "Please forgive me. That's never happened to me before: it must have been the whisky."

'Bella smiled and said: "All right, I'll forgive you this time, but only on condition that you stop talking and fuck the arse off me instead."

‘ “With pleasure,” grinned Manfred, cradling his quivering cock in one hand whilst he rubbed her nipples up to erection with the other as he told Bella to sit up and swing her legs over the side of the bed.

‘This request puzzled her but, as he moved off her, she shrugged her shoulders and obediently followed his instructions, sitting on the bed with her legs dangling down and her feet on the floor. However, all became clear when Manfred moved between her legs and she took hold of his colossal chopper and gently placed the tip of his knob at the entrance to her cunney. Then he whispered something to Bella and, sliding her bottom forward, she raised her legs high in the air and hooked her ankles around his neck as he eased his glistening shaft into her clingy love channel.

‘ “Oh yes, that feels terrific!” Bella cried out and she begged him to fuck her as deeply as he could, whispering fiercely: “I want every bit of your fat cock inside me, right up to the balls!”

‘ “And that’s just what I’m going to give you,” he responded as he raised her legs a little higher so that Bella could rest her calves on his shoulders as he drove his thick prick into her willing wet cunt until his thatch of curly brown pubic hairs became entangled with Bella’s fluffy blonde muff. Her yells of ecstasy were accompanied by the sound of the slap of his balls against her peachy bottom as they coupled, uncoupled and coupled again.

‘Manfred’s simple but effective mode of fucking was to pull his shaft completely out of Bella’s cunt before driving it back in between her puffy pussy lips. Now, I happen to prefer my lovers to leave a little cock inside my cunt on the outward stroke, but Bella did not appear to be unhappy by Manfred’s total withdrawal of his tool before it came plunging back inside her juicy crack.

'Manfred certainly put his heart and soul into fucking the sweet girl. Bella's buttocks were raised off the bed by the power of his thrusts and they both enjoyed their love-making to the full until suddenly he growled: "Bella, brace yourself, I'm going to spunk!"

' "Come on, then," she urged him. I must say that Manfred tried his best to ensure that his partner would reach her spend with him for, despite his own mounting explosion, he caressed Bella's breasts and buttocks to heighten her pleasure – and this did the trick, for in seconds the randy pair were gasping with joy as they climaxed together. I felt a delicious wave of pleasure run through my own cunney as Manfred drenched Bella's cunt with spout after spout of frothy spunk from his wildly jerking prick.

'Oooh, just talking about that night makes me tingle all over,' concluded Natasha, licking her lips at the memory of this raunchy episode. I myself had been so carried away by this erotic story that I grabbed hold of her hand, placed it on my throbbing shaft and said: "Well, can you imagine how frustrated you've made *me* feel? Please, Natasha, you must do something for my poor cock! Do you think we might—'

'Hush now, Master Johann! I know we have our own private compartment but supposing the conductor comes round to ask for our tickets?' she scolded me as she removed her hand from my rock-hard penis. But she offered no real resistance when I slid my hand inside her jacket and deftly undid the little white buttons of her blouse.

'Oh, you are a naughty boy,' she murmured as I slipped the straps of her chemise down her arms so that I was able to cup her uptilted bare breasts, pinching the nipples until they hardened up under my touch.

Meanwhile, Natasha's hand had strayed back to my lap and I helped her unbutton my trousers. My stiff naked cock sprang up to display itself before her, vibrating with unslaked desire. This was the first time we had romped together since our initial meeting back in Jaschnitz and, as she wrapped her fingers around my bulging prick, she said mischievously: 'My God, Master Johann, how your cock has grown since I last took it in my hand. Have you had the luck to find another girlfriend since then or are you having to exercise it by yourself?'

'That would be telling,' I laughed as I threw up her skirt and slid my hand up her leg. Natasha gave a little jump when my fingers reached her pussy and she murmured softly: 'Johann, Johann, the blinds might be down but what will you do if someone knocks at the door?'

'I'll just tell him to go away and come back in ten minutes,' I answered as she lifted her bottom to allow me to tug down her knickers. Then the sultry dark-eyed girl lay down across the seat and parted her legs whilst I climbed on top of her. Pushing her skirt up around her waist, I carefully placed my knob between her yielding love lips and eased myself down to let my yearning shaft be slowly enveloped inside her squishy slit.

'Ahhh! How lovely! Come further into me,' she breathed as our lips mashed together and her warm wet tongue snaked a passage between my teeth and into my mouth. I pistoned my prick to and fro inside Natasha's close-fitting honeypot as we kissed with an increasingly urgent passion. Hers was one of the snuggest little cunts one could wish to fuck, but without any discomfort to either of us. I worked my way in until her neat little clitty was rubbing against my cock. When my cock was fully inside her and my balls were slapping against her bum, I paused for a moment to enjoy to the full the delicious clinging tightness of her cunney muscles around my cock.

Then I began to pump my shaft in and out of her luscious cunt and she panted: 'H-a-r-g-h! H-a-r-g-h! H-a-r-g-h! Goodness me, you might not yet be sixteen, Master Johann, but you've a grown man's cock on you, that's for sure! Oh, to think that when you get married, some lucky girl will be able to spend every night with a big thick prick like yours up her crack!'

Naturally, this compliment spurred me on to pump away even more fervently whilst Natasha offered up her nubby raspberry nipples for my delectation. I sucked on each tittie in turn and my hands slid underneath her to clasp those seductively rounded bum cheeks. We were both content to fuck at a leisurely pace and glorious ripples of sheer delight ran through every fibre of my body as my cock slewed its way in and out of her juicy cunt.

Indeed, by now her cunney was so well lubricated that my cock was slipping faster and faster up and down the length of her love funnel and soon I could feel the stirrings of an inevitable spend. However, I wanted to prolong this exquisite friction so I deliberately slowed down the pace of the fuck and, from sliding my shaft to and fro, I changed to fucking her with a series of short jabs, pushing not much more than the knob-end of my twitching tool into her sopping snatch.

'Oh, Johann, I'm not there yet! Please try to stop yourself from cumming!' she pleaded with a note of desperate anxiety in her voice, and so I slowed down almost to a standstill, continuing to let just my knob-end slide into the red chink between Natasha's puffy cunney lips. Happily, the train had also slowed down and I was able to continue fucking her in time to the rhythm of the wheels as they click-clacked over the joins between the rails. I was able to relax and prolong the fuck at a slow, even pace especially as we did not try and move ourselves into a more adventurous position. Natasha lay back along the plush upholstery and her hard, erect nipples rubbed sensually against my palms as my cock slid in and out of her pulsing pussy in time with the motion of the train.

Of course, all good things must come to an end and when Natasha finally felt the approach of her climax, she began to pant and jerk her hips. I responded by filling her cunt with my rampant love truncheon and she clutched at me, her fingers digging into my back as I felt her body tremble with the first shuddering spasms of her orgasm. This whole scene was so exciting to my mind that I had difficulty in holding myself back any longer and I flooded the depths of her cunney with a fierce spurt of jism, filling her to the limit whilst her lithe body writhed underneath my weight.

'Oooh, what a lovely cum! Quick, give my titties one last squeeze before you pull out your cock!' she begged, and I duly obliged. Then Natasha picked up her knickers from the floor and carefully wiped her pussy and my cock before stuffing the underwear concerned into her handbag.

Whilst we dressed ourselves I said to her: 'Now remember, I am going to tell my father about Manfred's little game. I'm sure he will dismiss him once he hears how he has been blackmailing a poor defenceless girl.'

Natasha frowned and said: 'Oh, I would feel terrible if Manfred lost his job. Yes, it's true he has been pressurising me, but since that night with Bella, he's never actually threatened to speak to Herr Dachsmann about us.

'And I do rather like him,' she confessed with a little smile. 'I just want him to leave me be for a while and let me make up my own mind whether or not he can fuck me.'

I raised my eyes to the ceiling and readers will probably guess the passage from Virgil's *Aeneid* which flashed across my brain – *varium et mutabile semper femina! [Woman is always fickle and changing – Editor]*. I took a deep breath and said slowly: 'Look here, Natasha, is Manfred blackmailing you or is he not?'

She replied with a pout: 'Yes, I mean, no, not exactly, that is. You see, I'd love to be fucked by Manfred if only he didn't try to force me into it!'

In despair, I ran my hands through my hair and said crossly: 'Well, do you or don't you want me to say something to my father? He could simply warn Manfred not to pester you but wait and let you make up your own mind though, for the life of me, I don't see why you couldn't do that yourself.'

'Because it just wouldn't be the same, coming from me,' said Natasha firmly. 'Believe me, he would listen much more carefully to a rebuke that would in any case come much better from an older man, especially from someone like your father whom I know that Manfred greatly respects.'

'So you really just want him to woo you,' I sighed. She fumbled in her bag as she went on: 'Yes, that's exactly what I want and, quite honestly, I don't think that's too much to ask.'

'No, I don't think it is,' I agreed. Natasha brought out an envelope from her handbag and passed it to me as she said: 'Take a look at this love letter, Master Johann. It's from Albert, the young under-butler at Doctor Hildebrand's house who is very keen on Bella. It arrived last week and, though I can't read it myself, of course, I asked Bella if I could borrow it as I was thinking of showing it to Manfred and telling him that this would be the sort of letter I would like to receive from him. At least, I think I would, because she never got round to reading it to me.'

My ill-temper evaporated instantly as she looked pleadingly at me. I gave a grunt and said: 'All right, Natasha, I'll read it to you.'

And then, as a joke, I added: 'But I doubt if it will be as fruity as that letter from that Russian Princess to Doctor Hildebrand that I read to you when we first met!'

Natasha smiled and sat back to listen as I cleared my throat and began to read to her what turned out to be quite a *billet doux*! Not that I minded all that much, of course! Be that as it may, Albert's letter read as follows:

My Darling,

Just a quick note to say how much I am looking forward to seeing you next Sunday afternoon. If the weather keeps fine, perhaps we could go for a picnic and with any luck we'll then find somewhere quiet for a kiss and cuddle away from the crowds.

My sweet Bella, I simply cannot tell you how frustrated I feel as we've never been to find ourselves alone for more than five minutes. As I have told you again and again, you are the most beautiful girl in Vienna and I can't wait to make love to you. Just day-dreaming about your pretty face and silky tresses of golden hair makes me go weak at the knees and every night, when I settle down in my lonely bed, my cock thickens up at the thought of holding you in my arms.

Shall I tell you my favourite fantasy that floats into my mind whilst I slide my hand up and down my throbbing tool? We are both lying naked in bed and I am caressing your divinely rounded breasts whilst I lick and lap your gorgeous strawberry nipples until they are standing proudly erect like two tiny red-coated soldiers. And, as I am paying homage to your titties, I am playing with your pussy, making you squirm with delight as I dip my forefinger in and out of your juicy cunt.

'Oh Albert, you are dreadfully naughty but that's so nice! Now kiss my cunney, you rude boy,' you breathe as you open your legs wider and I move my face downwards from your breasts, all the while licking your satiny soft skin, until I reach the golden thatch of hair at the base of your belly and I bury my face inside the damp patch of silky curls. You let out a squeal of delight as I begin to lick your pink pussy lips with long lascivious swipes of my tongue. Soon they part and I can feel your little stiff clitty rolling around inside my mouth.

'Y-e-s-s! Y-e-s-s! Y-e-s-s!' you cry out, your lovely breasts jiggling as you thresh from side to side and then, wrapping your thighs around my neck, you cry out: 'Suck me off, darling! Make me come with your tongue!'

Without further ado I suck away faster and faster, rolling my tongue round and round your clitty, now and then nipping it with my teeth which makes you moan in ecstasy whilst I clutch your bum cheeks to keep your pussy pressed tightly against my lips. Then you begin to shudder and, as you start to spend, a fine creamy emission spurts out of your cunney and floods my mouth. I gulp down this tangy love juice until you shiver into limpness as the delicious crisis melts away and you whisper in my ear: 'Please fuck me, Albert, my pussy is aching for your big stiff cock!'

By now my shaft is twitching wildly and I have to wrench my hand from my shaft or I would shoot off before I have had the chance to oblige you. I turn you over and you scramble up on your knees to present your peachy bum cheeks to my throbbing tool. I slide my cock into the crevice between the fleshy spheres and as my knob slips between your love lips into your welcoming wet quim, I lean forward and play with your erect stiff nipples. I only have seconds to dream of how delicious it would be to pump my prick in and out of your juicy snatch when I can feel my shaft tensing itself for the first spurt of sperm to come gushing out of my knob, and I have to finish myself off, shooting my sticky jism into a handkerchief.

Dearest Bella, how I would love to spend a whole night fucking and sucking with you! Alas, at present this is only a fantasy – but who knows what the future may hold?

All my love,
Albert

'Well, well, Albert doesn't mince his words, does he? I wonder whether Bella will transform his fantasies into reality,' I remarked to Natasha as I folded the sheets of notepaper back into the envelope. 'From what you have told me, Bella would seem to prefer girls to boys in her bed.'

'Oh no, she thoroughly enjoys a good fuck but, as Bella says, occasionally she likes to vary the menu,' replied Natasha as there was a loud rap on our door and a voice shouted: 'Your tickets, please!'

I pulled back the bolt and the black-uniformed conductor stepped into the compartment. I passed him our tickets which he clipped and gave back to me, saying: 'We're running on schedule, sir, so we'll be at Pinczow in exactly two and a half hours.'

This allowed us time to eat a light luncheon in the dining car and when we returned to the compartment Natasha soon dozed off. I picked up the newspaper but even whilst I was reading about the latest squabbles in the

Balkans, my cock swelled up and remained painfully stiff because lewd thoughts of romping around in bed in a lascivious threesome with the blonde Bella and the raven-haired Natasha refused to leave my mind. However, I resisted the temptation to ask the gypsy girl to bring me off again, though in the end I was forced to visit the cloakroom and call upon the services of Mother Thumb and her four daughters to relieve my feelings.

As the conductor had promised, we arrived dead on time at Pinczow station. I had already arranged for our cases to be taken off the luggage coach and, as we alighted from the train, I looked around for my father. To my surprise, he was not on the platform to greet us, but a burly young man dressed in a white peasant's smock and black baggy trousers came up to us and, doffing his hat, enquired in a heavily accented German whether I was the son of Count Gewirtz.

When I nodded my head, he saluted me and said in a warm, friendly fashion: 'Welcome to Pinczow, sir. My name is Stefan Solodowski and I work for your father when he comes here on a business trip. The Count sends his best wishes and looks forward to seeing you this evening, but unfortunately he was too busy to meet the train and so he asked me to drive you and your servant to the house.

'I have a horse and cart waiting outside,' he added as he called for a porter and gave the man instructions in Polish, presumably to bring out our cases to the station yard. 'Follow me, please. Don't worry, I'll make sure that the bags are all loaded onto the cart.'

'Thank you, that will be helpful,' I said. Natasha and I followed him out of the ancient old cart in the station yard. We sat up on the wooden driver's seat on either side of Stefan who seemed to be a very amenable kind of chap.

I asked him whether he farmed or worked at the lime and cement works which my father had told me had recently been established on the eastern borders of our land.

'No, sir,' he answered. 'My family works a small farm on your father's property, but I am studying medicine at Warsaw University. It's a great struggle for my parents to keep me there, but when I come home in the summer your father kindly gives me a month's work helping to prepare his overseer's annual accounts.'

Now I had heard my father mention that one of the reasons for his trip was to check whether this overseer had been carrying out his instructions so I asked: 'His overseer? Would that be Herr Basler?' Stefan's amiable expression immediately changed into a cold scowl and he muttered: 'Yes, that's the man.'

Natasha looked across at him and said dryly: 'It's obvious that you don't like this Basler fellow. My parents are gypsies and if he's like any overseers we came across when we were employed to help harvest the crops, I can certainly understand why you feel that way.'

'Well, I don't,' I said, a little crossly. So Natasha explained that more often than not the gypsies had to haggle with the overseers as to how much they would be paid for harvesting, for example, three fields of cabbages. 'He would pay us so much a kilo, but we always suspected that his scales did not show the true weight. Because of this, I admit that, to compensate for this trickery, our men sometimes put stones in the bottom of their sacks. But I never blamed them because there were so few overseers that you felt could be trusted.'

'Is Herr Basler honest in his feelings with our tenants?' I asked Stefan bluntly, but he looked away from me as he replied: 'It's not my place to say anything about Herr Basler, sir.'

I drew breath to speak again but Natasha put her finger to her lips to silence me and I followed her advice and did not question the clearly troubled Stefan any further about our overseer, though I made a mental note to speak to my father about the man.

Instead, I looked at the large quarry on our left. My paternal grandfather Franz Ferdinand Gewirtz had discovered a huge deposit of chalk and had built great kilns and sheds for the preparation and warehousing of the snow-white lime. A small village had grown up around the mining operations which gave work to a sizeable number of men, but I noticed that everything in the immediate neighbourhood of the quarry was powdered with a spectral coating of chalk-dust, like a layer of hoar-frost. All the adjacent buildings were covered by this mineral 'flour' which gave the place the strange, chaste appearance of an isolated world made of porcelain.

'It looks like snow has fallen in summer,' I observed and Stefan nodded and said: 'Yes, sir, the dust isn't usually so thick but quite a strong wind blew up early this morning.'

'That must be hard on any women who put out washing,' commented the practical Natasha but, as I found out in later life, the Poles are a moody people and the malign spell of Herr Basler had so affected Stefan that he said little more until we reached the cottage where my father stayed since he had managed to rent out the imposing manor house.

Stefan brought in our luggage and asked if he could be of further service, but Natasha said that she would unpack our cases. Stefan said: 'Very well, but if you need me, I can be found at Herr Basler's house. Turn right as you leave here and then at the crossroads turn right again and it's the first house on your left about a hundred metres up the road.'

'Something doesn't ring right about this Herr Basler. I'm going to find out more about him,' I vowed as I picked up a note from my father which he had left on the dining room table. He had written:

Dear Johann,

Sorry I couldn't meet you myself at the station. I'm spending the day at the quarry but will be back at about eight o'clock. Wanda, a nice girl from the village, is coming in at about five o'clock to prepare supper for us. Now, as you see, the cottage only has two bedrooms so you'll have to bunk with me so that Natasha can have her own room. Looking forward to seeing you very soon.

Much love,

Papa

I read this out to Natasha and commented: 'Not as exciting as the letter I read to you on the train, I'm afraid,' and she chuckled: 'Just as well, perhaps: this isn't the time or the place to get randy. But really, there's no need for you to share with your father. I can easily sleep on this sofa.

'See, it's quite big enough for me,' she added as she lay down on it, using her hand as a pillow. 'Honestly, all I need is a blanket or two and I'll be perfectly comfortable.'

'Well, thanks, that's very kind of you,' I said gratefully, for I had no wish to sleep in the same room as my father, if for no other reason than that, as we had entered the cottage, it had struck me what fun it would be to creep out of bed for a midnight liaison with Natasha!

I helped her unpack and I had just finished having a wash and brush-up when someone knocked on the back door. 'Damn, that must be the girl who is coming to cook supper for us,' I muttered as I quickly towelled my hands and face, for I had seen Natasha go out to the privy at the back of the garden. I threw the towel around my bare shoulders and walked through the kitchen to open the door.

However, my irritability disappeared in a flash when I opened the door, for there stood a stunning girl, nearer sixteen than twenty, with light honey-blonde hair, a pale face and big blue eyes. She was tall and high-breasted with a lithe, slender body and I would have wagered a thousand marks that her long legs hidden under her skirt were as stylish as I hoped.

'Herr Johann Gewirtz?' said this delicious creature in a sensual sibilant voice as she bent down to pick up the two bags she had been carrying. 'Good evening, my name is Wanda Dienst and I've come to cook dinner for you.'

'Oh yes, please come in,' I said and moved to one side to let her pass through into the kitchen. 'I'm glad you speak German. I'm afraid that my Polish is very limited.'

'Well, it's no matter for I speak both languages as my mother is Polish and my father was born near Eberswalde, a small town not very far from Berlin,' she explained. 'He is an engineer and came here to set up some installations at the chalk quarry. But he stayed on to work as a supervisor and shortly afterwards married my mother. We speak mostly German at home, but most of my friends are Polish so I have to switch from one language to another all the time.'

'I also find myself in that situation occasionally,' I said as I watched the gorgeous girl pull out a bag of potatoes from one of her bags and plonk it on the rough-hewn kitchen table. 'My mother comes from the Netherlands and she taught me a little Dutch but my parents often speak in English – usually when they want to talk about something private in front of their children! Of course, my sisters and I were keen to know what was going on so we paid great attention to our language studies. Come to think of it, it was probably all a cunning ploy by our parents to make sure their children learned English!'

'I would love to learn English because I want to go to America,' said Wanda eagerly. 'Did you find it very difficult?'

'No, not really,' I said slowly. 'Though it's not a logical language like German. There are many words which sound alike and some are even spelled the same but have two meanings – and a lot of the spelling doesn't make sense. You just don't know when to pronounce the letters. For instance, the English word for *schere* is "scissors" spelt s-c-i-s-s-o-r-s. God knows why there is a "c" there!'

'How silly,' she giggled and I went on quickly: 'But if you've any free time tomorrow or the day after, I'll gladly teach you some English.'

'Would you really?' Wanda answered joyously. 'Oh, how nice of you to make such an offer. I can see that you're a kind man, just like your father.'

I blushed and asked what time would be convenient. She said: 'I could be here at ten o'clock tomorrow morning – if that's not too early.'

'No, that would be fine,' I said and, suddenly realizing that I was standing there bare-chested, I added: 'Now I'll finish getting dressed and then perhaps I can come back and give you your first preliminary lesson whilst you prepare our meal. What are you cooking, by the way?'

'It'll be a very simple supper, I'm afraid,' she said apologetically. 'Just vegetable soup and roast chicken followed by fresh fruit.'

'Sounds absolutely delicious,' I said with a smile. 'Give me five minutes to put on my shirt and then we'll start your first lesson.'

I was as good as my word and when I returned I watched Wanda cook our dinner whilst I taught her to say: 'Good morning, my name is Wanda Dienst and I am eighteen years old,' in perfect English.

So began a most exciting evening although the excitement actually began five minutes later with Stefan returning to the cottage with the news that my father would not be able to join us for supper – and indeed would not be returning until the early hours – as he had completely forgotten that he had accepted an invitation to dine with the Wesolowskis, our tenants at the manor house, and the Mayor of Pinczow was coming out especially to pay his respects to him.

This left me in the enviable situation of being waited on hand and foot by both Natasha and Wanda and the two pretty girls seemed to vie for my favours which I was only too happy to bestow. After the delicious meal – and I insisted that the girls dined with me at the same table – Natasha suggested that I sit in an easy chair and finish my dinner with a glass of some '73 cognac that she had found in the drinks cupboard whilst she and Wanda washed up the dishes.

'Look, I don't mind giving a hand,' I said as I rose from my chair but Natasha protested: 'No, no, it wouldn't be right. Anyhow, it won't take ten minutes for Wanda and I to polish off these plates.'

'Are you sure?' I said, but Wanda also insisted that I rest whilst they clear the table. So I sipped my cognac and, as I scanned through the rest of the newspaper I had bought on the station in Berlin, I was pleased to hear sounds of laughter coming from the kitchen which clearly showed that the two girls had struck up a friendly relationship.

When they returned, Natasha brought in a pot of hot

coffee and we chatted away happily until I brought up the subject of the overseer, Herr Basler, and Wanda's face dropped and she exclaimed: 'Oh, that horrible so and so! He must be the most hated man in Pinczow.'

'Although Stefan Solodowski said nothing to us about Herr Basler, from the look on his face when Basler's name came up in conversation I'm sure he would echo those sentiments,' I commented as I wrinkled my brow. I added with some emphasis: 'What's going on here, Wanda? If this Basler fellow is throwing his weight around unfairly, then my father should be informed and he'll soon put a stop to any bullying.'

'Johann's quite right, you should tell the Count,' pressed Natasha as Wanda gnawed her lip in an agony of indecision. Then she raised her head and said: 'Yes, of course we should. As the Maccabees said, it is better to die on your feet than to live on your knees.'

She looked me straight in the eye and continued: 'All I ask of you is that if you don't think that your father can help, then please don't tell him or anyone else what I am going to tell you about Herr Basler.'

Isn't it strange how things work out? Earlier in the day Natasha had regaled me with her dilemma regarding Manfred the footman and now, not twelve hours later, a second pretty girl was asking me for my advice as to how she should tackle a difficult personal problem!

Of course, I was flattered by Wanda's resolve to share her secret with me and I answered: 'You have my word of honour on the matter, though I cannot believe that nothing can be done. After all, Basler is only an employee.'

Wanda sighed: 'True enough, but the situation is very complicated, Master Johann. The trouble all started three years ago when we suffered a most terrible summer drought which almost bankrupted some of the small farmers because the harvest was so poor. And as if this wasn't bad enough, the quarry had to shut down for eight weeks because of a slump in orders and then some new machinery was installed which meant that about a dozen men lost their jobs. That's when Herr Basler stepped in.

'He offered loans to all those families who were in trouble – but at very high rates of interest. Well, people tried everywhere to raise some money but in the end most of them were forced to accept Basler's terms. So since then everyone has had to struggle to keep up their payments to him. In fact, the terms of the loan were so high that it's all people can do to pay the monthly interest, let alone pay off their original loan.'

'What a filthy pig!' Natasha interjected and Wanda nodded her head and she went on: 'So, you see, it looks as though they will be indebted to Herr Basler for life.'

There was silence for a moment or two whilst I digested this news. Then I asked why no one had thought of writing to my father about their plight for I was certain that he would have helped his tenants in such an emergency.

'Unfortunately, your parents were in America most of that year,' Wanda answered gloomily. 'And anyhow, I am sure that his overseer's reports to your father painted a very different picture as to what was happening here. If anyone had complained directly to the Count, Basler could always have written that any problems your father might hear about were being caused by a few trouble-makers. Frankly, as he had never given any cause for complaint before, there was no reason for your father not to believe him.'

I exhaled a deep breath and said forcefully: 'Well, I don't see why I can't tell my father about this swine now. He'll sack Basler immediately.'

'Ah, well, you see, it's not quite so simple as that,' said Wanda. Her cheeks flamed crimson as she lowered her eyes to the floor. She paused for a moment and then continued: 'After a year had gone by, Basler let it be known that there were other ways open to pay off the debt. He always swaggered around with a cane in his hand and he told my best friend Suzi that if she and any other of her chums would play a game of "Naughty Schoolgirls" with him, he would remit part of their families' debts.'

I shook my head in surprise. 'I could understand it if he simply wanted to fuck the girls, though it's vile to pressure them in that way, but what's all this about playing "Naughty Schoolgirls"?'

Natasha gave a hoarse chuckle and said: 'You're still an innocent, Master Johann. "Gypsies, tramps and thieves!" they used to shout at us in some of the places we stopped, but every night men came round and laid their money down for our favours. I wasn't interested but I heard what they wanted – some wanted to whip us and others wanted to be whipped.

'Strange world, isn't it?' she added, but at only approaching sixteen years of age I had little experience of the foibles and deviances of the bedroom. So I scratched my head in amazement and muttered: 'You can say that again. Anyhow, I want to know what happened to the girls that Basler propositioned. Wanda, did what's-her-name, Suzi, take up his offer?'

Wanda nodded her head and replied: 'Our parents don't know but quite a few of the girls did. And yes, I did too and I'm not a bit ashamed of having done so. My poor parents were working all the hours God sends to pay back this dreadful man.

'I don't mind telling you what happened and you can tell the Count about it, too. A month or so after Suzi told me about Basler's suggestion, I told him that Tanya Kozalin and I would like to take part in one of his games. His eyes lit up and he rubbed his hands and said: "Good, come to my house at about eight o'clock tonight."

'Suzi had warned us what to expect so that evening we told our parents we were going out to a party. On Suzi's instructions, we took off our knickers before we left home and at eight o'clock sharp I knocked on Herr Basler's door. He opened the door himself and, as he ushered us in, he said: "I've given my servants the night off so we won't be disturbed."

'He plied us with cakes and glasses of vodka and then, after a while, he said: "Now it's time for some *real* fun. I want you two to go into the next room and pretend that I am your school headmaster and that you are two naughty schoolgirls who have been sent to my office by your teacher for misbehaving in class."

'We tried our best not to giggle as we walked through to the dining-room and I whispered to Tanya: "I hope this won't take too long, I said I might go for a walk with Stefan Solodwoski later tonight."

'Well, we didn't have long to wait. Herr Basler swept in and glared at us. "Now then, you bad girls, what have you got to say for yourselves? I warned you only last week about how I would punish you if you continued to talk in class and be rude to your teachers."

'We remembered what Suzi had told us to do, so we looked very shamefaced and begged his pardon. But he shook his head and, after giving us a lecture on our bad behaviour, he concluded: "It's too late to say you're sorry. I am going to give you both a good tanning. Now, who is going to be first?"

' "I will, sir," I said meekly and Herr Basler licked his lips wolfishly as he put three chairs together in the centre of the room. Then he sternly ordered me to lie down at full length upon the chairs and pull up my skirt to receive my well-deserved punishment.

'As I obediently bent over the chairs I saw a bulge appear in the front of his trousers whilst he brought up a fourth chair upon which he would sit so that he could administer the smacks without having to stoop. Then the rogue bared my bottom, smoothing his hand along the crevice between my buttocks before beginning the spanking.

'He rested his left hand on the small of my back and started to smack me with hard firm slaps, but only on the right cheek, which made me wince. But after half a dozen or so smacks, he stopped and said: "My word, what a beautiful contrast the lovely bright scarlet of your spanked bum cheek makes with the untouched white one.

' "Still, I must not neglect my duty," he sniggered as he set to work on my left cheek, giving it a series of sharp smacks which made it match the other in colour. Following Suzi's directions, I wiggled my smarting bottom from side to side and begged for mercy in piteous tones, crying out: "Oh! Oh! Oh! No more, I have had enough. My poor bottom is burning like fire!"

' "No, I think you should have another round of three smacks on each bum cheek," he said, but when I turned my head towards him and saw that the bulge in his trousers was now sticking up even more noticeably in his lap, I moved my left arm up and deliberately brushed my elbow against his stiff cock as I pretended to wipe a tear from my eye.

'This startled Herr Basler so much that he pulled his restraining hand away from my back and I was able to wriggle free and stand up. I went quickly back to Tanya who was standing against the wall. I said quietly: "If he really hurts you, give his hard-on a rub. That should stop the dirty rascal."

'Now, I should mention here that Tanya is a most attractive petite girl with a pretty little face which was almost hidden by her long, flowing tresses of glossy, soft, auburn hair. Herr Basler was clearly smitten by her feminine charms because he called out angrily: "It's your turn now, Tanya. Now, you've been even naughtier than Wanda so I'm going to whip you."

'This frightened my friend and she moved to the door but then he added: "Don't worry, I'll make it worth your while. Submit to a whipping and I'll cancel the payments on your family's loan for the next three months."

'She hesitated for a moment but the lure of his bait was too strong. So she nodded her head and walked up to him. "Good girl, now you're being sensible," he growled. Then he strolled over to the cabinet and took out a short, slender little birch-rod. Then he came back and, sitting down on his chair, he told Tanya to take off her skirt and bend herself over his knees. I thought she might refuse, but Tanya wanted to release her parents from Herr Basler's clutches, so she unbuttoned her skirt and silently laid herself over his thighs.

'I must confess that my heart began to beat faster when he exposed her perfectly proportioned rounded bottom. In the same way that he had held me down, he placed his left hand upon her back and, with a smile on his face, he raised his right arm high in the air. Then the rod hissed down and fell with a swish on Tanya's plump white bottom, instantly marking her bum cheeks with red weals and making the poor girl cry out in pain. A second stroke of the rod made Tanya throw back her head with a jerk, and toss her long hair all over her face as she uttered a loud, shrill squeal as the twigs raised another set of weals on her quivering backside.

'I had not realised that the little whip could hurt her so much, especially as, to be fair, Herr Basler did not birch Tanya too severely. Nevertheless, she wriggled and kicked her legs in all directions as the rod swished down again and she shrieked out: "W-a-h-h! Y-a-h-h! Stop! Let me go, I'm not taking any more of this!"

'But he refused to listen to her cries and he held her down firmly whilst he slowly counted up to six as he completed her punishment. Surely he would now stop, I thought to myself, but he chuckled: "One more for luck," and the rod flashed one final time across Tanya's luscious young bum. She lay trembling across his knees, writhing from the smarting pain.

'After she had recovered, Herr Basler placed his hands under her shoulders and hauled her up. As her skirt was raised, when she turned towards me I had an excellent close view of Tanya's cunt. This was the first time I had seen a shaved pussy and I gasped with astonishment when I glanced at the tiny wisp of delicate brown down around her prominent pink love lips.

'Anyhow, as soon as Tanya had dressed herself we left Herr Basler's house and went back to my home. My parents were out with some friends and so we went straight up to my bedroom where we took off our skirts and knickers and washed our sore, red arses. I think Tanya's blood had also been fired by watching Herr Basler spank me, for she told me to lie down upon my bed and then she rolled me over onto my belly. She placed her hand on my bottom and said: "Wanda, has anyone ever told you that you have a ravishingly beautiful bum? The cheeks are so soft and rounded that I can hardly stop myself from pinching them."

' "Thank you for the compliment, but I think your

backside is nicer than mine. Your cheeks jiggled so invitingly when Herr Basler was birching you and you have such delicious dimples that his cock must have been sticking up like a flagpole whilst you were bent over his lap."

'She smiled ruefully and said: "Yes, I could feel it pressing against my belly and I jolly well hope that it was as uncomfortable for him as it was for me. Incidentally, I saw you looking at my pussy. You looked rather surprised – haven't you ever seen a shaved pussy before?"

' "No, I haven't," I confessed and, with a frisky gleam in her eyes, Tanya said: "Oh, but you must try it. It's so nice and cool in the summer but what's more important is that my boyfriend finds it terribly exciting to slide his cock into my quim and to be able to watch it see-saw in and out between my pussy lips."

'This interested me and I said: "Tanya, do you think that Stefan Solodowski would like to see my bare pussy?"

'She answered: "I'm sure he would, dear. In fact, you don't have to wait to find out – aren't you going for a walk with Stefan a little later? Let me shave your pussy before you go and you can show it to him. What have you got to lose? If he isn't too keen, it won't take more than a week or two for your pussy hair to grow again!"

'This was reassuring although I was still slightly wary about the idea. However, Tanya pressed home her argument by saying that my blonde bush would be easy enough to remove and that Stefan would be surprised and overjoyed to see my shaven mound. So I smiled and said: "All right, Tanya, it can't do any harm. As you say, if Stefan prefers a hairy cunt, it won't take very long for my thatch of pussy hair to reappear."

'Well, Tanya was quite right. At first Stefan was astonished when he pulled down my knickers and looked at my hairless mound but, as she had forecast, once the shock had worn off, he found my shaven haven very exciting and we had such a glorious fuck that my pussy was quite sore the next morning! But it would have been tiresome having to shave all the time and, in fact, Stefan said that he thought my blonde muff was very pretty and asked me to let it grow again. Still, I enjoyed the experience and, as I had expected, my pussy hair grew back very quickly.'

She giggled at the memory and Natasha was clearly fascinated by her story for before Wanda could continue she interrupted: 'A boy friend of mine once suggested that I should let him shave my pussy because it would make it more comfortable for him to bring me off with his mouth.'

'And did you, Natasha?' asked Wanda. But Natasha shook her head and answered: 'No, I rather fancied the idea but it would have been difficult to find the time or somewhere private to do it. Besides, even if I had been able to borrow my father's razor, I had never used one before and, to be honest, I was a little bit scared of cutting myself.'

'Well, if you would like to find out how it feels, you must come round to my house tomorrow night and I'll be happy to shave your pussy for you,' said Wanda kindly. Emboldened perhaps by the cognac, I blurted out: 'Why wait till then? You can use my shaving tackle. I've a pot of Roger & Gallet Heliotrope Shaving Cream and a new Wilkinson's razor which my father bought for me in England.'

Natasha laughed and said: 'That's not a bad idea, Master Johann. And afterwards you must give me your honest opinion about whether you prefer my pussy hairy or bald. Now you get out what's necessary from the bathroom and I'll boil up some hot water. Is that all right with you, Wanda?'

'Oh yes, by all means,' she answered excitedly, although I think she was somewhat surprised that Natasha was keen to include me in the little game, not realizing, of course, that the voluptuous gypsy girl and I had been frenetically engaged in the most lascivious love-play during our train journey only that very morning!

Anyhow, on Wanda's instructions I brought my shaving set and a towel out of the bathroom. When Natasha came back from the kitchen with a bowl of hot water, we were ready to proceed. Natasha pulled off her clothes and my cock immediately hardened up at the sight of her proud young body in which were joined the incisive lines of a lithe, lissome girl with the provocative ripeness of a Rubenesque model. For her slender waist accentuated her large breasts with their wide areolae and proud erect nipples – and, although I was looking forward to seeing Wanda shave Natasha's mound, it did seem a shame to do away with that glossy carpet of luxuriant black hair. This hair formed a perfect setting for the glowing red slit which looked so inviting when, using a cushion as a pillow, Natasha lay down on the floor in front of the fire, pulled her puffy pussy lips apart and provocatively ran her forefinger all down along her long crack.

'Please be careful with that razor,' said Natasha nervously. But she need not have worried for Wanda showed that, with tuition, she could have been as good a barber as Zimmel Goldberg, the tubby little Jewish hairdresser patronized by my father back in Vienna. First she carefully clipped Natasha's bush with a pair of nail scissors. Then, after thoroughly dampening the remaining hair with hot water, she spread a generous amount of shaving cream around Natasha's pussy and, with long sweeping strokes, shaved the lot away, not once nicking the soft skin around the outer cunney lips, until Natasha's cunt was totally devoid of its hirsute covering.

I handed Natasha a small mirror and she squealed with delight as she peered down at her hairless quim. Wanda finished by rubbing some lightly perfumed oil all over her pussy and by this time I was feeling so randy that my stiffie was fairly aching for release. Fortunately, Natasha had been similarly stimulated. She looked up and spread her legs invitingly as she said: 'What are you waiting for, Johann? I want to know whether you think Wanda's work makes it even nicer to make love to me.'

Now, I was only too delighted to find out the answer to this question – although I could hardly imagine that anything could top the ecstasy of pleasure I had experienced whilst first fucking Natasha on the grassy knoll in the woods near Jaschnitz some six weeks before or the sensual delight of that very morning in our compartment on the train from Berlin to Pinczow. But one *can* enjoy one bout of love-making more than another, although in my opinion there are only two kinds of fuck – the good and the great! And even the merely good ones are memorable. For as my dear old Scottish pal Jack Webster, the Laird of Duntocher, wittily asked the company at a dinner party recently: 'What is the difference between an egg and a fuck?' Jack kindly provided the answer: 'You can beat an egg!'

Of course, this philosophising was far from my mind as, notwithstanding the presence of Wanda, I tore off my clothes and lay down next to Natasha on the rug. After a brief but passionate kiss, my mouth slid lower and lower down her trembling body until it was pressed against her outer labia. I was hardly experienced at eating pussy and at first I licked her tentatively, drawing the tip of my tongue along her sopping slit as I explored the manifold furrows of this exquisite flower that was opening out in front of me.

'Yes, yes, tongue me out and make me cum,' Natasha moaned in delight and this gave me the confidence to start slurping with a fully uninhibited vigour on her moist quim which had been made deliciously aromatic by Wanda's perfumed oil.

'Oooh, that's *so* nice,' she gasped whilst I inhaled this sensual bouquet and darted my tongue between her pussy lips to roam inside her juicy cunt.

I placed one hand underneath Natasha's jouncy bum cheeks to press her cunney even closer to my mouth, which I opened wide to allow my tongue to probe her inner recesses, and in seconds I found myself licking the nub of her erect clitty. After rhythmically circling it with the tip of my tongue, I nibbled and sucked the hard little love button until she spent copiously over my face. I swallowed up her pungent cuntal juice before I scrambled up and substituted my knob in place of my lips at the entrance to her dripping love funnel.

Natasha eagerly hauled up her hips as my shaft slipped into her dripping crack. She threw her legs across my back and heaved up and down in time with my robust thrusts as we enjoyed a most excellent fuck. Despite the outpouring of her own cuntal juices, Natasha's cunt was exquisitely tight, holding me in the sweetest vice imaginable. But her juices were now flowing so freely, oiling her cunney walls so well, that my further thrusts were made even easier as my cock buried itself within the luscious folds of her shaven slit.

'H-a-r-g-h! H-a-r-g-h! H-a-r-g-h!' Natasha cried out as she spent again whilst I made one last lunge forward, my balls banging against her bottom as, with a hoarse cry of triumph, I shot a stream of hot frothy spunk into her clingy cunt. I wriggled my prick inside her sated snatch while the seed continued to gush out of my knob in great jets as we writhed around on the rug, enjoying this magnificent fuck to the full.

As might be expected, watching this erotic drama which was unfolding just a footstep or two away from her had made Wanda unbearably randy and in a trice she had shed her clothes and was kneeling beside us in the nude. I withdrew my glistening wet cock from Natasha's cunt, and I must say that it was exciting to be able to see my heavy semi-erect shaft sliding out from between her swollen love lips.

However, Wanda appeared to be more interested in Natasha's breasts which she began to kiss, moving her mouth from one nipple to the other. Then she raised her head and whispered: 'Although he went too far, I must confess that I found being spanked by Herr Basler rather arousing. Would you like to give me a smack-bottom, Natasha?'

'Of course I will,' answered the gypsy girl with a flashing smile and, after Natasha had sat up, Wanda placed herself over her lap, exposing her tight, rounded bum cheeks to my lascivious gaze.

Natasha then began to smack the two beautiful white hemispheres of Wanda's backside, saying: 'This will teach you to shave my pussy, madam – there, you naughty girl, take that and that and that!'

But she only slapped with a light touch and their lithe naked bodies gleamed as Wanda wriggled whilst Natasha's hand rose and fell, her large strawberry nipples also rising and falling with each stroke.

It was clear that both girls were enjoying themselves

and Natasha cooed: 'Oh Wanda, I love the way your bum cheeks jiggle whilst I spank you. Your lovely backside is blushing so beautifully! It should always be this pinky shade, don't you agree, Master Johann?'

'I'm not really bothered either way,' I said huskily as Wanda reached up and grabbed hold of my thick swollen shaft. At her request, I knelt down beside her so that she could clamp her wide red lips around my rampant rod and she began bobbing her head up and down my twitching tool to the same rhythm of the slaps which Natasha was administering to her tingling bottom. She lashed her tongue around my prick which was now thudding away like a steamhammer and I worked my hips backwards and forwards as her pliant tongue washed over my bared helmet. I closed my eyes for a moment to wallow in the ecstasy of this superb sucking-off.

I heard Natasha whisper something and I opened my eyes to see that she was pushing Wanda off her lap. Natasha positioned Wanda so that the petite little blonde was kneeling in front of me whilst she continued to suck my cock with undiminished relish.

The reason for this move became clear when Natasha raised herself up on her hands and knees and locks of glossy black hair tumbled down over her face as she lowered her pretty head and kissed the soft ripe cheeks of Wanda's bottom. Then, turning onto her back, Natasha slid her head between the other girl's legs and, holding on to her thighs, began to worry her tongue around Wanda's corn-coloured muff of pussy hair which I was sure was already damp with cuntal juice.

Wanda gurgled as she gobbled furiously on my cock whilst Natasha teased the tip of her tongue between her pouting pussy lips and then inserted her thumb into her juicy snatch. Then Wanda suddenly pulled her mouth away and gasped out: 'Go behind and fuck my bum, Johann!'

Luckily, I had enough *nous* to spread a liberal amount of my expensive French shaving cream on my cock before kneeling behind Wanda and directing my purple domed bell-end into the crevice between her tight little buttocks. With her left hand, Natasha helped guide my tool towards the tiny star-shaped entrance to Wanda's rear dimple whilst with her right she carried on finger-fucking the pretty girl's cunt. The shaving cream greased my tool very nicely and, with only a minimum of discomfort for Wanda, I found my prick firmly ensconced inside the narrow canal of her back passage.

For a brief moment I rested and then slowly I began to pull my prick in and out of Wanda's arsehole whilst I slid my arms under her shoulders and squeezed her breasts as I rubbed her stiff engorged titties. She began to shake all over at this double stimulation and at the feeling of Natasha's tongue washing over her clitty whilst the gypsy girl drove her thumb and two other fingers in and out of Wanda's wet cunney, diddling her own cunt with the fingers of her free hand.

This lewd three-way love-making was so arousing that I soon flooded Wanda's bottom with a copious deluge of lubricating jism which enabled me to work my cock back and forth so that it remained stiff. With a "pop" I uncorked my knob from Wanda's backside and she yelled out her joy in a frenzy of lustful glee as she shuddered to a climax and discharged a flood of pungent cuntal juice over Natasha's lapping tongue.

Dear reader, you must forgive me, but I do wish to record the fact that, after we collapsed in a heap on the soft rug and lay recovering our senses, I was complimented by Wanda for remembering to coat my cock with shaving cream before sticking it up her bottom.

She said: 'That was very thoughtful of you, Master Johann. As the Poles say: *Pryzamya dupre* which, roughly translated, means that one up the back way won't hurt you. Most girls enjoy being bum-fucked now and then, but only when the boy takes the trouble to grease his cock like you did.'

Incidentally, ever since that memorable evening I have heeded these words and always keep a jar of cold cream handy for this purpose.

Be that as it may, the three of us were quickly fired up again and we engaged in some splendid licentious embraces, pressing our lips together and waggling our tongues in each other's mouths in the most sensual possible way. Now, after two fucks one after the other, even my eager youthful cock could do no more than dangle limply over my balls, but Natasha placed her hand on top of my head and, drawing it down to Wanda's golden bush of pussy hair, she said quietly: 'Now I know you're not up to another fuck, Master Johann, but I'm sure that Wanda would really appreciate it if you licked out her cunt.'

'Oh yes, that would be wonderful,' Wanda panted with a gleam in her big blue eyes as she laid herself flat on her back. Parting her thighs, she splayed open her cunt with her long fingers. 'Natasha has brought me off already and my pussy is bursting for another spend.'

'Your wish is my command,' I said gallantly and I began by rolling on top of her soft curves and drawing my body upwards until my tongue was level with her superb pointed nipples. I nibbled on her titties, sucking on their rubbery hardness until they were sticking out like two little raspberry stalks and then I let my tongue travel down the velvet skin of her tummy, briefly pausing to encircle her belly button before sliding further down into the smooth golden hair that veiled her pussy.

Like a snake I slid myself down between her legs and gently parted her lightly scented pubic bush with my fingertips to reveal her swollen clitty. As I pressed my mouth against the long gash of her cleft I breathed in the appealing cuntal aroma, a fragrance which from this day till now I have always found most exhilarating.

Wanda sighed with pleasure as I breathed deeply and then placed my lips directly over her clitty and sucked it into my mouth, where the tip of my tongue began to explore it from all directions. I could feel it growing even larger as her legs started to twitch along the sides of my body and her heels began to beat a tattoo on the rug. I nibbled delicately on the fleshy morsel until I managed to send her off into a intense orgasm. She shivered all over as the exquisite force of her climax spread through her body.

'M'mmm, what a dreamy spend,' Wanda breathed softly as I licked up the creamy cum from her cunt. 'It was almost as good as actually being poked by a real cock.'

I took this remark as a compliment, even if it was somewhat back-handed, but Wanda furthered my sexual education by informing me that boys naturally preferred straightforward fucking 'because they always cum sooner or later, but girls have to work to achieve a climax.'

'Yes, finding a considerate lover with staying power isn't so easy,' observed Natasha as she idly flipped my dangling cock over my thigh. 'One of the most disappointing experiences I ever had with a boy was last year when we were setting up camp at the big fair in Leipzig. My father and brothers never have any problem finding work there and my mother usually does very well with her fortune-telling stall. However, I had little to do on the morning before the opening day, so I wandered out for a walk and I came across some men putting up the big top for Professor Ardi Gluck's International Circus.'

'Professor Gluck, did you way? Why, what a coincidence, that's the circus which was playing in Stettin when we met each other,' I exclaimed and the memory of how I lost my unwanted virginity to Christa the tightrope-walker made my cock twitch as Natasha went on: 'Really? I hope they had good audiences there: the Professor's very popular with travelling people because when he needs extra hands he always pays them a fair wage. Anyhow, as I walked by them I came across a troupe of acrobats rehearsing their act and I can tell you that I found it quite a turn-on to see these five muscular young men with their rippling muscles, broad chests and tight bums working out in their tights and leotards.

'There was one handsome blond chap who especially caught my eye, and when they finished their rehearsal I sauntered over and congratulated them on their act. We got to talking and I was delighted to find that Kurt, my good-looking blond bombshell, seemed especially keen to continue the conversation. When the other lads saw that I reciprocated his obvious interest in me, they tactfully melted away, leaving us alone. "Natasha, I'm so hot from all that exercise that I was going to the river for a quick dip," said Kurt. "Would you care to join me?"

' "Thank you, Kurt that will be very nice, but don't expect me to go swimming: it's not warm enough for me yet," I said. We chatted away gaily whilst we strolled along the bank of a nearby stream until we found ourselves in a wooded clearing away from prying eyes.

' "I'll just wash off all the perspiration," said Kurt whilst I took the towel he had brought with him and as he began to undress he looked up at me with a flushed face and muttered: "Er, Natasha, I don't have a swimming costume so if you might want to go behind a tree for a couple of minutes—"

' "Oh, that's all right, you can't live in a gypsy camp without seeing people in the buff," I said cheerfully as I sat down on the river bank and watched him pull off his tights. But Kurt appeared to be bashful about letting me see his cock, because he turned away from me as he tugged down his briefs – although this did of course, give me a view of his taut, muscular bum cheeks. He ran into the stream and splashed around for a while. Then it became clear that Kurt really was a shy boy because he came out of the water sheepishly covering his cock and balls in his hands!

' "Here's your towel," I said, trying hard not to giggle as he took one of his hands away from his crotch to grab the towel – which he immediately wrapped round his waist. But not before I had the chance to peep quickly at what looked like a very large prick dangling between his legs!

' "Let me help dry you," I said but he politely declined my offer, saying that he preferred to let his body dry off in the sun. I squinted up to the sky and went on: "It isn't that warm, Kurt. You'll catch cold if you're not careful. Here, give me that towel and I'll give your back a good rub."

' "Honestly, that's not necessary," he protested, but I wasn't going to take no for an answer – at least, not until I had taken a peek at the interesting bulge under the towel which was drawn tightly over his lap. "No, I really want to, Kurt," I said firmly as I started to unbutton my blouse, adding: "I'll just take this top off in case I get it wet."

'He gaped at me as I shrugged the garment off my shoulders. I was wearing such a low-cut slip that, when I bent down to place the blouse on his pile of clothes, I gave Kurt a grandstand view of the swell of my breasts. This made him give a nervous gulp and his cheeks reddened when I cupped my hands underneath my tits and said sweetly: "Do you like my breasts, Kurt? You can feel them if you like."

'Kurt said nothing but just sat there open-mouthed. So I pulled the straps of my chemise down over my arms and my bare breasts tumbled out as I leaned over to him and gave him an encouraging kiss on the lips. He began to tremble and asked if he could fondle my nipples. "Of course you can," I cooed. His warm fingers made them swell up and I could feel my knickers getting moist with excitement. Then I moved my face forward and kissed him on the lips whilst I gently pulled the towel from off his lap.'

Natasha paused to take a sip of the cognac which I had left in my glass and Wanda chuckled: 'I bet his prick was as hard as a rock – don't you agree, Master Johann?'

By now my own tool was starting to thicken as I answered with a grin: 'I should say so!' However, Natasha shook her head and said: 'You would think so, wouldn't you? But, though Kurt had a thick meaty cock, it was only standing at half-mast, although it did swell to stand up firmly against his belly when I slid my fingers around his shaft and, after jamming down the foreskin, gave it a friendly stroke. "That's better," I murmured as I fisted my hand up and down his pulsating pole. "Now let me just take off the rest of my clothes and you can make love to me."

'Well, would you believe it, he actually turned me down! In fact, his cock actually started to soften whilst he looked at me in a very embarrassed sort of way and mumbled: "I'm dreadfully sorry, Natasha, but I don't go all the way with girls."

'Well, I hadn't thought that a lad like Kurt, who

admittedly was no more than seventeen at most, could still be a virgin, especially living in the free and easy world of a travelling circus. Perhaps he had suffered one of those dreary religious upbringings where boys are warned that if they play with themselves their cocks will drop off, so I didn't storm off in a huff but decided to encourage him by actions rather than words.

'So I knelt down in front of him and held his cock flat against his belly so that I could lick the underside, from his balls right up to his knob. This made Kurt's prick perk up again and I could feel it throb as I swirled my tongue over his uncapped helmet. Then I held his shaft tightly and flicked at it with the tip of my tongue before opening my mouth and cramming as much of his thick cock as I could manage between my lips whilst I smoothed my free hand over his thick thatch of blond pubic curls.

'Kurt grunted softly as he shut his eyes and he was undoubtedly visualizing some kind of fantasy whilst I gobbled his cock as if I hadn't tasted anything sweeter in my life, sucking so hard that my cheeks hurt. I couldn't get enough of it and sucked again and again till he was ready to come – but to my amazement he then jerked his prick out of my mouth and began tossing himself off so fast that his hand was a blur until he came, letting out a guttural cry of triumph as he spurted great globs of jism over my face whilst he lay back against a tree-trunk massaging his balls.

'I was so shocked that, without a word, I simply wiped off his cum with the towel which – then passed to Kurt to dry his cock. He bit his lip and said: "I'm sorry, Natasha, I owe you an apology for my strange behaviour. I should have told you that I have a steady partner and we promised each other that we wouldn't fool around with anybody else. As it is, I'm sure someone the troupe will tell Christa and I'll have some awkward questions to answer when I get back to her, but at least I can swear on my word of honour that I hadn't been unfaithful."

' "Huh, that's being somewhat economical with the truth," I commented in some anger. "*Your* cock was in *my* mouth and *you* let *me* suck it and quite frankly I don't think it matters that much that right at the end you brought yourself off."

'He hung his head and admitted: "That's true enough, but I just couldn't resist you, Natasha, you're so pretty and, believe me, it was all I could do to stop myself taking up your invitation to fuck."

'Well, what could I say? To be fair, I had made all the running and if there had been any seduction, it had been on my part, so I gave him a quick smile and said: "No hard feelings, Kurt. I just hope that your lady love will forgive you. If you bring her over to the gypsy encampment in the park, I'll tell her that nothing naughty happened between us." '

Now, of course, I was wondering whether this Christa was the same Christa as the circus performer who had helped me through my rite of passage into manhood. So I asked Natasha if she knew anything about Kurt's *amorata* and she replied with a shrug: 'Yes, I think she was a tightrope-walker. But why do you ask, Master Johann?'

'Oh, there's no particular reason,' I answered airily. 'It's just that my friend Carl Hildebrand and myself went to the circus in Stettin and I wondered whether I had seen the girl perform. As it happens, I think I do remember there was a high-wire act by a girl called Christa but I can't really recall anything about her.'

'Come on, I bet you can, young sir,' said Wanda roguishly as she gently slapped my shoulder. 'Those girls don't wear a great deal and the state of your cock is telling me that you remember more than you're letting on!'

I looked down at my cock which had indeed thickened up during Natasha's raunchy confession but as I moved across to return the slap on Wanda's cheeky bum I let out a yelp as a sharp twinge of pain suddenly shot across the small of my back.

'Ouch!' I yelped and I clapped my hand to my back. Fortunately, though, the pain went away with equal swiftness, and when I explained what had happened Wanda said: 'It's all the unaccustomed exercise you've had tonight, Master Johann. How would you like a nice massage?'

'That would be very welcome,' I said, and the three of us (for Natasha naturally wanted to watch) scrambled to our feet and made our way to my bedroom. When I laid down on my bed Wanda commanded me to turn over onto my belly before she jumped up onto the eiderdown and straddled me, with her knees between my parted legs. Then she placed her hands on the back of my neck and began to massage me slowly, not too fiercely but at a firm, sensual pace, beginning at the top of my back and working her way down my spine, over my buttocks and thighs, right down to the backs of my knees.

'There, doesn't that feel better?' she asked and I agreed that my muscles felt wonderfully relaxed under her skilled hands.

Then she worked her way back to my neck and ran her fingertips lightly down my body. But when her fingers reached my bottom, she slid her hands back and forth across my buttocks and then she moved further down the insides of my thighs. My cock was now as stiff as a board as she gently caressed my ballsack from behind and then told me to turn over.

'I could easily get used to this,' I said as I rolled over onto my back. Wanda smacked her lips as she looked down at my throbbing boner which was sticking up high in the air, but when I reached up to squeeze her luscious breasts which dangled so temptingly above me, she giggled: 'Now, now, keep your arms by your side – there'll be time enough for a bit of rumpy-pumpy when I've finished!'

I was in no mood to argue so I closed my eyes and settled down to enjoy the sensual feel of Wanda's hands pressing and kneading my muscles. Though my shaft was now aching for relief, she teasingly kept her hands away from my frantic cock.

But relief *was* soon at hand for, once she had completed the massage, Wanda lowered her mop of silky blonde hair and planted a smacking wet kiss on my lips. With difficulty I restrained myself and kept my arms resting on the eiderdown as she worked her tongue down my body, stopping briefly to circle my nipples before at last descending to my aching cock. She licked all round the ridge of my helmet and then sucked in as much of my straining shaft as she could manage, stroking my length with one hand and teasing my balls through the pink wrinkled sack with the other. Wanda's head bobbed up and down as she treated me to a most delicious gobble and, once she had thoroughly anointed my pulsing prick before she climbed aboard for a ride, she whispered: 'Master Johann, I'm now going to sit on your lovely thick prick and feel it glide into my wet little cunt.'

As she leaned over to move her knees, her jaunty red nipples brushed my chest and this time she raised no objection as I slid my hands around them and rubbed her big titties between my fingers whilst she slowly impaled herself on my quivering chopper.

This was to be a short, sharp fuck but memorable for its intensity, for her cuntal muscles clung tenaciously to my cock as I jerked my hips up and down to slide it up and down her tight but juicy sheath. I thrilled to the feel of the clinging cunney wall, one hand clutching a jiggling bum cheek as Wanda bounced up and down on my twitching tool.

Then I felt a fresh electric stab of desire speed through my body as she took my tightening scrotum in her hand. The soft feel of Wanda's fingers sent me over the top and I came straightaway, shooting my seed deep inside her cunt and flooding her love funnel with a real torrent of sticky spunk.

'Ahhhh! *Wunderbar, wunderbar!*' she gasped as she reached her climax whilst the jism poured out of my knob as Wanda milked my cock of the last drops of my copious emission.

I found it impossible to fight against a delicious but overpowering drowsiness that made me close my eyes and fall into a welcome light sleep. It was not surprising that I was *hors de combat*, not just from the effort of a third spend in less than ninety minutes, but also from the effects of the long journey from Vienna, not to mention the earlier excitement of the unexpected lewd fucking with Natasha on the train.

'Poor Master Johann, he looks absolutely all-in,' I heard Natasha say as she helped Wanda cover my body with the eiderdown. 'I'll bring his clothes in here and then we had better get dressed before his father comes back.'

'I dare say you're right,' sighed Wanda. Then she broke out into a fit of giggles as she went on: 'On the other hand, can you imagine the expression on the Count's face if he were greeted by two naked girls who offered to help him undress before tucking him up in bed!'

This thought caused Natasha to burst into laughter but I must confess to a sense of relief sweeping over me when she replied: 'Well, I'm sure the Count is a red-blooded gentleman and would be more amused than offended if we invited him to fuck us, but it wouldn't be right to tempt him with forbidden fruit. From what I can gather from the other servants, he was once known as one of the horniest men in Vienna before he married Johann's mum, but since then the Count's rarely strayed from the straight and narrow.'

I could hardly believe what I was hearing – surely it could not be true that my father once behaved like Doctor Hildebrand who I had been shocked to discover was regularly shagging his lusty housemaid Sonia!

'What do you mean by "rarely"? Doesn't he fuck any of the maids back in Vienna?' demanded Wanda with a note of disbelief in her voice. Natasha chuckled: 'Well, no, not that I know of and, as I understand it, he's always been true to his wife in his fashion, but for instance when he travels by himself to England on business, his old valet Alfred told me that the Count often invites the Prince of Wales *[the future King Edward VII and a notorious libertine who at his Coronation in 1902 set aside a special pew in Westminster Abbey for his mistresses – Editor]* to wild parties at his house in London.'

Wanda brightened up at this news and remarked: 'Is that so? Well, you tell me all the juicy gossip about them whilst we get dressed.'

I would have liked to have heard more about these orgies myself but I was so tired that I fell fast asleep and did not wake up until almost nine o'clock the next morning.

As I heaved myself up there was a knock on the door and Natasha came in carrying a mug of steaming hot coffee. 'Good day, Master Johann, how are you this morning?' she asked brightly as she set down the mug on my bedside table. 'My, you were so tired that you didn't hear your father come in last night, did you? Well, I'm afraid you've missed him this morning: he left about half an hour ago. But he said he would return by noon – and Wanda will soon be coming back from the village shops and she is going to help me cook a nice lunch for the pair of you.'

'That'll be nice,' I said as I reached over to take hold of the mug and take a refreshing gulp of coffee. I only had a small sip but a warmth swept immediately through my body.

'Wow! What kind of coffee is that?' I spluttered and Natasha smiled: 'I don't know but I poured a dram of cognac into the mug to give it a kick.'

Now, as usual I had woken up with a tremendous erection and perhaps the cognac emboldened me for after I had downed a further larger gulp I pulled the gypsy girl down upon the bed and stroked her glossy black hair which now tumbled freely over her shoulders. In a trice we were entwined in each other's arms exchanging the most ardent of kisses as Natasha slid her hand under the eiderdown and rubbed my straining shaft which was standing up like a thick little telegraph pole between my thighs. Then she released it to unbutton her blouse as she whispered: 'Help me off with my knickers, there's a good boy.'

I needed no second bidding and in no time at all Natasha lay naked beside me. Even though I had seen her naked before I still stared in wonder at her lush, exquisitely proportioned uptilted breasts capped with their big biteable nipples and her smooth white belly below which now lay, unencumbered by any covering of hair, the prettiest pair of pouting cunney lips imaginable.

She slid her arm around my neck to cradle my head and

we kissed again, our tongues meshing together as I let my hands drop onto the jouncy cheeks of her bottom as I pressed her eager body against my rock-hard cock.

We rolled from side to side on the bed until Natasha broke the embrace to grab one of my pillows and insert it under her back so that her thighs and cunney would be positioned at a perfect angle for my bursting prick which she held in her hand. I lay on top of her, nudging her knees a little further apart as she guided my knob directly into her sopping crack.

I was already so worked up that I pumped in and out of her juicy cunt at some speed whilst Natasha moaned with delight as I slewed my sinewy shaft in and out of her tingling love channel. She pressed up to meet me at every stroke as she gasped: 'Oh Johann, I've cum already! You can shoot your load whenever you want to, you randy young man!'

Nothing loath, I increased the pace until I was pistoning in and out of her squelchy quim at a great rate of knots, my balls slapping against her thighs as she wrapped her legs around me. I cupped her breasts, pinching the erect nipples between my thumb and forefinger whilst my cock sluiced back and forth as we moved into the final stages of this voluptuous coupling. Natasha's lithe frame twisted and bucked at the approach of a second spend which came just as I sent a powerful stream of spunk into her saturated cunt and the uniquely delicious warm feelings of delight spread out from my cock to every fibre of my body.

We lay together panting with exhaustion but then Natasha threw back the eiderdown and jumped out of bed and she said: 'Come on, Master Johann, I've plenty of work to do before Wanda comes back with the shopping. Now, shall I boil up some water for a nice hot bath before your breakfast?'

'Yes please, that would be very nice,' I said as I drank down some more of Natasha's special coffee and then added with a naughty smirk: 'You're very welcome to join me, Natasha. I could soap your shaved pussy and you could wash my cock and balls.'

'I'm afraid there's no time for any of that,' Natasha answered briskly as she stepped into her knickers. 'Wanda will be here soon and I still have to tidy up the bedrooms.'

It suddenly struck me that it must have been quite late when I fell asleep the previous evening and I wondered whether Wanda had in fact stayed the night – and if so, where had she slept! This was a delicate matter but I decided not to beat about the bush so whilst I was eating my breakfast I said bluntly to Natasha: 'I heard you talking to Wanda about my father before I dozed off last night. No, it's all right, I won't tell him. But answer me truthfully, was Wanda still here when he returned? Was he greeted by the pair of you in the nude?'

'Yes, Wanda did stay the night,' she grudgingly admitted but then added emphatically: 'But I promise you that almost nothing untoward happened between your father and Wanda.'

There was an obvious loophole in this observation and I shot a question through it. '*Almost* nothing, Natasha? Come on, don't hold back, I want to know exactly what happened here during the night.'

'It's as I say, nothing that would concern you,' the gypsy girl hotly asserted. 'Still, if it makes you happy I'll tell you that your father, being a perfect gentleman, said that it was too late for Wanda to go home but he refused to let her doss down on the floor and insisted that the pair of us sleep in the bed whilst he slept on the sofa. Now are you satisfied?'

I replied: 'No, not really, because although that does

sound more like my father, there's clearly more to be told. Come on, out with it, Natasha!'

She threw back the long strands of dark hair from her face and heaved a sigh as she said: 'I'll tell you everything, but you must swear not to tease your father about it.'

'You have my word of honour,' I promised her and she continued: 'Well, if you must know, after the lights went out Wanda and I were playing with each other's pussies. Not to put too fine a point to it, I was finger-fucking Wanda up to a spend and she began to groan so loudly that she woke up your father who must have thought there was an intruder in the bedroom.

'When I heard your father moving around, I pulled my fingers out of Wanda's cunt. But by the time he came dashing in stark naked with the poker in his hand, Wanda had begun to diddle herself and was so far gone that she began to moan: "Ahhh! Ahhh! I'm cumming, I'm cumming!"

'I pretended to be fast asleep but I saw Wanda, who was quite overcome by the waves of her climax, throw out her arm and clasp your father's cock, holding on to it for dear life whilst she brought herself off. Of course, his shaft swelled up in her hand and she gave it a little rub before letting it go. Then, lying back, her eyes fluttered open briefly and she said: "Oh, I've just had the most amazing dream!"

'With her eyes again apparently closed, Wanda fell back on the pillow and began to caress her breasts whilst she slept as she mumbled something about needing a big thick cock to fill her tight little pussy,' Natasha concluded and smiled when I commented: 'Do you believe that she was really asleep?'

'No, to be honest, I think Wanda knew exactly what she was doing, but your father clearly believed that she was guilty of nothing more than having a very exciting dream, but he simply tip-toed out of the room and retired back to the sofa.

'There, now you have the full story, Master Johann – nothing of consequence actually happened, but I don't want the Count to hear a word about it or Wanda and I will both be in trouble.'

'Your secret is safe with me,' I laughed, for I was amused rather than angry at this anecdote of an unsuccessful attempt to seduce my father. 'But why did Wanda want my father to fuck her?' I asked, for I thought I had given the nubile young blonde a good seeing-to the previous evening. However, Natasha informed me that I should not take her desire to be poked again as a personal affront. She said: 'Poor Wanda's problem – and you must also keep this between ourselves – is that after she told Stefan Solodowski about what happened at Herr Basler's he became so angry about how the overseer's lust and financial greed was ruining so many people's lives.

'And what was worse, there was nothing he could do about it because if he complained to your father about Herr Basler, he might lose the work he desperately needs if he is to complete his studies in Warsaw. Well, the long and the short of it is that this has affected Stefan so badly that he can hardly get it up any more. Wanda's tried everything, rubbing cream on his cock, sucking his balls and sticking her fingers up his bottom but even if he does manage a stiffie, it's usually gone by the time he slides his shaft into her cunney. It's all very sad.'

This melancholy story reminded me of the unfinished business with my father's overseer and when Wanda came in with the food she had bought for our lunch, I told her and Natasha to sit down for a moment to help plan our campaign against the tyrannical Herr Basler. I was all for just telling my father straight out what the villain had been up to but this worried Wanda who said: 'No, please don't do that, Master Johann. Look at the situation from your father's view. Basler is an efficient manager who, to be fair, is probably more honest than many others in Galicia. It'll be his word against ours and besides, there is something else that you should know.'

I listened intently as she took a deep breath and went on: 'I was ashamed to tell you both before, but I'm not ashamed of what I did. The fact is that my little sister was taken quite ill earlier this year and we had to call the doctor to come round and give her some medicine. Doctor Kochanski only charged us half his normal fee but I knew this meant there was only one way we would be able to pay the next instalment of Basler's loan. This would be to sell my mother's only piece of jewellery, a brooch which had been given to her by her grandmother. So I went round to Basler's house and told him that he could smack my bare bottom again if he would waive half of the monthly payment which was due.

'He said to me: "No, I'm not interested, there are any number of girls who will submit to discipline for a much smaller reduction of their families' debts." Then he looked me up and down and said: "On the other hand, I'll let your father off the entire amount of what he owes me this month if you'll let me fuck you."

'What was I to do? I agonized about whether or not to accept the offer, but my mind was made up for me when my sister fell ill again and we had no other course but to ask Doctor Kochanski to return and examine her. Thank goodness, she recovered but now I knew I had no choice so the next night I went back to Herr Basler's house and agreed to his terms.

' "You've made a very sensible decision, my dear," he

sniggered as I followed him upstairs into his bedroom. "Why, if you please me we might come to some kind of regular arrangement which would help your family's financial situation no end."

'This idea revolted me but now at least I knew that if we found ourselves in dire necessity again, I could do something to help. Anyhow, we both undressed but then, to my horror, I saw him take a slender stick out of his wardrobe. "You said nothing about birching me," I protested but he added scornfully: "Bend over that chair, Wanda. Did you really think that I would let you off an entire payment for a mere fucking? Anyhow, this isn't a birch, it's only an ashplant with which they punish naughty children in English schools."

'With tears in my eyes I did as he demanded, but despite what he had said, the caning was no laughing matter. In the long wall mirror I could see him swing the cane high above his head, poise it in the air and then bring it down with a fierce sweep onto my defenceless bare bottom. Slowly spacing the strokes, he marked my skin with six thin red lines as I looked over my shoulder at him with an imploring expression on my face and beseeched him to stop hurting me.

'At last he stopped and, throwing down the cane on the floor, he smoothed his hand over my poor bottom which was covered with a network of weals. I could see that my tormentor now had a huge cockstand as he said with surprising gentleness: "I'm sorry, Wanda, I didn't mean to flog you quite as hard. But I'll now put some cold cream on that tempting little backside and that should ease your discomfort."

'Herr Basler then told me to lie down on my tummy on the bed. I could see that he had a huge cockstand as he knelt behind me and rubbed the cold cream onto my burning bum cheeks. When he had finished he wiped his hands and exclaimed: "Good, that will stop the throbbing. Now, I've been looking forward to this next part of our arrangement all day and I can't wait to fuck you now that my prick has stiffened up so nicely."

'But when he pulled my buttocks apart to make room for his cock in the cleft between my cheeks I squealed with pain and gasped: "You can't fuck me doggie-style, sir, it hurts too much. I can't bear the slightest pressure on my bottom."

' "H'm, I hope you're not trying to weasel out of our agreement, because I don't think we'll be able to manage it on our sides, face to face," Basler said gruffly. However, I think he knew that I was not play-acting because he did not press the matter further but added: "Well, there's only one thing for it, Wanda, we'll have to fuck in a different way. It'll be a bit awkward for you but my cock is almost bursting and I'm damned if I'm *not* going to poke you. We shall have to get off the bed to do it in the wheelbarrow position. Come downstairs and we'll have a good shag in the living room."

' "Oh, I don't care what position we do it in so long as you leave my sore backside alone," I said as we walked back downstairs and he assured me that I wouldn't have to lie on my bottom and that he wouldn't have to touch it.

'I was puzzled but Basler soon enlightened me. Lifting me in his arms, he turned me upside down with my feet in the air and with my hands resting on the floor at the full extent of my arms. Then he made me put my legs around his neck whilst he held me round the waist with his hands clasped upon my belly so that he supported my weight and took the strain off my arms.

' "Try and keep still," he advised as he lowered my body, manoeuvring it into a slanting position. When my bottom was uppermost my pussy was on the same level as his cock. Then, by slightly bending his knees, he was able to slide his thick prick inside my cunt. He began to fuck me by moving his hips backwards and forwards. It was by no means the best fuck I have ever had, but I was grateful that my bottom was never touched nor rubbed against in any way. After Basler had spent, he put me back on my feet and asked me if I had enjoyed myself. I thought it best just to thank him for being considerate and said: "Well, you managed it very nicely, but it isn't very comfortable as it's made all the blood run into my head."

' "Yes, I suppose it would – so next time we'll fuck first before I cane you," he said and I was tempted to tell him that no way would there be a next time. But he surprised me by showing me that he was a man of his word, for he brought out his account books and in front of my eyes he wrote down that the monthly payment of the Dienst family debt had been made.'

Wanda gave a short, sardonic laugh and sighed: 'Fool that I was, I really believed that there might be a spark of decency in Herr Basler.'

'Well, far be it from me to defend him,' I said with some hesitation. 'But if I had to be Devil's Advocate, I would have to say that at least he tried to make amends for flogging you so severely and he didn't trick you by refusing to cancel the debt.'

'No, but he *did* trick me, Master Johann, because I soon discovered that the swine had deliberately inflicted such a cruel beating. Not only did he enjoy doing it but the whole purpose was to get me into that wheelbarrow position – for, unknown to me, his servant was standing behind the curtains in the living room with a camera and now Herr Basler has a set of rude photographs of me which he has threatened to show my parents if I don't continue this arrangement every month. Of course, you can't recognize Herr Basler from the pictures and he said quite openly to me: "I'd rather fuck you than collect the instalments on your family's debt. You see, I don't need the money, I've now got quite a nest-egg stashed away in the bank." '

'What a villain! Master Johann, we must tell your father,' exclaimed Natasha, but Wanda shook her head and went on: 'I'm afraid that wouldn't help me. You see, Herr Basler also warned me that he would make sure that my photographs were plastered all over Pinczow. So this afternoon he wants to have his way with me again and I just don't see how I can refuse although I am genuinely worried about Stefan. As I told you, he is so depressed about things that he can't get a hard-on any more, but now he has told me that the only way out for us is for him to murder Herr Basler.

'And believe me, he means it! Only this morning I met Stefan in the village and he had a strange gleam in his eyes when he said to me: "Wanda, I mean what I say about Basler. If I can't get hold of a gun, I'll throttle him with my bare hands." '

The room fell silent for a while and then Natasha snapped her fingers and exclaimed excitedly: 'Wait a moment, there might be a much better way to deal with Herr Basler ourselves. Master Johann, did the Count say whether he was taking any of his cameras with him before he left home last Monday?'

I said: 'Yes, as it happens my father told me he was looking forward to trying out his new Neild Double Quarter Plate Camera on this trip.'

'Good, and do you know how to use it?' she demanded. I looked at the gypsy girl quizzically and replied: 'Of course I do: the Neild camera is so simple to operate that a child could take photographs with it. But why do you ask, Natasha?'

'Because if you are agreeable, Master Johann, I think we could give Herr Basler a taste of his own medicine,' she said firmly. 'Look, this is my plan – this afternoon your father told me he will be at a directors' meeting of the limestone quarry company. Now, so long as he doesn't take his camera with him, I propose that we borrow it and set it up inside Basler's house so that you can take secret photographs just like his servant took those pictures of Wanda.'

From the puzzled expression on our faces, she could see that neither Wanda nor myself understood what she was driving at, and she laughed: 'Well, don't you see? Can you imagine Basler's face if he receives a note from Wanda saying that she and her friend Natasha would like to play some frisky games with him this afternoon? Only this time, we'll make sure that any photographs will show just what your beloved overseer is really like: we'll also photograph his accounts book to show the Count.'

'Gosh! What a clever girl you are,' enthused Wanda. Natasha smiled her thanks, then looked at me and added meaningfully: 'Of course, it all depends on whether Johann agrees to help us.'

I wrinkled my brow as I pondered over the plan. If we were found out and Basler reported us to my father, there could be all hell to pay. Not only would the overseer show Wanda's parents the rude photographs of their daughter and extract even harsher terms for the repayment of their loan, but Natasha would probably be dismissed and doubtless I too would suffer the consequences of my father's anger.

However, the operation was in a good cause and, as far as I was concerned, if things went wrong – well, this was a risk I was prepared to take. I said to the girls: 'Count me in! The only problem we have is how we can sneak into Basler's house without being seen.'

'I don't think we'll have too much trouble there,' said Wanda thoughtfully. 'When Stefan was talking so wildly to me this morning about doing away with Herr Basler, he happened to say that today would be the best time to kill him, because old Otto, his servant who took the photographs of Wanda, always spends Wednesday afternoons at the market in Brodnica and doesn't usually return until about six o'clock.'

'Thank you for a delicious lunch, ladies,' said my father, giving his ample stomach a gentle pat after downing the remains of his glass of cold beer. 'However, I had better be on my way to the quarry offices. It wouldn't look good for the chairman to arrive late for the annual general meeting.'

Then it seemed as if all our plans were to be dashed when he rose from the table and said to me: 'Johann, would you please fetch the camera from the bedroom? I might have time to take a few shots of the quarry to show your mother when we get home.'

I could see Wanda's jaw drop at his words but I remarked: 'Father, surely it would be better to have some photographs taken of us at the quarry tomorrow morning on our way to the luncheon the Mayor is holding in your honour. Mama would be much more interested in pictures with us in them.'

My heart was in my mouth as my father considered this observation but happily he nodded his head and said: 'M'm, you're probably right. It will only take a few moments to set up the camera so that all Stefan has to do is to stand behind it and press the button.'

The girls and I breathed a collective sigh of relief as my father picked up his case and said: 'One of our biggest customers is coming to the quarry later this afternoon so I don't think I'll get away much before five thirty. So prepare my evening suit for seven o'clock sharp, please, Natasha, because Johann and I have been invited to dine at the Grand Hotel with Ignace Rydz, an old Berlin University friend of mine who owns a large timber mill in Brodnica.'

Naturally my father did not realize how Natasha, Wanda and myself were all silently urging him to be on his way as he fiddled with some documents in a large green folder. I let out a sigh of relief when he finally slid the papers back in the folder which he placed under his arm as he walked over to the door.

'Good-bye, everyone,' he called out. We chorused back our farewells and then watched impatiently whilst he had a short chat with Stefan Solodowski who was driving him to his meeting. 'Come on, father, come on, you were saying just before how bad it would look if you were late,' I murmured until at last Stefan shook the reins and the black horse trotted out to the road.

The Neild camera was surprisingly light and Wanda carried the tripod for me as we made our way to Herr Basler's house. It was easy enough to break in, although I felt like a burglar as, after opening wide a kitchen window which had been left slightly ajar, I gave Natasha a leg-up and she crawled through with little difficulty.

She opened the back door for us. There was no problem setting up the camera, for even though we had to close one set of curtains to hide my presence, there was still plenty of light coming in the room from the other windows for me to take my photographs of the accounts book. When I announced that all these had been completed,

Natasha said: 'Right, make yourself nice and snug, Master Johann. Wanda says she knows exactly where to find our prey. I'll go with her and bring him back here straight away.'

'We'll probably be back inside twenty minutes,' said Wanda. This forecast proved accurate almost to the minute and my heart began to beat faster as I heard a key turn in the lock. Through the gap in the curtain from where my lens was peeping out, I saw Herr Basler enter the living-room with Natasha and Wanda in tow.

'How about a little drink to get us in the mood for our fun?' proposed Wanda. Herr Basler rubbed his hands and said: 'An excellent suggestion, my dear. Would you fetch a bottle of sparkling wine out of the ice-box in the kitchen whilst I put out the glasses?'

The sun was beating down on my back and although I knew what the wicked overseer had in store for them, I must admit that I envied the girls their refreshing glasses of bubbly whilst I waited for the action to begin. Luckily, I didn't have long to wait for, after they had finished the best part of the bottle, Natasha and Wanda were giggling away as though they were quite tiddly and I saw Herr Basler pull at the slight bulge in the front of his trousers and say: 'Time to go upstairs, girls.'

'Oh, Baldur – you don't mind if I call you Baldur, do you?' Natasha pouted prettily. 'It's far too hot to climb all those stairs. Why don't we stay down here?'

Before he could object, she moved across to Wanda and murmured: 'Aren't you too warm in all those clothes, darling? Let me make you more comfortable.'

Now my cock started to thicken as I watched Wanda make no effort to resist the eager groping which led to her skirt being unfastened. She lifted her body off the sofa so that the garment could be slipped off completely, leaving her clad in only her chemise and knickers. I could see Natasha working her hands inside the chemise. The slender blonde beauty eased the way by sliding down the straps and then lifting her arms high so that Natasha could pull it off.

'M'mm, don't do that, it makes me too excited,' Wanda murmured as Natasha bent her head and planted a series of wet kisses across her bare breasts. Her nipples were sticking out like two hard corks as Natasha ran her palms over them and then cupped her perky white globes in her hands.

'Oooh, you bad girl, you're making my knickers all wet,' murmured Wanda and the dark-haired gypsy girl muttered: 'Well, we can't have that. Lift up your bum again and Baldur can take them off.'

They looked across to the overseer who gave a short laugh as he strode over and tugged down Wanda's knickers, revealing her inviting flaxen thatch of silky pussy curls. Whilst Natasha stood up to begin undressing herself, he knelt down at Wanda's side and frigged her sweet little cunney with his finger whilst with the other hand he tweaked her luscious titties, making her wriggle madly under this twofold stimulation.

Now naked, Natasha knelt down beside Herr Basler and her hand wandered between his thighs to feel the protrusion in his trousers. One by one she delicately undid his fly buttons. Then her soft tapering fingers took possession of his naked cock which had swelled up under her touch to a meaty thickness, although I noticed that his shaft was not yet fully erect.

It was fascinating to watch this erotic scene through the viewfinder of the Neild. I wished I had another camera with me so that I could take some close-up shots, especially when Herr Basler moved away to throw off the rest of his clothes whilst Natasha moved up over Wanda. She teased the blonde girl's quivering pussy, pulling open the cunney lips and rubbing her knuckles back and forth across the entrance to her honeypot.

But when the now stark naked overseer returned to the fray, they stopped this playful fondling and laid him on his back on the sofa. Natasha took hold of his beefy boner and rubbed it between her palms until it stood smartly up to attention, waving slightly in the air.

'*Gott in Himmel!*' he cried out as Wanda licked his hairy pink ballsack and Natasha gobbled on his uncapped purple knob. I busied myself taking exposure after exposure whilst the girls changed places and Wanda now lapped on his mushroom bell-end, savouring the salty pre-cum which had formed around the 'eye'. There was time for me to snap one more excellent shot as Wanda slid her lips down his shaft. His wiry pubic bush must have tickled her nose for she suddenly pulled her head back and gave three violent sneezes.

'Atishoo! Atishoo! Atishoo!' went Wanda. Natasha released Herr Basler's balls from her mouth and said gaily: 'Tut-tut, Wanda, I am reliably informed that *The Ladies' Book of Etiquette* expressly states that it is considered extremely rude to sneeze whilst sucking a gentleman's cock.'

'In that case, I had better express my apologies,' laughed Wanda. She straddled Herr Basler and, taking hold of his thick blue-veined tool, guided his prick into the red chink between her puffy pussy lips. She wiggled on his tool until she was fully speared upon it. Then, with a tiny yelp, she began to fling herself up and down on his vibrating todger. Her breasts jiggled merrily up and down as she clamped her knees around his thighs.

My own cock was now aching so much that I ripped

open my trousers and released my throbbing stiffstander. It throbbed stiffly in my palm as I fisted my hand up and down my hot shaft.

Natasha now joined in and swung herself over Herr Basler's head, facing Wanda and with her hairless pussy poised directly above the overseer's mouth. 'Will you lick me out?' she asked him and he panted out 'Yes! Yes!' She sat down carefully upon his mouth. I could hear him slurp his tongue inside Natasha's juicy cunt whilst Wanda continued to bounce herself up and down on his cock.

Fools rush in where angels fear to tread, says the old English proverb, but, as the Europeans say, when the cock stands up, common sense flies out of the window. I found this voluptuous scene simply too inviting for me to remain hidden behind the curtains, so I whipped off my clothes in record time. I rushed out from my hiding place to stand beside Natasha who, carried away by the sight of my palpitating prick, immediately turned her head to swirl her wet tongue over my smooth-skinned ruby knob.

Of course, the sudden appearance of a naked youth joining in the fucking greatly startled Herr Basler who pulled his face away from Natasha's groin and croaked out: 'My God, who the hell are you?'

'Don't worry, Johann is a friend of ours,' gasped Wanda as she reached out with her hand to cup my scrotum whilst Natasha took hold of my cock and bobbed her head to and fro along my swollen shaft.

No doubt it was the lascivious sight of Natasha sucking my cock whilst Wanda played with my balls which brought Herr Basler off so quickly.

'A-h-r-e! A-h-r-e! I'm cumming, I'm cumming, I can't hold back!' he wailed, but Wanda panted: 'It's all right, I'm almost there too – shoot off when you like, you randy fucker!'

These lewd instructions sent the pair of them whizzing past the point of no return. Although Wanda was only shagging the overseer for an ulterior motive, she gloried in the delight of an unforced mutual spend. She reached down with her free hand to diddle her clitty as her love channel swiftly became awash with a flood of her own cuntal juices and Herr Basler's copious emission.

'I think I'm going to spend, too,' I panted. Natasha began to swallow in anticipation as, sure enough, the surge of a powerful cum coursed up from my balls. She quickly gulped it down as I drenched her mouth with a torrent of creamy seed.

After she had milked my cock dry she released my still semi-erect shaft and smacked her lips, saying: 'M'mm, I really enjoyed gobbling you, Johann. Nothing tastes as clean and fresh as a squirt of frothy spunk straight from the cock and your jism has a delicious salty tang.'

'My word, his prick is still nice and thick – do you think you could carry on?' asked Wanda as she slid out her hand and began to slick her fist up and down the length of my twitching todger.

'Certainly I can,' I answered confidently, although I assumed I would not be called upon to perform whilst Herr Basler's mouth was still pressed against Natasha's pussy lips.

However, Wanda had another plan in mind. As she gently frigged my stiffening shaft she murmured: 'Then why don't you fuck Natasha's bottom, Johann? I know she would enjoy that very much, wouldn't you, sweetie?'

'Oooh, you wicked girl, what a naughty idea!' squealed Natasha. But it was clear that Wanda's proposal appealed to her for she lewdly thrust out her buttocks as Wanda slipped off the sofa and, pulling me by my cock, positioned me behind the trembling gypsy girl. Then she wedged my knob in the cleft of Natasha's backside and whispered: 'Stay there a moment, Master Johann, I'm just going to get something from the larder to spread on your cock. Don't you move, now. I'll be back in no time!'

'I'm not going anywhere,' I answered breathlessly. The thought of Natasha being bum-fucked whilst he brought her off with his tongue also greatly excited Herr Basler, but the overseer was now too tired to continue. His head fell back onto the arm of the sofa, so that he had a bird's-eye view of Natasha's shaved cunney and arsehole and the underside of my throbbing tool as it waited patiently to begin its slide forward into Natasha's bottom.

Now Wanda came running back with a small bowl in her hand. She smeared my shaft with butter before pulling apart the firm, curvaceous cheeks of Natasha's backside to enable me to slide my greased bell-end into her alluring little back passage. Despite Wanda's assistance, I was very much a novice at this form of fucking, and found it difficult to achieve the correct angle to enter the tiny star-shaped rosette. Natasha wriggled her body, shifting her buttocks back towards my belly and, reaching back with her hand to guide me, she deftly introduced my knob inside the ring of her anus. Then she edged slowly backwards to completely engulf my shaft inside her rear dimple.

When she was fully impaled on my cock we commenced a short, sharp bout of erotic play. Natasha began to ride me, squirming slowly so that I could see everything: the sensuous jiggling of her buttocks, the stretching of her sheath by my shaft as the sphincter slid up and down my length in a way that produced the most excruciating pleasure.

This might have been ecstatic for me, but Herr Basler found it uncomfortable to be squashed underneath my added weight. He struggled out from underneath us and rolled off the sofa onto the carpet. Meanwhile, I leaned forward to fondle Natasha's breasts. Soon my balls were aching for release as I jerked my hips to and fro, pumping with wild abandon into her luscious bottom. My cock slithered to and fro inside her narrow sheath, plunging in and out of the now widened rim, and soon I cried out: 'I'm going to shoot, Natasha. Do you want it up your bum or in your cunt?'

'In my cunt!' she cried out. I pulled out my prick with a 'pop' from her bottom and slid it inside her pussy as I continued the fuck doggie-style, looking with relish at my glistening shaft see-sawing in and out of her puffy pink cunney lips, above which the brown rosebud of her arsehole quivered and winked with each push.

'Wow!' I gasped as the muscles of Natasha's love channel tightened delightfully around my shaft as it pounded anew in and out of her juicy cunt until, with a gigantic whoosh, a torrent of sticky spunk burst out of my cock into her eager quim. Gush after gush spurted deep inside her while the walls of her cunney squeezed my shaft. I jetted a veritable fountain of thick, gruelly seed inside her sticky wetness before rolling off her and crashing down onto Herr Basler who was still lying there after his fall from the sofa.

Now, I have always maintained that, according to my own empirical observations, the old saw about women being the weaker sex is based on a fallacy – and an early example of this was manifest that afternoon. For, after two cums, my cock was as limp as Herr Basler's shaft which was flopping forlornly over his balls after only one climax.

Nevertheless, the girls were still game for more fucking. When they could see that we were unable to continue,

Natasha and Wanda cuddled up together. The sultry dark gypsy girl ran her finger through the fluffy blonde thatch of Wanda's pussy hair and said throatily: 'Oooh, your cunney's all lovely and wet, darling. Let me suck out Herr Basler's spunk and your quim will tingle and throb as I slide my tongue all along your crack and swirl it around your clitty. Would you like that, Wanda? Would you?'

For answer, Wanda simply moved her hand to take one of Natasha's elongated nipples daintily between her slender fingers, rubbing the red berry which rose and hardened to her touch. Natasha smiled as she gently pushed Wanda down upon her back until her head was resting comfortably on the arm of the sofa. Then she knelt between her legs and kissed each delicious rounded breast, sucking the engorged red nipples before kissing her way down the snow-white flesh of her midriff, past the small indenture of her belly-button until her lips buried themselves in the soft bush of fluffy blonde pussy hair.

Wanda gurgled with pleasure as Natasha positioned her head on her thigh. Natasha slipped one hand under the blonde girl's bottom and used the other to spread open her coral cunt lips, using her thumb and forefinger.

I scrambled up to see Natasha place her lips over Wanda's swollen clitty – which was protruding from her cunt – and suck the fleshy love bud into her mouth.

'M'mm, the mixture of Herr Basler's jism and your pussy juices tastes like nectar,' mumbled Natasha indistinctly whilst she continued to frig Wanda's cunney with her fingers. Then she dived back again and ground her face right into the blonde girl's mound which made Wanda purr with pleasure as she arched her body upwards. She called out: 'Darling, move across me and I'll lick you out at the same time.'

There was a gleam in Natasha's eyes as she lifted her

head. Then she swung herself over and around Wanda, facing her feet and crouching on her knees and wriggling down until she had brought her hairless pussy down upon Wanda's lips. Natasha bent forward to resume licking out Wanda's pussy and this new position gave the other girl a chance to caress Natasha's tight peachy bum cheeks. She splayed open the two rounded spheres to make room for her lips to lick and lap between the luscious dimpled globes. She tickled the rim of Natasha's tiny puckered arsehole with the tip of her tongue before moving her lips down to the smooth crease of her cunney. Natasha's love lips opened out under the probing of Wanda's insistent tongue which slithered into the juicy orifice of her quim.

'Oooh! Oooh! Oooh!' squealed Natasha as she leaned forward to allow Wanda's tongue further access to her dripping love channel. 'That's really divine, Wanda. Keep on! Oh, keep on and don't you dare stop until I spend!'

I could see the tremors of desire shivering across Natasha's lithe body as she bent down and completed the pattern, forming a perfect *soixante-neuf* as, after pausing a moment to savour the musky cuntal aroma, the gypsy girl began to ream out Wanda's pretty blonde-fringed pussy with long slurping laps of her moist pink tongue.

Wanda too was quivering with lust and she panted out: 'Natasha! Oh yes, you're licking me out beautifully! I can feel your tongue fluttering inside my quim . . . can you feel mine? Wait, I'm going to slide it right inside your sweet cunt as far as it will go . . . There!'

Oblivious to everything but each others' juicy quims, the girls' bodies tensed with the onset of their orgasms. They moved together in perfect unison, pleasuring each others' pussies by licking and lapping the slits of their dripping cunnies until the tribadic twosome finally shuddered into their longed-for climaxes.

However, the girls quickly recovered when Herr Basler clapped his hand to his forehead and gasped: '*Mein Gott!* I've just remembered that I promised to give the latest accounts to Count Gewirtz at the quarry office at four o'clock sharp. I must be on my way or I'll be late.'

'Oh dear, but there's no need to worry, Baldur, we're all honest and wouldn't steal anything from you. We can let ourselves out as soon as we've dressed ourselves,' said Natasha comfortingly whilst the overseer hastily pulled on his trousers and grunted: 'No, the three of you stay and wait for me, I'll only be gone for about twenty minutes. There are some questions I want answered when I come back.'

Then I caught his eye and, as he slipped on his shirt, he added grimly: 'For a start I want to know more about *you*, young man.'

Once we saw his horse clip-clopping at a steady pace down towards the quarry, I too began to pull on my clothes. Natasha suggested that Wanda should also dress herself and help me take the camera and the plates back to the house where I could start, there and then, to make up the prints.

'If you say so,' said Wanda as she stepped into her knickers. 'But won't Herr Basler be furious to find out that we've scarpered?'

'Perhaps, but so what?' retorted Natasha with a short laugh. 'Anyhow, he'll be even more furious when I tell him that the young man here this afternoon was taking photographs of what was happening before he couldn't contain himself and joined in the fun.'

'Are you going to tell him who I am?' I enquired. I must confess to feeling slightly relieved when Natasha shook her head and answered: 'No, not at this stage and it might never be necessary if he agrees to our terms. But I shan't tell him anything except that you and Wanda can be found in the Count's cottage – and it's my bet he will come storming over straightaway with me in tow. Now, you will only have to mention the fact that you have taken photographs of his secret accounts and I'm damned sure that Herr Basler will accept our terms without any quibbling.'

'But suppose he doesn't?' asked Wanda anxiously. 'What do we do then?'

'In that case, we must go ahead and show the Count the photographs,' said Natasha slowly. 'For there's no point in holding back, you'd only be back in the same position – no, worse, in fact, because Herr Basler will be so furious he'll try to punish you and your family in some way.'

'Yes, you're right, of course,' sighed Wanda as she buttoned up her skirt. 'And, talking of punishment, it's just occurred to me that he didn't flog us first before the fucking. Who knows, there might be a better side to him after all?'

'Maybe, but I wouldn't bank on it,' Natasha replied darkly. 'Remember, he still has compromising pictures of you that he might still send to your parents even if he agrees to wipe off all the debts. Now get off back home, you two, I'm sure I'll see you back there very soon.'

Even if I had had the necessary chemicals with me, there were no facilities for developing my photographs, so I hid the plates under my bed and after replacing the Neild back in my father's room.

Natasha was right, because within the hour Herr Basler was knocking on the front door. Wanda opened the door but there was no sign of Natasha as Herr Basler strode in and snapped: 'Right, now the Count has told me that he won't be leaving the quarry till six o'clock at the earliest and I want to know exactly what's been going on before he comes back.' Wanda ignored this outburst and asked quietly: 'Where is Natasha?'

'She's tied to a chair in my living room and old Otto, my servant, is guarding her,' he answered curtly, but seeing an expression of concern cloud Wanda's face he went oh: 'Oh, Otto won't hurt her. In case you didn't know, his preference is for stable-lads.

'But on the other hand, I won't release her till I get some answers,' continued the overseer firmly. 'Now, how does that old rhyme go? *Fucking is a funny thing, it makes a man a fool/It takes away his appetite and wears away his tool*.

'Well, fucking made *me* foolish all right this afternoon! I got so carried away by you and your friend that I didn't even ask what he was doing there – besides joining in the rumpy-pumpy, of course.'

I decided that the best way to resolve the situation was to come clean about my identity. Frankly, whether or not Herr Basler knew my true identity was not a matter of great importance because if agreed to our demands, there would be no need to tell my father, and if he refused – well, I would have to convince my father that I had acted in the best interests of the estate and with luck the photographic copies of Basler's accounts would back me up.

So I hauled myself out of my chair and said: 'Herr Basler, we meet again. As we never had time to be formally introduced, let me do so now. My name is Johann Gewirtz. I don't think I need tell you that you are, of course, well acquainted with my father.'

I went on: 'And you wouldn't have met me this afternoon except that, like you, I behaved unwisely when presented with the sight of two pretty naked girls who were clearly eager for cock! I should not have joined in the fun but stayed behind my camera.'

The overseer's face went white as he repeated shakily: 'Behind your camera? What camera? I don't understand.'

'You *should* understand, Herr Basler,' I said with growing confidence. 'As *I* understand it, you have been taking certain photographs yourself and blackmailing girls like Wanda with them.'

'I don't know what you're talking about,' he blustered but I said calmly: 'Oh, I think you do. Only the difference between my photographs and yours is that mine will show the identity of the man involved.' I paused for effect and then said slowly: 'But before you arrived with the girls this afternoon, I also took some even more interesting shots of your secret accounts books.'

He looked at me silently and said: 'I suppose you're going to tell your father all about this sordid business when he gets home and demand that he gives me the sack.'

I shook my head and said quietly: 'Not necessarily, Herr Basler. What I suggest is that you give your books to Stefan Solodowski and he will calculate just how much of their original loans each family has paid back to you. Once they have paid back the full sum, you must release them from any further obligation. And, naturally, there must be no more harassment of the village girls.'

'And you must release Natasha at once and bring her back here straightaway,' Wanda chipped in. For a few moments there was silence as he considered these proposals. Then he nodded and gulped: 'And if I agree, nothing will be said to your father?'

'You have my word on it and also that none of the girls whom you have been fucking will breathe a word to their parents,' I assured him. Then, remembering how my father (who was a great believer in the principle of *noblesse oblige*) always maintained it was far more important to be respected rather than feared, I said: 'And I'm sure that the tenants will be so pleased to have this terrible burden lifted from their backs that you'll find it far easier to manage the estate in future. So what about turning over the page and making a fresh start?'

The overseer threw his hands up in the air. 'You leave me no choice. I'd find it very difficult getting another position after being dismissed by Count Gewirtz without a reference.'

Then he gave a rather sad little smile and said in a low voice: 'Don't think too badly of me, Johann. I know I've been a bit of a cad and deserve my come-uppance. But my wife ran off with one of the managers at the quarry five years ago and I've been very lonely and become all bitter and twisted inside. I never used to want to whip girls but since she ran off I suppose I wanted to punish all women for my unhappiness.'

Well, as my mother is fond of saying, there is more than a spark or two of goodness in most people, and I felt tremendously pleased about how (if only by accident) I had changed for the better the lives of all the tenants on our Pinczow estates – and of Baldur Basler himself. He may have lost out financially but he gained far more because, when my father went back to Pinczow the following Spring, he found that the overseer was no longer living alone but with an extremely pretty young woman whom he later married.

All went well for Wanda, too, because Stefan's cock soon recovered and within the year the Dienst and Solodowski families were also joined in marriage.

As for Natasha and myself – well, she was a quick

learner and soon after she had completed her basic education, she left our employ to take up a job at the Grand Hotel in Vienna. The last I heard of her was that she had obtained a position as the assistant manageress at the Hotel Splendide in Przemysl *[a city in South East Poland – Editor]*.

But what grand memories I have of fucking that sultry dark-eyed gypsy girl. The very thought of those youthful adventures makes my still stalwart shaft stand up again. I must put down my fountain pen and open my fly buttons before calling in my private secretary to suck me off!

Count Johann Gewirtz
Villa d'Argent
Cannes
May 1911

THE END OF
VOLUME ONE OF
EROTIC MEMOIRS

TONY ANDREWS

IN THE PINK: STRIPPED FOR ACTION

Here, in the IN THE PINK series of inside revelations so shocking that they could only be told as fiction, you will discover the sexual secrets of the exclusive, hidden lives of the men – and women – who produce the world's top-selling girlie magazines. Learn the erotic inside stories – in more ways than one – of the girls who take their clothes off for money, and of the men who take the photographs.

Join Tony Andrews behind the steamy scenes at the photographic shoots where inhibitions are discarded as recklessly as the clothes are. Learn the amazing facts about the popularity of the 'readers' wives' sections of men's magazines. Read the explicit details of the girls who like it rough – and of those who just want to be loved.

'Tony Andrews' is the pen name of one of Britain's most experienced girlie magazine editors and publishers, with over 25 years in the business in both Britain and America. You'll be fascinated – and maybe shocked – by what he has to tell. This raunchy, uninhibited and above all honest exposé is not for the prudish . . .

HODDER & STOUGHTON PAPERBACKS

TONY ANDREWS

IN THE PINK 2: SIN CITY

In this instalment of his erotic escapades, Tony Andrews experiences the sensual delights of New York at its raunchiest. As a red-blodded Brit, he's got several advantages over the local men: like the frustrated NY ladies says, 'New York men are either gay, married or sexist pigs.' Tony's none of these things, so the Big Apple is his Bit Oyster – and for him, there's an 'R' in every month! From singles bars to video dating agencies and the sex clubs where anything – but anything – goes, Tony's going to take a big bite out of the Big A at its juiciest . . .

HODDER & STOUGHTON PAPERBACKS